KATE A. BOORMAN

AMULET BOOKS   NEW YORK

Library of Congress Cataloging-in-Publication Data

Names: Boorman, Kate A., author.
Title: Heartfire / Kate A. Boorman.
Description: New York : Amulet Books, 2016. | Series: Winterkill ; 3 | Sequel to: Darkthaw | Summary: Emmeline fights the Dominion to save her adopted home in the land of the First Peoples.
Identifiers: LCCN 2016004360 (print) | LCCN 2016023809 (ebook) | ISBN 9781419721243 (hardback) | ISBN 9781613121832 (ebook)
Subjects: | CYAC: Fantasy. | Survival—Fiction. | Love—Fiction.
Classification: LCC PZ7.B64618 He 2016 (print) | LCC PZ7.B64618 (ebook) | DDC [Fic]—dc23
LC record available at https://lccn.loc.gov/2016004360

ISBN: 978-1-4197-2124-3

Printed and bound in U.S.A.
10 9 8 7 6 5 4 3 2 1

Amulet Books are available at special discounts when purchased in quantity for premiums and promotions as well as fundraising or educational use. Special editions can also be created to specification. For details, contact specialsales@abramsbooks.com or the address below.

ABRAMS The Art of Books
115 West 18th Street, New York, NY 10011
abramsbooks.com

1

THE FOREST IS RAVENOUS.

It opens up its jaws, swallows us whole.

The trees blur, blending one into the next, shadows bleeding black to blacker. No sun, no sky within this place. But despite the perils—the creak and snap of beasts unseen—these dark woods offer us one thing:

Escape.

Muscles straining, lungs burning, I skirt tangles of brush and duck under green boughs, dragging my bad foot. My heart thunders in my ears.

I feel my pursuer behind me like a hot breath on my neck. As I labor over a fallen log, a thin branch whips my cheek. I bite back a cry.

And now, a flash of blue to the left. A boy my age—one of Matisa's kin, mayhap—fleeing like me.

For a split second I see his eyes—they're bright, determined; like he's sure he'll get away. Echoing my thought, he picks up speed and disappears. I want to follow but no, that's foolish. I'm not fast like him; I'd only lead them his way.

I stumble to a halt and rethink my escape. Could I double back toward Matisa's village and hide? I turn to the northwest, planning to carve a long arc and retrace my path. There's a sound behind me.

I glance back and find nothing but a row of trees, but deep down I know: I've been spotted.

Hurry.

Desperate, I scan the woods. Several strides to my right the moss floor disappears as the earth dips into a steep ravine. A cluster of spruce with low, bushy branches clings to the hillside. There's nowhere to run beyond it; the descent is far too steep—I'd fall and break something, surely. If I hide there, I'm trapped.

But I've run out of time.

I dart behind the trees and drop to the earth, trying to flatten myself below sight lines.

I hold my ragged breath.

Silence.

A line of sweat itches at the back of my neck, under my braid. My palms, too, are slick. I wipe them on the moss and risk a sip of air. My heartbeat slows from a gallop to a trot.

Silence.

Did he run past?

Real cautious, I draw my head up.

"You're dead."

My heart stutters. *Where—?* I push to my knees, scanning the trees. A figure shifts at the corner of my vision.

Tom is staring down the barrel of his beloved rifle, not ten strides away.

"Bang," he says. And smiles.

I frown up into his blue eyes. "Aren't you supposed to touch me?"

"You're plain in my sights. Don't need to."

"That thing's not even loaded."

"Course it isn't. You're still dead."

I curse and push myself to standing, dusting soil and spruce needles off my hands. "I'm not fast enough for this game."

"No," Tom agrees, relaxing his aim and bringing the rifle to his side. "But you were quiet. I had to look for your traces."

I glance at my bad foot. The boy who passed me will last far longer against his opponent, but I suppose it's something that I wasn't loud.

I remember chasing through the woods like this near our settlement, three seasons ago. That day, the day everything changed, I crashed into the forest after Matisa, tearing and shredding my way through the brush like hail through squash blossoms, while she darted ahead, silent as a sunbeam. Living with her people, *osanaskisiwak,* these past weeks has taught me to move quieter. And I've learned to listen better, to observe.

But you need speed and strength to become one of their warriors.

I cross through the trees toward my best friend. His cheeks are flushed, though probably more from excitement than the chase, since I didn't get far.

"Thanks," Tom says. "That was good practice."

I snort. "Hardly."

"Every little bit helps." He says it so earnest.

I tilt my head. "Not sure I recognize this Tom."

3

"Which Tom?"

"The one obsessed with his battle skills."

"Just want to prove them. I'm hopeful I won't have to use them."

"Sure you are," I tease, a smile pulling at my lips.

"I am. Been enough death around here lately."

My smile fades.

He's talking about the Bleed—the sickness that lives in the "little waters." This summer it's claimed over a dozen of Matisa's people.

"The rumor's gaining strength," he adds, his voice soft.

A familiar unease settles in my chest.

Battle preparations began as a precaution when, weeks ago, I arrived here with Matisa, Isi, and Tom with news that the Dominion—the people who rule in the east—are fixing to settle out this way. Matisa's people have long been wary of that group, who overthrew and slaughtered First Peoples in the east. But her people have also always had the upper hand against invaders: a remedy for the Bleed.

The healers' circle Matisa belongs to has guarded that remedy for years, planning to use it to negotiate peace with invaders. It's their best hope against the brutal weapons of the Dominion, and it's a secret the circle has dedicated their lives to protect.

The recent deaths from the Bleed have one of two explanations: either the victims weren't taking the remedy, or the rumor Tom speaks of is true—the remedy no longer works. If it's the latter, there'll be no negotiation, and Tom'll end up proving his skills in a bloody war.

We all will.

I change the subject. "What's next?"

"After this? Target practice."

I roll my eyes. "Like you need practice."

He grins. "Come on," he says, tugging at my arm.

We find a ridgeline, climb it, and head back toward the village, taking care to keep the turtle-shaped mountain directly before our right shoulder—the way we were taught. Deep in these crevasses the woods are so thick, it's easy to get turned around, lost. There are many hazards about: crumbling cliffs, large predators. Accidents aren't common; Matisa's people know the land well. But Tom and I are new here; it'd take far longer than a summer to understand this place.

Matisa's brother, Nishwa, is waiting on the training flats. He raises an eyebrow as we emerge from the trees. "Back so soon?"

"Tom needs faster prey."

"Ah." Nishwa runs a hand over his partially shaved head, a hairstyle that indicates his new rank: trainer. The position was his reward for stopping the *osanaskisiwak* hunters before they left on their yearly trip. He'd warned them of the approaching danger and urged them to stay and defend the valley. His shaved head should make him look fierce, but his round face is too open, his grin too easy. "Good. That means you can compete as well as the others." I don't feel slighted by his words; I'll always be too slow, too awkward, to be a warrior.

My gaze is drawn to the lake. A rider on a smoke-white horse is coming along the shore. Eisu, Matisa's cousin.

I nudge Tom with my elbow. "Use Eisu next time."

Tom's eyes dart toward the handsome scout and away.

I hide a grin. Tom's in a spell over Eisu. He hasn't said as much, but I can tell.

"It'd be a more fair matchup," I amend.

And now I see Matisa, emerging from a line of trees on the far side of the flats. She shields her eyes against the setting sun and beckons.

"I'll see you later?" I say to Tom.

"Thanks again, Em." But Tom's eyes are fixed on Eisu.

I turn away, unable to hide my smile this time. I know what Tom's feeling. I know what it's like when your skin ignites at a person's touch, when your heart races when he speaks your name . . . I draw a breath and shove sudden thoughts of Kane—of the days of travel it would take to reach him—away.

I focus instead on reaching Matisa and notice an animal skulking in the shadows of the trees near her. It's a thin dog, all ribs and mangy fur. Matisa extends her hand, a scrap of something in it. The dog darts close to take it into its jaws and retreats just as quick.

I keep my distance. "Whose dog?" Dogs are new to me, and they look too much like wolves for me to feel comfortable around.

Matisa shrugs. "It seems she does not have a home. Perhaps she was run out of her pack."

I watch the dog gulping the scrap. It pulls its head up, eyeing Matisa and licking its chops. "You're not worried it'll bite you?"

"She won't bite me," Matisa says. "She is just looking for a friend." She tosses another scrap, which the dog snaps out of the air. My heart skips a beat. "A friend with food."

"You wanted me?"

"Yes," she says. The dog creeps forward again, but Matisa's hand is empty. "We need more healing salve."

"Oh?" I mix pastes and tend to wounds the warriors get during war practice, but there are other people who can do what I do; my work is never urgent.

"And I wanted to tell you about my dream."

Oh.

I fight to keep my thoughts from my face. Inside, I'm weary. The dog cocks its head.

"This one feels different," she ventures.

Feels different.

I swallow a sigh. Matisa believes she and I are the ones her legend speaks of: the dreamers from two different times who can prevent disaster for her people. It's the reason she searched for my settlement last fall, and it's why we journeyed together to her people. And the fact that our dreams led us to one another then, and again when we were split up during our trek to this valley, made me believe it, too. I always figured arriving here would lay our purpose bare.

But for weeks her dreams have been the same: she is searching through a forest, a pile of her slaughtered people nearby. Mine are of me burying Matisa in the soil at my settlement.

Seems our dreams foretell death, so how they can help us prevent it is something I can't figure.

Matisa is waiting for my reply.

"Course." I force a smile, but her brow creases—she always knows what I'm thinking—and there's a flash of desperation in her eyes. My heart twists. She's changed since the day she found my settlement last fall. Back then she appeared from nowhere, a bright-eyed savior full of mystery and new possibilities. Now, worry spiders along her features, draws her shoulders down.

I chastise myself for adding to that worry, square my shoulders, and offer my hand. "I want to hear all about it."

Her face relaxes. "It's almost dinner." She takes my hand and gestures at the village. "We can talk while we eat."

I watch the dog out of the corner of my eye as it falls in beside us. It slinks along, wary-like, but peers at us all hopeful. It reminds me of someone . . .

The thought vanishes as two boys on horseback approach. They pass by at a quick trot. I stop and turn, watching as they dig their heels into their horses' sides, urging them into a gallop. They tear across the flats toward the lake. So strong. So fast.

Matisa is studying me. I turn my head. "What?"

"I have been thinking," she says. The dog moves closer and lifts its nose to nuzzle her hand, licking the salt from her palm. "Perhaps you should try again."

"Riding?" Matisa tried to teach me earlier this spring before we set out for her home. Back then, I was sure I could learn. I was sure about a lot of things: how exciting our journey would be, how my new life with Kane was just beginning. But our journey was a disaster, and Kane is now caring for his motherless little brothers in the safety of a newcomers' village—days from here and under the attentions of a pink-cheeked girl named Genya. Things didn't turn out the way I was dreaming they would; being terrible at riding is the least of those failures.

"We were rushed before," she says. "You could learn on a gentle horse, from a better teacher."

I consider this. I do love those beasts: all sleek lines and strong muscle, their smell so good and earthy, their eyes so kind. I remember feeling alive when we galloped through the drylands, trying to outrun the rain. But I also recall bumping along on Matisa's mare, the insides of my legs screaming after two days of practice. I remember how exasperated Isi was with his beloved Matisa for persisting in trying to teach me. He's a dear friend to me now, no more scathing looks, but that notion my lessons were useless sticks in my mind like a burr.

I sigh. "Not sure anything or anyone could help me."

"Matisa!" The shout draws our eyes. A young girl is hurrying toward us. She pulls up, out of breath, and launches into a stream of chatter in Matisa's tongue. As Matisa listens, her eyes scan the farmlands and the banks of the river.

"What is it?" I ask Matisa.

"Another sick girl."

I don't need to ask if it's the Bleed; the urgency in the messenger's tone and eyes say as much.

"The rest of the circle is harvesting today," Matisa says. "They would want to come, but I do not have time to summon them."

I can't offer to go find them for her; the healers' circle is out in secret places, collecting the remedy plant that is supposed to prevent the Bleed from taking hold. Once it's harvested, they'll mix it with other herbs to mask its identity in order to control the truth, to ensure the knowledge doesn't spread—by accident or someone's ambition—to newcomers. Like me.

Matisa chews her lip. "The girl will only be awake a short time."

"I'll come with you." I won't be allowed in to see the girl, but I want to be there for my friend.

"Let us go quickly," Matisa says. "She is being kept at the place of silence."

I struggle to keep up, following her west into a setting sun that crowns the mountain peaks with a blood-red glare, my skin prickling with anticipation. Or mayhap it's dread.

Dying from the Bleed is a short and grisly matter, over in half a day or night at most. Matisa isn't hurrying to heal the girl or even to ease her suffering. She hurries because if she can speak with her before she slips under the curtain of fever and pain, we might determine the cause of her death. We might learn whether it's like the circle *wants* to believe, that she failed to take the remedy. Or if it's true that the remedy no longer protects us.

My thoughts race alongside my heart as we climb toward the dying girl.

The rumor's gaining strength, I remember Tom saying.

A chill touches the back of my neck.

I pray to the Almighty it isn't true.

2

THE FOREST GIVES WAY TO CRAGGY CLIFFS. A small lodge sits before us, domed and made of a wooden patchwork, like a beehive—like the other huts that are built into the mountainside, resting places for those who need silence and privacy. We are no more than a five-minute walk from the village's constant pulse of laughter, song, the cries of children, the barks of dogs; the rich smells of woodsmoke, roasted meats, horses, sweetgrass—but up here, it all feels very far away.

A young man—brother or cousin to the sick girl?—stands outside, like he's waiting for us. His shirt is the sky-blue color Matisa's people are so fond of, with a line of beading along each sleeve that glints in the setting sun. Usually Matisa's people wear their hair braided, sometimes adorned with colorful strips of leather or feathers. This man's is loose and long—a sign of mourning. He, too, knows Matisa's not here to help the girl.

They exchange words in their tongue. When he opens the

door and light floods out, I can see a form lying on skins and furs inside.

Shivering.

And suddenly I'm grateful I'm expected to stay outside.

Matisa turns to me. Her face is unreadable.

"I'll be right here," I say, and put a hand on her arm.

She disappears inside, and as the door is pushed shut behind her, dusk falls around us once more.

I look to the man and offer their greeting: *"Tansi."* He acknowledges me with a polite incline of his head and turns his eyes away. I follow his gaze, tracing the route Matisa and I climbed.

From here, the glimmer of the village is visible over the treetops; several thousand people's homes nestled in the shadows of these impossible mountains. Farmlands lie at the far end of the valley, next to a glistening lake. The walls of rock create barriers near impassable to the stranger who doesn't know this land, and the east entry to the valley is guarded by a long stretch of sentries. From a distance, this place is a picture of strength and beauty.

But from up close, it's under attack, one person at a time.

A murmuring of voices comes from beyond the door. I picture that girl in there, trying to speak around a swollen, bleeding tongue, and all at once I want to clap my hands to my ears and flee back down the mountainside.

Shame courses through me. My fear helps nothing.

Still, some days it creeps into my mind and muddies my thoughts until I don't know up from down. Those days, I miss Kane so much, it feels like a part of me has been ripped away and thrown to the winds. Those days, I dig for memories of him, desperate to remember his face, the sound of his voice, the touch of his hands. I struggle to light my heart-fire, which once burned so bright for him, I thought it might burst.

I rub my hands together, not so much for warmth as for something to do, and stand in strained silence beside the man, thinking, not for the first time, that I must seem dimwitted. Can't speak but a few simple words in Matisa's tongue, and I'm forever gaping at her people's ways. They're a mix of two different groups, like we were in my settlement, but they've learned one another's tongues—something we never did. And not everyone here speaks English perfect, but most understand it. Learning the language and weapons of the Dominion helped *osanakisiwak* understand the danger their dreams foretold. Being protected from the Bleed was supposed to ensure their survival.

I stare out at the glimmering valley, reaching for a feeling of peace.

It drifts beyond my grasp, like a torn leaf in a breeze.

An eternity passes. Matisa reappears. She places a hand on the arm of the man, giving him a look of condolence, and gestures for me to follow her.

Once we're well into the forest, out of earshot, we stop to speak. In the twilight her eyes are shadowed, giving her a haunted appearance.

"She rode out yesterday to find her younger brothers, who were hunting goat in the ravine," she says. "She forgot her waterskin and drank from a small creek."

"And her brothers?"

"They had their skins, filled with the water from here."

"They didn't drink from the creek like her?"

"No."

"So it's the same as the other deaths." The handful of families we've spoken with said their loved one was out beyond the reaches of the village before he or she became sick.

"No," Matisa says. "It is not the same. Her mother has been ensuring they take the remedy each day."

"All the victims' loved ones say they were taking the remedy—the circle believes they say that to save face."

"I asked the girl. The fire in her eyes spoke her truth."

"But . . ." A sliver of fear jabs at my heart. *The remedy no longer protects.* "But how can this be? When your people discovered the remedy all those years ago, bringing it here was the reason you survived. You said my settlement using it unknowing is the reason *we* survived."

"That is what happened."

"Then how—?"

Matisa shakes her head and is quiet for a long moment.

"My dream last night," she says finally. Her voice is halting, like she's trying to figure her words as she says them. "I am in the woods on my hands and knees, searching for something, as before. I come upon a great fire of the remedy plants. They all burn until they are ash." She closes her eyes. "And then I am buried in the dirt near your settlement." I draw in a breath. It's like *my* dreams. "The feeling I have, when I am buried . . ."

"What?"

Her eyes open and find mine. "It is one of peace."

I chew on my lip. "It doesn't mean what you think." But my voice quavers. Been worried for weeks that my dreams foretell Matisa's death.

She offers me a faint smile.

I take her hand and grip it tight. "We'll figure it," I say, fierce.

She nods, untangles her fingers from mine, and starts down the mountain.

I follow her home, to our beds.

But I know she won't sleep tonight.

The dead in the river sing out. I turn my head to look at the shining waters, where the sun is glinting so bright, it near blinds me. I want to hush them, want to clap my hands to my ears, block out their song, but I can't move.

The fortification walls cast long shadows on the Watch flats where I stand. I see the figure lying in the dirt.

It's Matisa, her skin mottled and bruised, swollen with blood.

In her hand she holds the remedy plant. She crushes it, letting the dust drift from her slack fingers.

I fall beside her and dig, pulling up handfuls of soil and pressing them to her, covering her in earth.

A rush of hoofbeats comes. Gunfire. Horses. Screaming.

The voices of the dead call out.

Make peace with it.

The morning light peeks through the window in the wall above me, and dust dances in a long line, streaming to the wood floor. I push the soft bison blanket down and sit up on my bed. I know without looking that Matisa's bed is empty: I'm alone.

That dream leaves a chill of unease on my skin each time, but this morning it coats me in dread.

I pull on my moccasins and dress quick in the sleeping space Matisa and I share. Our beds sit opposite one another, and an unlit, strange-looking hearth sits at the far end of the room. Its chimney is a long cylinder, and the fire is contained in a metal box shut behind a small, heavy door.

Matisa was raised here in the healer's lodge, away from her family. New members of the circle are chosen as children, and an elder healer raises each child selected. Sokayawin, both a healer and Matisa's aunt, raised Matisa. Oftentimes the new members are family, since ties of blood ensure loyalty, but being chosen so young to such an honor pretty well guarantees loyalty, as well. Everyone protects their vow fierce.

Everyone except Matisa.

She told me about the remedy when we left my settlement. She knew I wouldn't leave without being reassured my people weren't at risk from the Bleed, and she believed we had to stay together. By then, she'd already disobeyed the circle by searching for me. They didn't share her dreams, so she left of her own accord, which was rebellious but not unlike her. Even as a child she'd tested the circle's patience: asking questions about every little thing, wandering off to think on the answers, and skipping her chores.

Sokayawin loves Matisa dearly, so she tolerates her willfulness. It's clear Matisa's always had her own mind. Even if that means risking people's favor.

And mayhap that's why I feel a kinship with her, why we're so connected.

I find her sitting outside, facing the river. I've slept long; the sun is already visible over the far peaks.

I stand before her, my shadow casting her in shade.

"You told the circle about the girl?" I ask.

She raises her eyes and nods. "Meyoni will conduct a quick burial. It is not proper, but it is the way of things now." The circle is sacred, so they oversee such things as sending people to their Peace. Matisa told me there used to be rituals that lasted days; lately there've been too many deaths for that.

"But what did they say about the remedy?"

She shakes her head and stands. "Sokayawin was not in the hall, and I want to tell her first." I raise my eyebrows; it's custom that the circle speaks on important things all together. "And I would like you to come with me." She starts walking.

We're halfway through the village when Tom and Eisu approach. The boys are walking close together, and Tom's wheat-blond head is bent toward Eisu's chatter. Eisu's long, dark hair is pulled back, away from his handsome face, and he's gesturing with something in his hands.

They don't notice us until we're near right on top of them.

"Eisu's showing me a spot in the lake where you can catch bull trout," Tom says in a rush, before I can ask where they're headed.

I raise my eyebrows, and his cheeks pink.

"Make sure you show him how not to lose his line to the

trees on the far side," Matisa says. "If you know how to do that?" She's teasing.

Eisu's mouth pulls up in a smile. "His aim is perfect," he remarks. "He won't lose his line." Tom ducks his head, pleased.

Matisa rolls her eyes. "Go before the day gets hot." We watch them pass, and once their backs are turned, she shares a knowing look with me. I wait until I'm sure they're out of earshot. "Do you think Eisu . . . ?"

Matisa has a gleam in her eyes. "I have never known him to share his secret fishing spot."

We find Sokayawin checking the vine tripods in the gardens, a short distance into the fields. The farmlands stretch out lush behind her, stalks and vines heavy with all manner of vegetables. Matisa says this valley is special, that most soil in the mountains would not grow such things. Here, though, the summers are longer and the winterkill not so deadly. Animals journey to this place for shelter during the harshest months of *La Prise*.

Matisa's people once roamed the prairies, following the great herds and gathering sustenance from the forests and grasslands. When they united with groups to the south and moved here, their manner of living changed. They shared ideas, found new ways of existing. Lots of the plants they grow I've never seen before, and their tools are also new to me. At my settlement, we hauled buckets from the river to water our meager gardens. Here, the water is drawn up from the river by a kind of wheel and brought through a series of ditches to feed the thirsty plants. And they have a couple of strange plowing carts for when they plant and harvest—like the ones we saw in Genya's village. They have tools to sort seeds from dirt and debris, and a building where they gather the crops and clean them for their food storages. Some of these tools run on their own, powered by the river, or, as Matisa tried to explain to me, by water becoming air.

The rhythmic clanking of those tools used to spark fear in me. Seemed too unnatural for them to be running without a hand to crank them or a beast to pull them, but over the weeks I've gotten used to the sound.

All their methods and ways of living are new to me. Different but good.

The gardens, glinting green and gold in the morning sun, stand in sharp contrast to my settlement's sparse harvest.

Sokayawin straightens when she sees us coming.

We cross through the soft soil, the heady scent of green leaves and dirt rising up. There are particular factions of Matisa's village whose tasks are planting, tending, and harvesting the gardens. Sokayawin is not one of them, but she loves to be out here anyway, fussing over the vegetables.

"The squash looks good," Matisa remarks—in English, for my benefit. "This spot was a good choice."

The old lady clucks her tongue in agreement. "It grows better now."

"You changed its planting place?" I ask.

"The soil tires after too much of one plant. They moved the squash from the west end of the gardens." Sokayawin takes a pinch of shredded root out of the pouch at her belt.

Matisa nods at the sprawling vines. "Soon you won't be able to contain it."

Sokayawin levels her a look. "I am used to that." Matisa pretends to study the vines. The old woman sighs. "But you are not here to discuss the squash." She places the shredded pinch in her mouth.

"Meyoni is overseeing the latest burial," Matisa says. "A girl my age."

Sokayawin is quiet, worrying the root with her teeth.

"She was taking the remedy."

Sokayawin's jaw stills. "You are certain?"

"I am."

The old woman holds Matisa's gaze a long while. She looks at me, like she's deciding something. Finally she gestures toward the lake. "Let us sit."

3

OUTSIDE THE GARDEN ROWS WE FIND A SPOT facing the lake. The wind blows strong, stirring up the impossible green-blue waters into white waves, but the sun is hot on our heads and bare arms.

Sokayawin settles back, waiting for Matisa to speak.

"The rumor is true," Matisa begins. "The girl was taking the remedy as we have always instructed. It did not protect her. And I have been trying to determine how this can be." She draws a breath. "Auntie, I believe the sickness has changed."

I squint at Matisa. "Changed?"

"I believe it is stronger now, and the remedy can no longer fight it."

Sokayawin tilts her head as if she is considering this, a worried look on her face.

"But how can a sickness change?" I ask.

"Over time, many things change to survive." Matisa waves a hand as she tries to explain. "Like the mountain deer. On the plains, deer are speckled so they can hide in the grasses from predators. Here in the mountains, their hides are shades of gray to match the rock. They have changed so they can better hide themselves. The sickness could be the same."

My frown deepens. "The sickness is an animal?"

"Not an animal, exactly." She rubs her brow. "But it is alive—we can kill it by boiling the water it lives in. And many living things change in order to survive. The sickness may have done the same."

"The sickness appears as it always has," Sokayawin muses aloud. "And the remedy, too. As long as we have been in this place, the plant grows strong."

"Whether things appear the same or not, something has changed," Matisa replies. "On our journey here, Em dreamt of me crushing the remedy plant to dust, then discarding it, like it is useless. I believe her dream foretold this trouble."

Sokayawin looks to me. The rest of my dream crowds into my mind: Matisa's bruised body in the soil of my settlement. I nod, my stomach knotting.

"Auntie, we must tell our people."

Sokayawin clucks her tongue. "Telling them the remedy is useless could be dangerous. They may lose trust, like *sohkâ-tisiwak* did."

My skin prickles at the mention of the group of abandoners from this village. They left a year ago, fed up with the secrecy of the circle. For reasons unknown to us, they were hunting for Matisa; we narrowly escaped them on our journey here.

"We have no choice. We must tell them," Matisa says. Movement along the shore interrupts her.

A group on horseback is making their way around the lake. As they get close, I can see by the leather breastplates and wrist guards that they are warriors. Huritt, their leader, is at the front. He's a huge man in dark leathers, his long hair pulled back all severe from his face, and on his tall black horse he makes a fierce picture.

"Day and night, they train," Sokayawin murmurs, watching them head west to where the river meets the lake.

"But our battle prowess will not be enough against the Dominion," Matisa says. "And if we have nothing to negotiate peace, the war I dreamt of will destroy us." A somber silence falls. We watch the riders wind along the shore until they are specks in the distance.

"I have been thinking about Em's settlement—the way it was when I found her." Matisa speaks, her voice halting. "Secrets kept her people captive and struggling."

My brows knit while I work out what Matisa means but isn't saying. She's drawing a parallel. In my settlement, one man's secret kept my people choosing fear for years. We guarded our walls against some spirit-monster, punished one another for failing our virtues.

"It's not the same," I say. "The secret in our settlement was created to protect one man's position, and it destroyed him." I can picture the face of our leader, Brother Stockham, the moment I revealed his deceit to my people. A heartbeat later, he ended his own life. "Your healers created a secret to ensure everyone's survival."

"Both were desperate acts."

"But at least yours was meant for good," I argue.

"No matter their reason, secrets can do harm," Matisa says.

There is a flicker of disquiet in Sokayawin's eyes. "You should say all you wish to say."

Matisa takes a deep breath. "Auntie, you tell me that our understanding of ourselves, our ability to see our path, comes from retelling our stories, one generation to the next. But what happens when those stories have been changed— when the truth has been concealed? The healers' circle has not dreamt our path in many years." She looks at me. "And I believe finding Em, learning that secrets kept her people in fear and desperation for so long, was a warning. Our secret was thought to be necessary for the good of our people, but I feel that it has disrupted our ability to see things clearly. Perhaps if we disclose the truth, more of us will begin to dream again, and our path will become clear. We need to tell our people what the remedy is and why it has been kept secret."

I risk a glance at Sokayawin. Her face is calm, but her eyes burn bright.

"You wish to break the circle," she says.

"No . . ."

"We are looked to as leaders because we protect our people with our methods. Disclosing such a thing will change that."

Matisa is silent.

Sokayawin rises to face the lake. When she turns back to us, her expression is grave but not angry. She speaks words in her own tongue to Matisa, turns, and starts back to the village.

I look at Matisa.

"She says I must speak to the rest," she says.

"That notion of breaking the circle won't sit too well with the others," I remark.

She draws her knees up, wraps her arms around them, and sits quiet a moment. "I have been thinking about *sohkâtisi-wak*," she says. "They were right, in a way."

"To abandon you?"

"No. To believe that the circle was not truly protecting our people."

"But you *are*. I mean—you're trying."

"We are failing."

"It doesn't mean they were right," I protest. "They have foolish beliefs. They think the woods outside my settlement are forbidden because they contain something powerful that the circle is keeping secret."

"The remedy plant came from those woods, and we kept it secret," Matisa points out. "Again, they were right, in a way."

"The woods are forbidden because your scouts disappeared there all those years ago. We discovered the truth when you found me—their deaths were at the hands of our settlement leader; it had nothing to do with the Bleed or the remedy plant."

"I know." She sighs. "But I can't help but wonder . . ."

"What?"

"If it was more than mistrust that caused *sohkâtisiwak* to desert us." She chews her lip. "Only one thing prompted *me* to leave the safety of this valley."

She's speaking on her dreams. "Matisa," I say. "They were hunting you—"

"But we still don't know why."

I'm quiet.

"I just wonder." She stands and dusts off her hands. "But these are thoughts I will not share with the circle. My ideas about our secrecy will be enough for today."

I watch her catch up to Sokayawin, my heart clenched tight. Can't figure her thoughts on *sohkâtisiwak*, but as she becomes a small form in the distance, her words from earlier drift through my mind.

Secrets can do harm.

Unbidden, an image of Kane standing on the hill where we said goodbye creeps into my heart. Not telling him what I knew about the Bleed was my attempt to protect him from knowing a dangerous secret. But if I'd been more honest with him, would we be parted right now?

A shadow creeps into the corner of my vision. It's the dog from earlier, lurking near a rock. Her ears prick forward when I look at her. Matisa says dogs were once used for helping to carry things, but ever since Matisa's people settled here, they've kept dogs as companions.

Almighty.

"No food here," I say, showing my empty hands.

She wags her tail.

"Shoo," I say.

She creeps forward, her belly low to the ground. She's so thin—just matted hair and bones. All bedraggled. Reminds me of someone I used to know.

Reminds me I've been deceived by appearances before.

Charlie, the outcast from my settlement, the boy who

betrayed us on our journey here and near got us all enslaved, looked vulnerable like this starving dog. My guilt clouded my good sense when I gave him a chance, took him with us. My anger overshadowed sense again when I punished him for betraying us and left him tied to a tree with small chance for survival. He was all alone . . .

I push the thought from my mind and step forward. The dog shies back a mite but—Almighty's grace—peers up at me, hopeful-like.

"Go on," I say.

I head back to the village. When I reach the outskirts, I look back. She's not following. I wind through rows of buildings, watching children chase each other around, passing by women and men who are doing all manner of work as they sit together in the sun: cooking large game, mending garments. But some of them are in their leathers, which means they've either just finished warrior training or are about to begin. A few people raise their heads and watch me as I pass. It's a bit unnerving, but I realized weeks ago their eyeballing was curious, not wary.

Still, their stares remind me I'm a stranger here, and not a particular useful one so far. I clench my teeth. Need to do something. Anything.

I cross through a gleaming network of buildings, built of large stones and timber, and head for the horse paddocks.

Three boys stand at the far end. I recognize Isi by the way he stands—straight and proud. If you didn't know better, you'd think he was always cross. But I'm happy to see his fierce face. His jaw loses its hard edge as I approach.

"Emmeline," he says.

I nod hello to the other boys, who are checking over their riding gear.

"You going somewhere?" I ask him.

He shakes his head. "Oiling the gear." He waves his hand at the leather effects before him. "Everything needs to stay in good order." For the warriors, he means. "What troubles you, *ankwaca?*" He's calling me squirrely; it's his way of saying I look preoccupied. I frown. My gaze drifts over to Matisa's horse—the one Kane's little brother Daniel named Dottie. She stands in the center of the herd. Matisa said I need a gentle horse . . .

"You wish to ride?" Isi asks.

"It's just . . . well, Matisa's busy right now, but she thought it might be good if I gave it another go. Trying to learn, I mean. She thought . . ."

"Ah," Isi says. "She believes you need a better teacher."

"Not real sure that's the problem. But yes."

"You are looking for me, then." I turn. A tall girl stands at the paddock gate.

"*Tansi,* Lea," Isi says. "Yes, Em is looking for you."

I study the girl—she's a head taller than me and seems a few years older, too. Her hair is pulled back into a tight braid, and her eyes are raven black and piercing. She looks like she could snap me in two in a heartbeat.

She jerks her chin at the horses. "If you wish to learn, I can teach you."

"Lea is restless," Isi says. "She is missing the hunt."

The hunt. Each year after the Thaw, the fastest and strongest *osanaskisiwak* go out in large numbers to hunt the great herds and are gone all summer. They have many other food sources, but the hunt is a treasured journey—sacred—and a way to keep up their skills. News of the Dominion kept them in the valley this year to protect their people.

"How many summers have you gone?" I ask Lea.

"This was to be my third."

"So she needs a challenge," Isi pipes up. "This is good."

I scowl at Isi. He grins. I shake my head. "I tried to learn once," I tell Lea. "Not sure I can be taught."

"Everyone can learn." Lea shrugs as she says this, as if it's common knowledge. She looks me over, and my cheeks grow warm, but if she thinks I'm unsuitable, she doesn't say.

I can feel Isi watching me.

"All right," I say. "Yes. I'd like to learn."

The sun is high as Isi and I make our way across the village. My legs are still shaky from the ride, and my hands are sore from gripping the reins too tight. Didn't go as smooth as I was hoping, but if Isi thinks the same, he doesn't say.

Riding quelled that antsy feeling for a time, but I can feel it starting back up. That feeling that I should know more. Do more.

"*Ankwaca*," Isi says. "What are you thinking?"

I shoot him a look. "Nothing. That's the problem."

He is quiet as we walk out toward a group of boys his age gathered on the flats. He's joining them to practice his sling on the training ground. It takes physical strength and speed; it's not something I can learn. That unsettled feeling rises. I turn to him. "What do you do when you feel . . ." I search for the right word. "Lost."

He raises his eyebrows. "Lost?"

"Just . . . when you don't know what to do next, but you feel like you should."

"I have never felt that way."

Course he hasn't. "But if you did? What would you do?"

He shrugs. "Wait for it to pass."

"But what if you can't wait? What if there's no more time, and people are depending on you to know?"

But he's distracted by something behind me. I turn.

A cluster of shapes is moving along the far shore of the lake. Moments later the blur of movement sharpens: six riders on horseback are coming along the rocky terrain at a fierce pace.

"Scouts," Isi says.

All summer they've been sending scouts out between here and the great river that winds past my settlement, wanting eyes on any newcomers. They sent the first group when we arrived with our news at the beginning of summer, a second group two weeks ago. A third group set out yesterday. Each group is meant to be gone three weeks.

"It's the second group," Isi says, surprised. "I see Keme's ribbons."

We're not the only ones to see the scouts arrive. People have left their tasks and are hurrying to greet the group. A couple of children race out along the flats, hoping to be the first to welcome them.

The six don't slow. They avoid the children by a large

margin and skirt the village, streaming past the gathering crowd.

"Where's the first? Why are these returning early?" I ask.

They ride hard for the west side: the weaponry and warriors' stables. Whatever news they're bringing, they're sharing it with the war leaders first.

Isi is never one for speculation. He watches them, his face grave. "Go get Matisa," he tells me. "I will speak with Nishwa and find out."

4

WE TUCK AWAY FROM THE BRIGHT SUN IN THE shade of tall spruce trees on the riverbank. Isi's eyes are dark and thoughtful. For once, he stands still. It is Matisa who paces, her moccasins whispering back and forth along the needles and grasses. Tom stands beside me, silent.

The scouts reached the Keep: the newcomer settlement Isi and I rescued Kane's brother from during our journey here. They brought news that the first group of scouts is being held captive there.

The Keep was built by men from a place in the east called the Cormorant Bay. They're laying claim to a bunch of land out here without the Dominion's say-so and killing people who challenge them. My skin crawls, thinking on the man in charge: Leon, with the handsome face and dead eyes.

The scouts aren't the first people he's imprisoned. He's keeping women from the east against their will, and he's enslaved some of the abandoners from this place—*sohkâtisi-wak*. Our rescue of Kane's brother was successful because more *sohkâtisiwak* showed up and laid siege to the Keep to free their kin.

"That is not all," Isi says. "They found a young man—pale and blue-eyed. He was alone and did not look well. He was searching for the Keep."

Blue-eyed . . .

"Charlie," Tom says.

Charlie.

I picture his ice-blue eyes pleading with me before I turned away and left him in that grove, tied to a tree. I left him not knowing if he'd survive.

Don't know if I'm relieved or dismayed that he made it.

"He asked for their help in finding it."

"And did they help him?" Tom asks.

Isi shakes his head. "They did not like the look of him."

I feel a pang. I know what Charlie's after. His sister, Rebecca, was taken to the Keep. He's probably thinking to free her. But knowing the kind of man Leon is . . . well, Charlie's got little chance of that.

Tom touches my arm. "Charlie's not our concern," he says.

I square my shoulders. "I know."

"Any sign of *sohkâtisiwak*?" Matisa asks. "I wonder how they fare."

Isi's brow darkens. "What do we care for those who abandon our people?"

"Their desertion worked in our favor," Matisa reminds him.

She's speaking on the fact that Leon's brother, Julian, waited for *sohkâtisiwak* instead of taking us straight to the

Keep. He'd caught wind of their belief about some woods up north harboring something powerful—he decided it meant a cure for the Bleed—and planned to trade Matisa to them in exchange for directions to those woods. The whole idea was foolish—the woods they were speaking on are just the ones around my settlement—but Julian believing it probably saved our lives. It gave Tom a chance to find us.

"That was only luck," Isi insists. "Their dealings with the newcomers could have ended in disaster for us."

"I only wish to know the situation."

"Whatever it is, Huritt will lead a rescue for our scouts. We will not leave them to Leon's mercy."

Matisa shakes her head. "I do not think Huritt will agree to such a thing. Not now."

"Why?"

"Because this valley will require all the protection we can muster." Quick, she tells Isi and Tom what we've discovered. I watch Isi's face grow troubled as she speaks.

"So you can no longer negotiate?" Tom asks.

Matisa nods.

"But can we be sure the Dominion comes to fight?"

"If they do not, they will turn to it once they realize our valley appears safe from a sickness that ravages them. And without being able to provide them the means to settle safely elsewhere and leave us in peace, we are at risk."

Isi's jaw works. "We must tell Huritt about the remedy," he says.

Matisa nods. "I have been in talks with the circle. Sokay-awin will be the one to share the news."

We are silent a moment.

"Come," Isi says to Tom. "We will be needed at training."

"We?" Tom asks in surprise.

"Huritt has a great appreciation for good aim. And we will need every able fighter." He crosses toward Matisa and puts his hand on the back of her neck. She leans into his touch. The gesture shouts their love for one another.

He and Tom go.

I turn to Matisa. "What did the circle say about the rest— about telling your people what the remedy plant is and how it came to be a secret?"

"They have protected its origins for decades," she says, "and we have only been speaking the morning. They need time." Can't tell if she sounds hopeful or defeated.

"But if it no longer works, you no longer have a secret to protect," I say. "Why are they so against the notion of sharing the knowledge?"

She sighs. "I believe it has more to do with admitting deceit. Sokayawin tells me that years ago, when our wise ones discovered the remedy, not all of them agreed that our people could not be trusted with the truth. But louder voices prevailed; they cloaked the remedy in secrecy and encouraged people to believe that only those chosen for the healers' circle could create it. We changed our story; we misled our people."

"And now you think you have to restore the truth to see your way forward?"

"Our world is changing," she says. "The arrival of the Dominion guarantees that. I feel, deep down, that we must know our true history and pass on *those* stories. Or risk losing ourselves in the changing new world."

She turns to face the lake. "I love this place," she says. "I cannot bear the thought of it being taken from us."

I reach out and take her hand. We stand in silence a long while, gazing at the bank where two domed structures sit— willow crossed in a web that creates a kind of shelter—used for important ceremonies I haven't yet seen.

"I'm needed at the circle," she says. She turns to start back to the village.

I can't help myself. "Matisa?" She stops. "Did the scouts say anything about *wihkwetinaw*?" I use the name the scouts gave the village where Kane and his brothers now reside, instead of naming Kane, like it will mask my true question.

"They did not pass by that way."

I nod, fighting a wave of disappointment as I watch her hurry back to the village.

Don't think about it.

A tiny flurry of movement draws my gaze to the ground: a blur, hovering at an orange flower near my feet. It's a bird, about the size of my thumb, with a bright red throat, its wings beating so fast, they're near invisible. It dips its bill into the throat of the flower once, twice. It ignores the bloom of another orange flower nearby and buzzes away.

Âmopiyesîs. That's its name. Isi told me the boys called Matisa that, on account of her being so busy she couldn't be bothered with them. He was wrong. She stayed still long enough to notice him. They haven't declared their feelings in public—there's been no time for that sort of thing—but their love for each other is plain. Reminds me of what I used to have.

And just like that, my heart goes inside out. I sit and pull my knees to my chest. Images of Kane wash over me. The way he looked when he was teasing me, his mouth pulled up in a telltale smile. Or when he was listening to someone else, bending his head to their talk. Or when we were alone: his eyes dark pools of desire, his breath coming quick.

I vowed I'd go back for him, but nothing has been easy since we arrived. And lately I've been wondering if he'll be waiting for me when I finally do return. The image of Genya, the settlement girl who was kind to us but who blushed whenever she looked on him, crowds into my mind. Glossy hair, a glow about her that comes from being loved.

Will he have moved on?

The thought starts a panic in my heart so strong, it feels like physical pain. And now I'm angry with myself. I'm being foolish—not because there's no chance Kane has moved on, but because there's nothing I can do about it if he has.

Still, right now, with Almighty knows what news coming our way, I'd give anything to have him near. I throw a desperate glance west, toward *wihkwetinaw*, where I left him.

The village was safe from the Bleed and well guarded; the journey forward, to Matisa's home, was risky. Kane was no longer willing to risk his brothers' safety, but I couldn't leave Matisa, not when I was so close to the valley of my dreams, not when she and I had risked so much to stay together.

It was the right thing to do.

I need to make sure it wasn't for nothing.

5

THERE'S A FERVOR IN THE VILLAGE NOW. THE readying for war increases, with men and women training all day and provisions for battle being made by all kinds of hands. Word goes out from the healers' circle about the need to take water only from the village source and to boil anything else. The news sets the village on edge, and there are many questions, but the threat of the Dominion waylays any immediate action: no one abandons the valley.

But Matisa believes they prepare for a war they cannot win.

I bury myself in my tasks, creating stores of salves and ointments, and spend my early mornings with Lea, before her war training, trying to ride.

This morning my body calls out its usual protest as I answer her curt knock on our door. Four days of riding and my body has never felt so broken; every muscle in my arms and between my shoulder blades screams out. My stiff legs twinge in agony when I'm not careful—as painful as my bad foot ever was. Early morning is an unpleasant time of day to be tortured, but I can't sit around and do nothing while everyone else trains.

Course, I might never ride a horse proper, neither.

My body creaks as if to echo that thought as I bump around the paddock, all unceremonious and full foolish-looking. Before me, the sun appears and burns away the blue of dawn.

"Keep your arms to your sides!" Lea calls from behind me. "Tuck your elbows, like this."

I throw a look over my shoulder. It upsets my balance, and I grab for the horse's black mane in a panic. The beast stops dead, and I near pitch off.

"Bleed it!" I curse. I right myself, my face flushed. "I told you," I say as Lea crosses the training paddock. "I can't be taught."

"It is not that," she says, shaking her head. She takes the horse's reins under his jaw and puts a hand on his white blazed brow. "He senses your fear. He knows you don't trust him."

I peer down at the ground from atop the enormous beast. "It's a long ways to fall," I remark.

"But that is the problem," Lea says. "You cannot think you will fall. If you think this, he will think it, too."

I raise an eyebrow at her. "Will he, now?"

She points to my leg. "You two are connected. You must act as one. This is why I tell you to look at where you *want* to go, not where you *are* going." She pats the horse's front shoulder. "If you trust, he will also trust. You need to feel the way he moves and move with him. Do not fight it." She gestures at the paddock. "Go again."

"You'll be needed at training," I remind her.

"I have time. Go again."

I click my tongue and squeeze with my knees, and the horse breaks into a quick walk. One more squeeze and he is jogging again. I keep my elbows pulled in tight to my sides this time.

"Give him his head," Lea calls.

I frown before I realize she means to ease up on the reins a bit—he's tugging at them, throwing his head forward now and again. I hesitate. Don't want to give control over like this, but I can also see that being held tight pains him. I loosen my grip, and my heart skips as the beast increases his stride from a trot to a slow run. I expect to pitch off straightaway—the ground is rushing past me at alarming speed—but all at once I realize that this pace is much easier to weather.

The hoofbeats pound out a regular, smooth rhythm instead of a jerky, three-beat trot, and I find my body moving in time with the gait, natural-like. I pull my gaze from the ground and do as Lea told me, fixing my gaze on the wall of a far lodge.

The horse lopes, following the fence line, and as the wind pulls at the loose hair around my face, I laugh with exhilaration. Instead of feeling like an unwanted companion perched atop, I feel us connected through my seat and legs—like we're the same big and powerful animal. The horse pulls us about, and we circle back to Lea.

I tighten the reins, keeping my hands low at the horse's neck as we slow to a trot and stop before her.

Lea grins up at me. "He could feel you trusting him."

I run a hand along his neck and give him a solid pat. He

turns his white-blazed nose back toward me as if to acknowledge it. Can't stop smiling.

"You see?" A voice comes from behind me. I swivel. Matisa is leaning against the fence, smiling at us. "You just needed a better teacher."

Matisa waits while I brush the horse, telling me she will walk me back to our lodge to break our fast.

"Feel like I should name this beast," I say. Matisa flashes an amused grin. "Doesn't have one!" I say, defensive-like. "I asked Lea already."

"You sound like Daniel," Matisa says. "Always naming." I smile. Suppose I do sound like Kane's brother. He named Matisa's horses and acted like they were his own. The mare we found at Leon's Keep—he named her Lucky. It suited her; it was more than fortunate we found her when we did. Mayhap I should follow his lead.

I meet her at the gate and we leave the paddocks, nodding a goodbye to Lea, who is heading toward the training flats.

"He's so big," I continue. "I think Beast might be a good choice."

Matisa pretends to consider this. She nods. "A fine name. But then I think you should name your other friend, too."

I frown. "Who?"

She tilts her head behind us. I stop and look.

The dog is back. She lurks behind us like a mangy shadow. When she sees me looking, she pulls her head up and wags her tail. I sigh. The dog must take this as a good sign, because she ventures close, stretching out her neck to greet me with her muzzle. I stand still and let her get close enough to put her wet nose in my hand.

Matisa chews her lip, again in mock-seriousness. "But what could it be? Beast is already taken . . ." Her eyes light. "You should name her something that describes your bond."

"Our bond?"

"Yes. Her name could be Loyal. Or Love."

"It should be Hunger," I say, frowning again. "And I was not the one who fed her."

"She must have a bad memory," Matisa says, watching the dog nuzzle my hand. I snatch it away. She wags her tail. I sigh.

"Perhaps her name is Hope," Matisa suggests.

"I like Hunger." I offer my hand again, and this time, when the dog comes near, I scratch her head.

"Hunger," Matisa agrees.

Something buzzes at our feet. Âmopiyesîs again: the delicate bird with the red throat. There are small yellow flowers growing up around a rock on the ground, and the bird hovers over the blossoms.

I point to it. "Speaking on names."

Matisa snorts. "They call me that because I seem busy and distracted. But some things must stay busy in order to live."

"They called you that because, until Isi, nothing kept you still." I watch the bird hum over the flowers and fly away. "You're just as particular; those flowers weren't good enough. It doesn't pick just anything."

"That is because it knows the sugars within are not worth the effort," she says.

"Exactly," I say with a bright smile.

A laugh bursts from her. The sound is wonderful; it's been so long since I've heard it. I look at her close. Her eyes are shiny. "You're different today."

She nods.

"You have news."

She glances around us, like she's making sure we're alone. "I think I've figured out my dream."

"Truly?"

"Truly."

"Well?"

"I realized what I am searching for, in those woods." She takes a breath. "It's a new remedy."

"A new remedy."

"Yes, for the changed sickness."

I frown. "But . . ." I say. "You mean, you expect to find it before the Dominion arrives?"

"Yes."

I chew my lip. The remedy was discovered by Matisa's people by observing animals over many years. Finding a new remedy in our lifetime, let alone soon, seems impossible. But the look on her face . . .

"How—how do you mean to find it?"

"As I've always known; we will dream it."

"Matisa . . ."

"If we are patient, the answer will come." She reaches out and grasps my hand. "Our dreams will connect to tell us what the new remedy is." She searches my face, hopeful.

My heart twists. My dreams have been the same for weeks. It seems full unlikely they'll change. But . . .

The notion that my dreams foretell her death isn't one I like to think on. I straighten my shoulders. Does no good to be skeptical, just like it does no good to let fear rule my thoughts. Believing we'll dream a new remedy gives Matisa hope. Better to share that hope.

"All right." I squeeze her hands. "I'll be patient."

6

DAWN WASHES THE VILLAGE IN BLUE LIGHT. THE lodges are silent, peaceful.

I make my way between them, heading for the horse paddocks as I have every morning for the past week. Used to dread these early risings.

But Lea was right: trust is the difference. Weeks ago riding was awkward for me, and horses were intimidating; it feels natural now. My muscles have healed; they no longer cry out when I ride, and it feels like Beast gives me the speed and strength I was always meant to have. On his back is now the one place I feel in control.

This morning I'm desperate for that feeling.

Days have passed with my dreams remaining the same: me burying Matisa in the soil. I told her I'd be patient, but I'm not like her in that regard. Matisa acts of her own accord but thinks it through first. I often find myself thinking on what I've done after the fact; patience isn't something I know too well.

There's been no word from the scouts about the Dominion, but surely their soldiers will arrive soon. And the thought of this valley at war is like a cold hand gripping my throat.

Mayhap that creeping fear explains last night's dream. It was an old one, one I dreamt many times on our journey to this valley. I'm on the Watch flats, my hands covered in soil. Matisa stands before me: herself and not. Glistening bones on one side of her face melt seamless-like into the other half, which is whole and beautiful. Her clothes on the skeletal half hang loose—her hand of jumbled bones that holds the plant is crushing it into dust. She holds out her fleshy palm, the one with the soil.

But last night, for the first time in this dream, she spoke new words.

You must go back, she said, and she blew the dirt into my eyes.

I press on toward the paddocks, uncomfortable questions crowding into my mind. Is my dream telling me to return to my settlement, where it's safe? Is it telling me to return to *wihkwetinaw* for Kane? Or am I so fearful now, so doubtful of my purpose here in Matisa's village, that I just wish it were?

Lea's not at the paddocks, so I take Beast out alone to the river, lifting my face to the breeze and trying to clear my mind.

As I get onto the training flats, I see a group of warriors near the lake. Lea, watching from a distance, waves me over. I urge Beast into a jog.

"What's going on?" I ask as we pull up beside her.

"Huritt is leading them in a training game."

There are a number of targets placed throughout the field.

The warriors are lined up one after the other, carrying weapons: bow and arrows, guns, slings.

They're in their war leathers: gleaming breastplates that cover their chests and backs and the very top of their arms, and leather wrist guards that extend the length of their forearms and end in lashings that cover the palm but leave the fingers free for fitting arrows and handling reins. Some of the warriors, women and men alike, have parts of their hair shaved, and some have cut the front short and stiffened it straight up with grease. Must be for battle, like the markings they've drawn, and sometimes cut and dyed, on their skin. I can see the black and red swirls and lines from here—snaking around their upper arms and up their necks as they rock back and forth or shake out their limbs in anticipation of the challenge.

"You're not taking part?" I ask.

"My group went yesterday."

I search the crowd and see that Tom's among them.

His hair is glaring near white among a sea of dark, and he looks real handsome in the war leathers. He has his two guns: a long bolt-action he took off a man who'd succumbed to the Bleed—found when he was tracking us—and a short pearl-handled one he took off our captor, Julian, when he shot him and rescued us. It bears initials on the handle— JL—but Tom scratched a line through those initials like he was erasing the memory of the man.

I stare at him, pride welling up inside. Before this summer, could never have imagined him taking a map from Henderson—the mapmaker who found our settlement after the Thaw—and coming out after us on his own.

Looking on him now, I can't imagine him not doing it.

A few warriors are outfitted like Tom, but most have chosen bow and arrow or knives. Matisa's people have stock-piled some weapons through trading with other First People in the east: guns that repeat their fire, hand-held explosives, launchers for poison gas. Despite the damage these weapons can do, *osanaskisiwak* are still partial to the quieter methods of attack that prove the warrior's skill.

I notice Eisu watching on the far side of the field. Scouts have different exercises and challenges than the warriors; he's here to watch Tom.

"What is the goal?" I ask Lea.

"They are meant to hit a variety of targets while they run through the course," Lea tells me. "Huritt watches to see which of them hit the most targets. Hitting the target while standing still does not count."

"Why?"

"Because the Dominion have weapons that can kill more than one man at once. Better to spread out and not be fixed targets."

"But why on foot?" I ask. "Won't they be riding?"

"Battle is not always fought on an open plain, like this. We are skilled at moving through forests, but horses cannot always negotiate them safely. It is a good idea to have warriors able to go quietly on foot with good aim."

She points to the first line. "They will go one at a time, moving sideways so they can practice never getting into one another's line of fire."

I watch as Huritt calls to the warriors. He raises his right arm and drops it, and the first warrior, a girl with half her scalp shaved, carrying a bow, darts forward to begin the course. Tom catches my eye and grins.

The girl moves with lightning speed, hitting her first mark, grabbing another arrow from her quiver and hitting the dead center of a barrel at least fifty strides away. She continues sideways, ducking, popping back up, and hitting a wooden circle that swings in the breeze between two posts. Huritt throws a disc into the air for her third target, and as the girl runs, she lets loose an arrow that nicks the side of it.

The next warrior sprints into the course—he's carrying a Westie. His shot nails the first target close to dead center, but he misses the next, the swinging target. He doesn't slow after his mistake, though, just continues, shooting as he moves. The boy after him is near as skilled as the girl with the bow, although for two of the targets he stops to get his bearings.

"Those will not count," Lea remarks to me.

And now it's Tom's turn.

He's a mite slower than the rest, and my heart skips when I realize this, but his first shot is dead on. After nailing the first target, he ducks down and pops up to hit the second and then does a spectacular dive roll into the third mark, rising up on his heels to hit the disc out of the sky. He spins and pulls the short gun from his holster, hitting the fourth and fifth targets in succession as he runs the length of the course. Slower but surer.

Lea and I look at each other.

"Huritt will be pleased," she says.

At the far end of the course, those who have finished are

catching their breath and watching the rest who have yet to have their turn.

One by one, the warriors are waved through. I watch as they dart through the course, running and leaping and firing at the same time. My heart races as I watch them.

When they're finished, Huritt approaches and speaks to them in words that Tom must understand little of. Huritt waves his hands, giving them leave to return to their individual training exercises. He stops a few of the warriors, the biggest of them included, to talk to them, and Tom is left alone as the group breaks up.

I see Eisu approach Tom, his face aglow. He touches him on the arm and gestures back at the course. It's a familiar gesture but speaks of something more. A couple of the warriors look at them and then at one another.

I stiffen, waiting for some kind of backlash, until I remember that's not the way of Matisa's people. The fact of two men together isn't a joke; it's the fact of knowing someone has feelings for someone else

As he passes by, the biggest of the group claps Tom on the back.

Tom ducks his head, pleased. He turns and smiles at me.

And my heart near swells to breaking.

Lea touches my arm. "I'm needed at the weaponry," she says.

I nod. "I'm going to take Beast out."

Tom and Eisu head back into the village together. I urge Beast forward, steering him around the remnants of the training exercise. Once we're past and well onto the flats, I push him into a run.

My pulse races as he stretches into a full gallop. I lower my head and watch the ground rush past beneath us, trying to lose myself in the thunder of his hooves, wishing the sensation could hammer out the loneliness in my chest.

As we reach the shore, Beast slows to a walk. It is a rare, calm day. The lake of my dreams lies peaceful.

I drop a hand to fiddle with the tail of my *ceinture fléchée*. Today's the first day I've worn it since we arrived, since I traded in the clothes from Genya's village for the ones Matisa gave me. Suppose I viewed the sash as a reminder of a life I'd left far behind, but there used to be a time I wouldn't dress without it. I remember Tom's ma weaving his pa a new one in the common room, the candlelight casting shadows on her serious face.

I feel a pang at the memory and frown. Surely I can't be pining for a place I was so desperate to leave. I remind myself how caged I'd felt inside those walls. How little we knew about the world outside. How much of our own histories we'd forgotten. I run a hand down Beast's neck—Matisa tells me horses do not succumb to the Bleed. So what happened to our beasts of burden, all those years ago? The true stories have been lost to myth, to fear.

And all at once I understand Matisa's desire to restore the truth of her people's history. Knowing where you've come from helps you understand where you are, helps you decide where you're going.

A shadow draws my eyes to the ground at Beast's rump. It's following us, slinking along. I turn my head. Hunger pads after us, her tongue lolling. She gazes up like she's reprimanding me.

"Sorry," I say, pulling Beast up short. "Didn't think to invite you."

Her ears perk up at my voice. She ventures close.

How can one small act of kindness have turned her into such a loyal friend? Doesn't make sense. I take the reins in two hands.

Hunger waits to see which direction we'll set off.

I urge Beast forward, and as Hunger's shadow stretches out long before ours, I realize, mayhap it wasn't me who was offering the kindness.

I drift about the paddock, brushing Beast and giving him bits of grass I pluck from the ground beyond his reach.

You must go back.

Matisa's words from my dream return and, with them, the questions. Back where? And why? I stroke Beast's neck, my brow knitted with worry.

"Em!" Matisa's voice breaks into my thoughts. She's beckoning from across the paddock. "I've been looking for you everywhere!" Her cheeks are flushed. "The third group of scouts is back. You have to come see."

"What—" But she is gone.

I race to the gate. She is already far ahead of me, headed off through the village. I secure the latch and limp after her, through the winding rows of houses, past the healers' lodge and toward the warriors' quarter. The third group went out only last week. If they're back already, the news must be urgent. But can it be good?

I labor to catch her, but she's moving too fast.

Outside the training paddocks, half the village is gathering. A hum of voices fills the air. There's a crowd around half a dozen horses—the scouts' horses, no doubt—and the scouts have dismounted. I see Isi's head and Matisa's *moshum*—her grandfather—and Tom.

Matisa pushes through the crowd, and I follow, stumbling over someone's foot and muttering an apology.

We get to the last row of people, and Matisa stops so abrupt I near run into her. She looks over her shoulder at me, a mischievous smile on her face.

I frown in confusion.

She steps aside and drops an arm back to usher me through, giving me full view of the horses and scouts.

A young man is standing with his back to me, short dark hair, rough clothes. But the way he stands . . .

He turns.

And I take two stumbling steps forward and throw myself into Kane's arms.

7

MY FACE IS WET WITH TEARS OF RELIEF AND JOY.
I press it into his neck, my hands grasping at his rough shirt.
I don't remember him feeling this strong. His smell is different, too—like forest and spice. And he's taller? No, his boots
make him taller. I pull back to get a better look at him.

His hair has grown in—short and soft, like dark chick
down. He's wearing those strange clothes from Genya's village—wide brown pants tucked into boots—and it's clear
he's been working outside these past weeks. His skin is
darker from the sun, and his shoulders are broader.

"What are you doing here?" I choke out.

My breath gets quick as he grasps the back of my neck
with one strong hand. Runs his thumb over my cheek. And
the sight of him, his dark eyes so perfect and familiar, weak-
ens my knees. He came. He came for me.

All at once I remember how many people are around, and
I glance at the sea of faces, a mite embarrassed. But I can't
stop my gaze from going back to Kane.

"So glad you're safe, Em," he says, and hearing his smoke-and-honey voice again, hearing him say my name—it's like summer bursting into my heart.

I look to Matisa. She's smiling, but her brow is furrowed. Like she's waiting on the bad news.

Because there must be bad news. Why else would Kane show up this way?

Kane nods at the group of scouts, who are surrounded by various members of their families. "They found us about a day out," he says.

"Us?" I ask.

And I notice the figure on the other side of the horse. She ducks under its neck and offers me a shy smile. Cheeks pink as ever. Shiny dark hair framing her face . . .

"Genya," I say in shock. I look around for the others—for Kane's brothers—but it's just the scouts. And Genya and Kane. I don't understand.

"They brought important news," Matisa says. She gestures toward the warriors' quarter. I crane my neck and notice an even larger crowd gathering there. There's a flurry of activity at the weaponry. I catch a glimpse of Huritt, can see him barking orders. Warriors are gathering. Nishwa is among them.

"What's happening?" I'm still trying to make sense of Genya, here. With Kane. I frown in the direction of the assembling warriors.

"They will ride out to defend our valley," Matisa explains.

Fear stabs through my confusion. I look from her to Kane. His face is grave.

"Against who?" I ask.

"The Dominion," Matisa answers. "Let us talk at the healers' lodge." She puts out a hand to Kane and Genya. "You must be hungry and tired."

Kane nods. He grabs a pack from the ground at his feet and attempts to shoulder it but winces and drops it again.

"Careful!" Genya's face creases with concern as she hurries to his side, putting a hand on his arm.

"You are hurt?" Matisa asks. I can't get my tongue to work; I'm too busy watching Genya touch Kane.

"It's nothing," he says. But he doesn't move away from Genya. "A small cut from a tree branch."

"Em will see to it," Matisa says. She gestures, impatient. "Come."

In the common area of the lodge, I set to grinding yarrow for a healing paste while Matisa finds food and hot tea for Kane and Genya. We have stores of the paste, but I need something to do.

Kane and Genya sit near the hot stove, looking as though their excitement at arriving here has passed and exhaustion has taken its place. Kane slumps in his chair and accepts a plate from Matisa with a grateful half smile. I'm nervous and distracted, and my hands are clumsy. Kane appearing this way, out of the blue, felt like a miracle. Felt like the answer to the question that's been burning in my heart. When I saw him, I thought he came all this way for me. But . . .

Genya watches him close and picks at her food.

I focus on my hands until Matisa clears their plates and explains to me that Eisu spotted Kane and Genya while patrolling the swamp forest east of the lake. The third group of scouts was returning, and he alerted them, bringing them to Kane and Genya's aid.

Kane fiddles with his cup of hot tea and, at Matisa's gentle prompt, begins to explain. He tells us that Genya's village fell under attack from pale newcomers, likely Leon's men. Dominion soldiers arrived and fought off the attackers. He tells us the Dominion have occupied the village now and are using it as a kind of base.

"They've heard about the men carving out their own law out here; they've been ordered to crush any uprising," he explains.

"Uprising?" I repeat.

"Anyone who doesn't abide by Dominion law. Anyone who's settling out here without their say-so."

"Their quarrel is with Leon, then," I say.

Matisa refills Genya's tea, shaking her head. "If they are ruling over land they have never even seen, their quarrel is with us, too."

"That's why Genya and I needed to get here before they did," Kane says.

I frown. "But if they're concerned with the lawless, shouldn't they be looking for the Keep?"

"Leon isn't their only concern." Kane sets his mug down. "When they arrived at Genya's village, they sent men to inspect every home. They were looking for sick people. They'd lost several men on their journey."

"The Bleed?"

He nods. "I think they were trying to contain the sickness, like we used to when people took fever in the settlement," he says. "It's obvious they don't understand it—where it is, how people get sick."

"So . . ."

"They're occupying Genya's village because it appears to be safe. They're real interested in safe places."

I look at Matisa. Her face is grim. "Like this place," she states.

"Genya's people didn't mean any harm," Kane says. "But the Dominion asked if they knew of anyone else in the area surviving the sickness."

"And Genya's people knew of this place because of us," I realize, thinking back to our night at that strange village.

"At first we think Dominion will help." Genya's blue eyes are sincere. "But maybe not. And Kane say they are danger to you. We come to warn." She looks at Kane, and her cheeks go pink.

But why "we"? Why did he bring you? I silence the caustic voice in my head and grind the yarrow harder, thinking instead of the warriors of this village preparing and setting out. Ready to fight. "Can you be sure they'll come with force?" I ask. "Why are they so determined?"

"From what I could tell from their conversations, they believe that the land out here is valuable. There are"—Kane searches for the word—"resources here. They don't want more people like Leon arriving here first. But they're getting desperate, losing men to the Bleed. They were planning to head this way, once they'd regrouped. So once it was safe for us to try, we got out."

"Got out?" I take a pan of boiling water from the stove and set it beside the yarrow.

"They're worried about deserters. No one's allowed in or out of the village."

"But then how—"

"There was a way out near the spring. Genya showed me."

I look at Genya. Her cheeks are pinker still.

"You helped him escape to come here?" I ask.

"And then I come with. To be sure."

Kane nods. He's looking on her with admiration.

"But D-D-Daniel? And Nico?" *Stop stammering.*

"My brothers are safe there, for now," Kane says. "They've taken to Genya's ma, Dorotea."

I should be grateful to Genya for helping Kane, but jealousy is stabbing through me, hot and unfamiliar. I wonder just how entwined Kane and his brothers are with Genya's family now. I turn away, busying my hands with a cloth. "Take your shirt off," I say over my shoulder to Kane.

"Thank you for this," Matisa says to Genya and Kane. "It is good that you came. Good that you warned us. Now our warriors can meet the Dominion before they enter our valley, and Huritt will decide what show of force is best." I know what she's not saying; without the remedy to bargain with, force is all our warriors have.

"When do they ride out?" I ask.

"They have already sent more scouts. Huritt will lead close to a hundred warriors to the valley's mouth the day after tomorrow."

"Will a hundred be enough?"

"Kane tells us there were no more than a hundred Dominion."

But I can hear the worry in her voice. I dip a cloth into the pan of cooling water and turn to Kane, who is half undressed. There's a cut on his shoulder and a bruise the size of my thumb blossoming under the tip of his collarbone. I'm full aware of Genya as I wring out the cloth in the pan and approach him.

When I press the cloth to his wound, he sucks in a quick breath, closing his eyes. "Sorry," I say. Why am I pressing so hard? I nod at the cut. "How did it happen?"

"It was foolish," he says. "That bog in the woods east of here. I tripped over some deadfall."

"*You* tripped?"

"I think he was not being careful," Genya says, looking on Kane with a fond smile.

"At least I didn't hide in a log when the scouts came."

Genya utters a sound of protest. "Big men on big horses! What should I think?"

"You were a trapped hare." Kane frowns, though it's clear he's teasing. "If they'd meant to harm us, you'd have packaged yourself for them real neat in that hollow fallen oak."

She narrows her eyes, but there is a smile on her face. She says a word I don't understand. It's clear Kane does. His smile goes wider, his mouth pulling up at one corner in that way of his. My stomach hollows out.

I set to my task, wiping aside the crusted blood as gentle as I can. I'm trying hard to keep my hands steady, but I'm staring at his skin—the skin my fingertips have touched so light, and then so desperate . . . my gaze traces the bruise along his collarbone to the curve of his chest . . . I turn away, back to the stove, and busy my hands scraping the yarrow together with the water, mixing it.

Matisa looks over my shoulder at the paste. "Good," she says.

"Course it's good," I mutter.

Out of the corner of my eye, I see Genya venture close to peer at Kane's wound.

I clear my throat and ask her, "What's the plan for returning to your village?"

She looks at Kane.

"It's not going to be safe to do that for some time," he says. "And they'll need help."

"Help?"

"Getting their village back," Kane says. "From what I've seen of the Dominion . . ." A shadow crosses his face. "Like Leon, they take what they want." His gaze flicks to Genya. My heart stutters.

Oh. I bite back the sound just in time.

"Matisa," he says, "do you think your people . . ."

"We will help you," Matisa says.

"We'd be grateful," he replies. And hearing that "we"— knowing I'm not included in that . . .

I force myself to step close to him again. I take some of the ointment on two fingers and pat the salve onto Kane's wound as gentle as I can. My hand shakes.

"Genya's village took us in after the drylands," Matisa says. "And you have helped so much, bringing this news."

"Kane is the best kind of man," Genya says. "He will always help where is need."

The best kind of *man.*

When did Kane become a man?

I speak to fill the gaping hole in my heart. "I'm sure it

wasn't easy to leave your family. I'm sure you miss them already."

She raises her chin. "I love my family," she says. "But they do not decide my life."

I feel a bit sick at her words, but looking at her face, flushed with hope, reminds me of the old me. She reminds me of that fierce girl setting out from the settlement, determined to carve a new path but hanging her hopes on the promise of someone choosing to walk that path with her.

When I left Kane at her village, it was because he couldn't go dragging his brothers out, chasing after me. For a heartbeat, I thought he'd made a different choice. He didn't. There's an angry throb in my chest, dark and ugly. I'm not thinking straight.

"I will speak to the circle," Matisa promises.

"Thank you." Genya smiles.

My heart's all upside down.

Focus on what matters.

What matters is that war is here.

"Genya may stay here, in the healers' lodge, for the night," Matisa says. "Kane, I will take you to my family."

Matisa returns from her family's lodge. She raises her eyebrows at me lying on my bed, staring at the ceiling. "You did not wish to walk with us?"

I don't answer. I made an excuse about a task I didn't have and left the common area soon as I bandaged Kane's wound. The wound he got because he "wasn't being careful."

I change the subject. "So, Huritt rides out soon."

"Yes."

"You're worried."

"Yes." She sits on the edge of her bed. "I will go to speak with the circle, but there is not much we can do. With nothing to negotiate with, I cannot help but think it will end in violence."

I lie silent, a niggle of despair eating at my insides.

"He came for you," Matisa says, out of nowhere. "That is one good thing."

Kane, of course.

I frown. "He came to warn your people."

"He could have sent word with the scouts and returned to Genya's village."

"He needed to ask for your help," I say. "Could hardly send that request with the scouts."

"You are not happy that he is here?"

"He brought *Genya* with him."

"She helped him," Matisa says. "And she wanted to come."

"Or *he* wanted her to come."

Matisa gives me a long look.

I flush. "It's . . ." I struggle to explain. "It's just—why else would he bring her all this way?" That look, when he talked about the Dominion taking what they want. "He could've told her no. Could've—"

"So ask him."

"Beg pardon?"

"Ask him why he came."

I stare at her. She says it like it's such a simple thing.

"Can't do that."

She studies me. "Do you feel the same for him as you once did?" Her eyes pierce into me, as though she's searching for the truth deep down in my heart.

I lie quiet a long while, staring at the ceiling and blinking back tears. I take a deep breath and meet her gaze. "No," I say, full truthful. "I love him more than before. So much, I'm not sure I can survive his answer." My breath hitches, and I turn my face away.

Matisa sits in silence for several moments.

"Do not let fear cloud your thoughts." Her voice is no longer mild. "The answer will be what it will be. But you need to ask."

8

I WAKE WITH A START, BLINKING AWAY THE dream.

It was the same as the night before. Matisa stands on the Watch flats, herself and not: glistening bones on one side of her face, the other side whole and beautiful. She reaches forward, blows dirt into my eyes . . .

I sit up and push aside my blankets. It's still dark.

Matisa's bed is empty, but I know this is because she went to see the circle after we talked last night and hasn't yet returned. I stare around our room. My hands fumble for the lantern between our beds, but something interrupts the quiet. A voice? It's coming from outside. Feels insistent. Like it's calling to me.

I forget the lantern. I pull on my moccasins and take my old cloak from its hook on the wall. Pushing open the door, I step out into the moonlight.

It's cooler tonight, and I wrap my cloak tight around me. I glance behind and see the healers' lodge lit from within, glowing warm and yellow in the black night.

The sound comes again, tugging at my thoughts.

It's distant, coming from beyond the village, to the east.

I wander out to the gardens through the blue stillness.

Whatever it is, it's out there.

I'm halfway through the vegetable tripods when it comes again.

A crackling sound. Soft. So soft, seems impossible it's the sound that woke me.

And a light now. Can see it between the rows and rows of tripods.

I push aside leafy squash vines and find a fire, crackling orange in the black of the field. Standing next to it, Matisa. She turns her head and regards me, unsurprised.

The flames are devouring a great stack of sacks. I know those sacks—they contain one thing. The remedy.

She adds another stick to the pyre, and the flames lap up the sides of the bundles, snapping and biting at the sacks.

A great plume of black smoke furls into the night sky.

I edge closer to her. She bends, and I think she is getting another piece of wood but she digs her hand into the earth and takes a handful of soil from the garden.

She straightens and looks at me, beckoning me closer. I force my feet to move to her side.

"We must go back," she says. She holds out the handful of dirt, leans forward, and blows.

I snap my head away, scrubbing at the dust in my eyes with my fists. I pull my hands away and blink, furious.

I'm staring at Matisa's empty bed. Our sleeping quarters are bathed in soft morning light.

‡

Send To: FRA

Title: Heartfire /

03/20/19 07:13PM
From: CEN

There are no remnants of a fire in the garden, no coals or ash.

The morning sun's rays creep along the mountain peaks. I stand in the midst of the tall green stalks and gaze about, a soft breeze pulling at my unbrushed hair. Matisa was burning the remedy in my dream, just like *she* dreamt.

We must go back.

Back. Not back to Kane, not to Genya's village. Back to my people's settlement, where I go in my dreams. Where I'm heaping soil on Matisa. Digging and covering her, desperate-like.

I bend and take a handful of dirt in my hand, thinking of Matisa crushing the remedy plant to dust, holding out the soil instead, blowing it at me.

We must go back.

Sokayawin was standing in this same place days ago when we talked about the plants. About the soil. About . . .

My eyes widen.

I run to find Matisa.

I find Genya instead, alone, in the common area of the healers' lodge. She's sitting near the stove, holding a bowl of porridge. She jumps up as I enter, relief crossing her features. "Good morning," she chirps.

"Where's Matisa?"

Her forehead creases. "They all go," she says.

"Where?"

She shrugs. "I think . . . to . . . pray?"

Pray.

"For the strong people. The fighting people."

The warriors. They're praying for the safe return of the

warriors, who are setting out tomorrow. They'll be at *mis-tasiniy*, the grandfather rock, a place they go for the most serious of talks, the most important of prayers. I shouldn't interrupt them, but I need to say what I'm thinking while it's fresh in my mind, while it's still making sense.

"Thanks." I turn to go.

"Em?" The concern in Genya's voice draws me up short. I look back at her with a hand on the door. "Where is Kane?"

I grit my teeth. The way she pronounces his name. *Kahn.* "Don't know," I say. "But if I see him, I'll send him this way."

I bang out the door and around the corner of the lodge. And near run straight into him.

"Whoa!" Kane holds up a hand so we don't collide. I draw back, trying to avoid the same, and stumble a step. "You in a rush?" The soft morning light is swallowed in his dark eyes. He looks clean and rested, and all at once I'm aware I look a fright. Matisa's youngest sister stands beside him, holding his hand. She looks pleased; likely she's been asked to help him find his way around.

"Sorry," I say, stepping to the side so I can pass. "I—I'll be back."

"Are you all right?"

"Sure. Just—just need to . . ." I reach for the dream, grasping for it. The meaning is starting to fray. "Just need to do something."

"Can I help?" He stretches his free hand toward me.

I don't have time for this. "No," I say. "I'll be back." I brush past him and say, absent-like, "Genya's looking for you."

I hold on to the dream, trying to keep it bright in my mind. When I get around the corner of the next building, I run.

The boulder stands on a bluff overlooking the lake, as though dropped there from the sky. The group is sitting near it, lakeside, away from the wind. Matisa sees me coming from afar and rises to her feet.

She looks to the four other members of the circle and back to me as I hurry toward them.

I slow and stop several strides from the rock, watching Sokayawin and Matisa speak in their tongue. I'm waiting for Matisa to come to greet me, but instead she beckons me forward. "The circle would like to hear your news."

"How did they know?"

"You looked as though to trample us. You must have news."

The women nod at me.

"*Tatawaw,*" Kisew, the oldest and frailest of the five, says to me. She's telling me there is room at this gathering for me, too.

I sit, trying to slow my breathing. A sweet smoke drifts on the air. I look around. "Is there a . . ." I fumble for the word. "A manner of speaking here? A way to go about it?"

"There is," Matisa says. "But I think this cannot wait." She watches me, expectant-like.

I nod. "I . . . I think I've dreamt the answer."

Matisa leans forward.

I take a deep breath. "It's the soil," I say. "It's always been the soil. It's the reason people are getting sick." Meyoni, another healer, frowns. I shake my head. "Sorry, no. I don't mean they get sick *from* the soil . . ." I try to sort my thoughts. I start again. "Matisa felt that something had changed. She thought it was the sickness. It's not. It's the soil." I am met with furrowed brows. My hands flutter up. I don't have the right words to explain it fully. *Start at the beginning.* I turn to Sokayawin. "Last week in the gardens, you talked about rotating the squashes?"

Sokayawin nods.

"That's because soil changes, right? Soil can change, depending on which plants have been growing in it and for how long. We did the same at my settlement: rotated the vines because they took too much from the soil if they were left growing in one place for too long. And . . ." I take another breath, and my hands churn as if I might conjure the right words from the air.

"You think the remedy does not grow here the way it should," Matisa says. Kisew raises her eyebrows at Matisa finishing my sentence. "You think the soil is wrong for it."

"Yes! The plant near my settlement protected you. But when you brought it with you to cultivate here, you brought it to the wrong kind of soil. *That's* what's changed—not the sickness!"

There is a silence. Matisa presses her lips together as she considers this.

Sokayawin shakes her head. "The reason we know to rotate the crops is because they begin to fail. They do not produce what they should. This has never been the case with the remedy. For as long as we have been here, it grows strong."

But I don't mean that it's *failing.* I try to think of another way to explain. "The bittersweet berries Soeur Manon taught me to avoid: those always grow underneath the deadfall of a spruce, and they're poisonous, and she said it was on account of the *soil*."

"I know this plant you speak of. And it may be poisonous because of the soil, but it also grows *only* in that soil," Sokayawin says. "There are no bittersweet berries growing elsewhere that are not poisonous."

"It's *something* to do with the soil," I insist, though all at once I'm less sure. I look at Matisa. "In my dreams Matisa is sick with the Bleed, and I'm putting soil on her. But I'm not burying her. I'm *healing* her. In my dreams Matisa either burns the remedy or crushes it and offers me the soil instead. Could be the remedy *looks* all right, but it's not . . ." I trail off, unsure exactly what I'm trying to say.

Meyoni frowns again, but Matisa has that faraway look once more. Like she's figuring something.

An insect buzzes near my ear. And the sound . . . my eyes light up. "*Âmopiyesîs*," I say. Matisa glances at me, puzzled. "The *bird*. You told me that tiny bird is always moving, so it has to eat all the time, but still, it doesn't drink from just any flower—it picks and chooses, even when the flowers look similar. So how does it know? How does it know which flowers have the best sugars for it?"

"It just knows," she says.

"But to us they all look the same, right?" I say.

Matisa thinks for a moment. Her head snaps up. "Like *maskwa*," she says to the circle, using their word for *bear*. She pushes to her feet and begins to pace. "Long ago, people believed *maskwa* ate tree bark. They observed the animals tearing into the flesh of the tree with their claws and snouts—they would spend much time doing this. But *maskwa* was particular about which tree, and always chose the same kind. Over time, people realized that it was not the bark the bear was after but the bugs beneath the bark. It was not the tree bark that was satisfying its hunger." She looks up at us. "Do you see?"

But I'm lost, and Matisa sees this on my face.

"The remedy is what lives *on* the plants near Em's settlement." Her voice rises in excitement. "Like *maskwa's* ants, but smaller—something like what *âmopiyesîs* detects in the flowers."

"So . . ." My head feels stuffed with wool. "At my settlement, when we eat the plant, we're eating that small . . . thing?"

"Yes! And that, whatever it is, prevents the sickness! You dream of the soil surrounding your settlement because the plant, growing *there*, is the remedy."

I stare at her in shock.

"This does not make sense," Meyoni interrupts. "We have been protected by the remedy, grown here, for decades."

"We *thought* we were," Matisa says. "But what if, when our people moved from the forbidden woods, we moved away from the sickness, too? What if we have always grown a useless remedy but did not know because the Bleed was never in the little waters of this valley?"

Meyoni's eyes narrow in thought.

"Our remedy has never left this valley," Matisa continues. "We never allowed people to own stores of it because we were afraid they would hoard it or trade it. Our hunters are instructed to boil their water on the hunt. But we were never at risk here. Our main source is large water—the river—which explains why we aren't all dying from the Bleed. But the sickness has spread to the little waters in this valley at last. *That* is what has changed!"

I suck in a breath. "Then you still have your upper hand," I say. "You can still negotiate with the Dominion."

My heart races. The *soil* at *my* settlement grows the remedy. We figured it. *This* is why we've stayed together, why we've journeyed all this way. I want to throw my arms around Matisa, but I notice the silence. I glance around. Kisew tilts her head, her long snow-white braid falling across one shoulder. Meyoni frowns yet again. The wind whistles through the spruce at the lake, bending them toward us.

Matisa's triumphant look falters. "*Nisikos*," she says, calling Sokayawin her people's word for *aunt*, "surely you feel the truth of this."

Sokayawin nods, but her eyes are troubled.

"What is it?" Matisa asks, looking around at the circle.

"We do not have the plant grown in the soil of the forbidden woods," Meyoni points out.

"No, but—"

"So we cannot be sure," Meyoni cuts her off. "Perhaps it is not that our little waters finally have the sickness. Perhaps it is still as we feared: the sickness has changed. Emmeline's people may be suffering like us. They could be dying right now."

"But they were fine . . ." I don't finish the sentence: *when we left*. That was months ago. A chill touches my neck.

"No," Matisa says, her tone firm. "They are not dying right

now. Our dreams have fit together." Her tone lifts the specter of fear ghosting around my heart. "Surely you can see that this is the path?"

"Still," Sokayawin says, "we cannot negotiate with something we do not have."

"But we can get it."

"Not in time. The warriors ride tomorrow," Sokayawin says. "They will not risk the Dominion entering this valley."

"So have Huritt pledge our return with the remedy."

"We cannot offer something we do not know works!" Meyoni protests. "If it does not, the Dominion will look for retribution."

Matisa's face darkens; her eyes burn with an inner fire. "Em and I have dreamed the answer," she says, slow and forceful. "The remedy grows in the forbidden woods."

There is a long silence.

Meyoni sighs. "Matisa," she says, softening her tone, "even if this is so, how will we secure enough? We would need control of the land, of the plant."

Matisa looks to me. And I see my chance. "We'll create an accord," I say. "You have many things; you know many things. My settlement would be happy to share in exchange."

"You believe your settlement will cooperate with us?" Meyoni asks. "Instead of their own kind?"

"The Dominion is not our kind," I say, but I don't feel as sure as I sound. When my settlement got word of people existing in the east, the place their ancestors had left all those years ago, there was interest in setting back that way, trying to find kin. My settlement was cut off for generations and became our own kind, but, compared to Matisa's people, we're hardly united. We always kept to our own, unless a Binding across quarters was necessary for bloodlines. We don't even speak one another's tongues. We're nothing like *osanaskisiwak*.

"There is also the issue of *our* cooperation," Meyoni points out. "Our leaders have long feared those woods, have long believed the people there would be a danger to us."

"But if we tell people the truth, that we discovered the remedy in those woods, they will see—"

"We cannot share the truth until we are certain of your claims!" Meyoni protests.

Sokayawin holds up her hand. "Matisa, I can see that your heart tells you this is true. But how will you, Emmeline, convince your people that they should share this important gift?"

I open my mouth to respond but can't find words. How indeed? My people were fearful and foolish for so long. Convincing them they need to share something they don't even understand will be no easy task. But if I am going to be of any worth to Matisa, I have to try. "They'll choose the right path," I say. "I just need time."

"Time is what we do not have."

9

MATISA AND I WALK BACK TO THE VILLAGE shoulder to shoulder, trailing behind the elders.

"I was right," Matisa says, her voice bitter. "Telling a false story has broken our good sense, our ability to see what is right before us."

A wave of helplessness surges up in me. The healers' circle needs proof of our claims before they will negotiate. We need at least two weeks to retrieve the remedy from my settlement. Huritt rides out tomorrow. Who knows if we'll return in time to stop an all-out war? The little voice in my head urges me to hurry. We need to pack, to plan. But all at once I am tired. Bone-tired.

Frustration rises in me. "Why now? If we're the dreamers, why did it take us this long to figure the answer? Why couldn't we have dreamt this before we left my settlement? Before . . ." I don't list all the things it would've spared us. All the heartache and death.

"Our journey assures me we have discovered the truth," Matisa says.

I frown, confused.

"When Isi and Nishwa and I left this place to find you, we did not bring the remedy with us. People feared *sohkâtisiwak* were planning to leave and barter with the remedy; I did not want the same accusation leveled at us. We stuck to the big rivers and boiled our water on our journey to you. When we left your people, we had the tea I made from the remedy plant at your settlement; that is why we survived."

"So our journey is the proof?"

"Not proof," Matisa says. "But perhaps necessary, to help us understand our dreams, to make us certain of them." She laughs, a sad, soft sound. "Or perhaps Tom is right. What does he say? About being able to see what is ahead?"

"It doesn't change what's coming," I say, my voice small. Meyoni's words ring in my head.

They could be dying right now.

The thought sends a deep pang through me. Always felt like I didn't belong at my settlement, always felt scrutinized and caged. And leaving that place was like a weight lifting from my chest. But thinking of them all succumbing to the Bleed . . .

No. We've dreamt the answer.

Matisa utters a sudden, rueful laugh.

"What is it?"

"*Sohkâtisiwak,*" Matisa says. "They *were* right about one thing: there is something powerful in the forbidden woods."

I think on this. "Would they know what it is?"

"I do not think so. They may not even know where the woods are. But perhaps *that* is why they were searching for me: to force me to show them."

As we draw close, the bustle of the village reaches my ears. I can picture Kane walking around this new, strange place and being amazed like I was my first weeks here. I want to show him everything—the farmlands, the lake, the horses. I want to show him how good it is here, but there won't be time for that.

And can I ask him to help us, to come along? I asked him to choose me once, and it near ended in disaster. Not sure I can risk that again. Then there's the matter of us going on account of our dreams—that's something he's never full understood, even though he wanted to. What will he think when he learns the healers' circle believes that Matisa and I are acting on our best guess?

Matisa has slowed to a stop. She points to a small scrubby bush several strides away with a humorless laugh. "We planted it everywhere to make it look like a natural part of the land," she says. "And we harvested it like we do the other plants, so as not to draw attention to it." Her voice contains a trace of scorn.

I stare at the gray-green feathery leaves. I know this plant. It grows wild everywhere near our settlement. Soeur Manon taught me many uses for it: poultices, soup, tea . . . And I realize I've always known. In my dreams I could never put a name to the plant, but seeing it here before me, I know.

I look at her in astonishment.

"You need to know what we are after at your settlement," she says. "In case I am not there."

My blood ices over. "You're not coming?"

"I am coming. It is not that. The legend tells us the dreamers must stay together to find an answer—"

"And we did. We are the dreamers from two different times. The legend says those dreamers will find a way to prevent disaster."

"Yes, but it does not say what happens to them once they do."

I search her face, panic eating at my heart. "What have you dreamt?"

"Nothing," Matisa says. "But we have seen the dangers out there; we know the risk we take."

The image of me heaping soil on her bloodied body swims up.

But . . . no. No. Those dreams are not about her death. I know they're not.

I push back against the fear, shove it way down deep. Our dreams showed us our path. Now we just need to follow it. I take her shoulders in my hands and turn her toward me.

"I know what happens to the dreamers," I say, fierce. "They finish their journey and save their people. And they grow old and lose their teeth and tell stories of their journey until everyone is tired of listening."

Matisa smiles, soft. But the look on her face tells me she doesn't share my conviction. "We need to speak with the others," she says. "Find Tom and Kane. I will find Isi."

Kane isn't in the healers' lodge. Neither is Genya. The idea of them exploring the village together doesn't thrill me, but I'm also a mite relieved I won't need to ask for Kane's help just yet. I find Tom at the paddocks and take him aside to tell him the news.

Straightaway, he tells me we should get packing.

We walk back to the healers' lodge. I listen as Tom lists off the supplies we'll need, but as I look around us, at this village and the people in it, it feels all wrong.

"You shouldn't come," I say, interrupting him.

He turns a frown on me. "That's a fine how do you do. The last time you set out somewhere, you were desperate to have me along."

"It's not that I don't want you along. It's just . . ."

"You'd rather I not go?"

I stop and take his hand. "You're happy here." I don't need to say what I mean; we both know what I'm speaking on. He gazes around us, at the village houses and buildings, at the hum of preparation and anticipation.

"Never imagined being outside the settlement could be like this," he says. "But you did. You believed it all along."

I shrug. "I was a daydreamer."

"You still are." He squeezes my hand. "And I intend to see your dream through with you." He says it firm, without a shred of doubt.

He tugs me forward. As we walk, I study him. He's changed so much in such a short time. It was always in him, this bravery, this hope. It's so much bigger, so much brighter, out here, though. Out where he can be who he truly is.

"And Eisu?" I venture.

"Mayhap he'll join us." But something in his tone, like he's playing at being easy, makes me think he isn't sure.

He touches the butt of his bolt-action rifle. "Anyway, I have to come. In case I have to save your life again."

I nudge him and look over, noticing that the pearl-handled gun with the initials scratched out is no longer in a holster at his belt. "Where's your other gun?"

"Gave it to Eisu."

"Why?"

"We traded tokens." He fishes inside his shirt and pulls out a leather cord. There's a white stone hanging from it, flat and polished.

"Oh. Well, I'm not real sure about a gun as a token. Not exactly romantic."

"Didn't have anything else," he protests.

I smile, thinking on him appearing out of nowhere, all fierce and determined. At the time, I wondered how he could've been so brave as to follow us, alone, with only the pack on his back and Henderson's map and a bundle of tea.

My thoughts stop there.

The tea. He told me he'd brought that tea so it would feel like I was with him. I'd made that tea for his ailing pa, and he brought it out into the wild and drank it every night, sitting under the stars . . .

Tom's voice floats nearby, asking something about horses, but my mind is racing.

The tea was made from the plant Matisa showed me yesterday. My breath leaves me in a rush. I turn to him.

"You remember that tea you brought? Do you still have it?"

"Don't know," Tom says, his brow creasing at the abrupt change in conversation. "I'd have to check my things."

"Can you do it right now? Can you take me to it? It's important."

He looks at me in surprise. "Why?"

"Because," I say, "I think it might be the proof we need."

The little creek burbles, sparkling fresh and clear. I kneel beside it and glance over my shoulder. The little boys who led me here have disappeared.

Now it's just me and Beast and the sun beating down. A form slinks along the bank toward me, her tail wagging all hopeful-like.

And Hunger.

I sigh and stretch out a hand as the dog ventures near. Stroking her head, I look back at the creek. Could use my hand to scoop the water to my mouth, but I'll need to take some back to the village anyway, for proof.

The girl who died from the Bleed recent; it's luck her brothers are too young for warrior training. I found them picking berries, their horses nearby, and we left the village unnoticed.

With everyone so busy with their tasks and distracted with Huritt's plan to ride out, the boys won't be missed for hours. I urged them to show me the creek their sister had drunk from as quick as they could, and they were thrilled to gallop their horses where the trail was flat and easy. I didn't ask them to keep our journey secret when they return— there's no need for that.

Either way, we'll have our answer.

"Here," I say, and I upend my waterskin onto a flat rock near Hunger. I watch her lap up the safe water from the village source off the hard surface. Don't know if dogs are like people when it comes to the Bleed, but I don't want to take a chance.

I look back at the creek, gazing at the polished rocks below the surface. Images of those who've died from the Bleed swim in my mind: blackened tongues, bleeding eyes, swollen faces. My gorge rises.

I sit back on my heels.

Focus.

Taking the remedy prevents the Bleed from taking hold. If it's in you, you won't get sick. Only one small thing gnaws at my resolve: I don't know for certain how *much* you need to take. I used near to all of what Tom had left—it made a strong tea—and kept a small amount to show the circle. I hope it was enough.

It was enough.

My throat is tight. The sun is high—it's past noon—and heat is rising up from the rocky banks in waves. The insects are loud; their humming blends with the burbling of the creek. It's so hot here, another hour and my thirst would compel me to drink. But I can't wait.

Tom confirmed my hunch: he told me that when he set out from the settlement weeks back, following our trail, he drank from the little waters. Can't believe I didn't think to ask before. Suppose I was too distracted with everything: running from *sohkâtisiwak*, finding Genya's village, leaving Kane.

Can't be certain those little waters he drank had the Bleed, but I know this one does. And he didn't ask what I planned to do next, so I didn't tell him.

But Matisa will figure it out. When she hears what I've learned and realizes I'm gone, she'll come after me.

I had no choice. She would've stopped me. She would've insisted on doing it herself; would've told me it's her duty to her people.

But I know this is why she found me, why we dreamt one another. *This* is how I can help. If there's a chance we're wrong about this, Matisa will need to be here to help her people. If we're wrong, they'll need her wisdom, her leadership. If we're wrong . . .

We're not wrong.

I left the settlement vowing to find a new life. I proved Discovery a new way when I followed my dreams and found Matisa. I've learned a new way of thinking on Honesty, about being truthful with yourself. And if I want to define my Bravery a new way and see this journey through like I always believed I would, then here's my chance.

My one chance.

I push the waterskin below the surface of the water and watch bubbles rise to the top as it fills.

I am Honesty. I am Discovery. I am Bravery.

That fire inside me grows as I pull the vessel, dripping, from the creek and heft its weight in my hand. I clamber to my feet and walk to Beast, who is stretching his neck to reach pockets of long grass on the bank. I run my hand over his neck and pat his shoulder.

He blows out his air around a mouthful of grass, flicking his tail at a fly, and his lack of concern is so at odds with everything I'm feeling in this moment, I smile. I find a rock and sit, looking at the waterskin. Hunger crowds my legs.

A sound in the distance reaches me. Hooves clattering over rock. Could be the goat the girl and her brothers were hunting that day, clambering around the rise.

Or it could be horses from the village.

Do it now.

I take a deep breath, tilt my head, and raise the waterskin.

Do it.

Water pours into my open mouth. All at once the coolness feels foreign and scaly, like a liquid snake. I fight the urge to stop it, to block my throat with my tongue, to spit it out. It's just my mind playing tricks. I squeeze my eyes tight and swallow, suppressing a gag. I drink again. And again. I wait.

The Bleed doesn't take hold for hours after drinking infected water. Still, I listen to my body, waiting for any small niggle of disquiet.

"Em!" Matisa's voice shatters the silence.

I lower the waterskin and open my eyes. She and Sokayawin are on horseback on the ridge above, staring at me.

"What did you do?" she demands, hopping from her horse and slipping down the bank. Hunger leaps to her feet and growls, like she's protecting me. Matisa ignores her and presses forward, grabbing the waterskin away. Her skin is ashen. "What did you do?" she repeats, though it's clear she knows full well. Her face is stricken, a mix of fear and anger and a fierce love.

I reach for Hunger with a reassuring hand. "It's all right," I say.

"It is not all right!" She looks like she's not sure whether she wants to hug me or slap me.

"Matisa, stop." Sokayawin's voice booms across the space. "It is done." She sits atop her horse calm, her eyes grave. "And now we will have our answer."

Matisa's hand hovers near the edge of my vision.

"You have to stop doing that," I say, batting it away. We're waiting in the healers' lodge, waiting for Sokayawin to return. She and the others went to speak with Huritt when we returned with our news. That was an hour ago at least, and every two moments Matisa pries one of my eyelids wide with two fingers, looking for any sign of the Bleed.

She grabs her hand back and clasps it in her lap.

At the creek, I showed her what remained of the tea, describing how much there was to begin with, and she confirmed straightaway that I took enough of it. But she was still angry with me most of the way back to the village. She softened when Sokayawin began to speak and likened my running off to the creek to Matisa running off to the forbidden woods last summer. She said we both think with our hearts too much for our own good. She said it's no wonder we found one another.

"I thought you believed our dreams," I tease her.

She sighs, gripping her hands tight together. "I do. It's just . . ." She shakes her head. "You should have told me."

The sun is setting against the lodges, painting them in a rose light. I've gazed at this village many times in the past few days in fear and apprehension, but right now I feel at peace. We can protect this place now. We can avoid the war Matisa's been dreaming.

"We should be celebrating," I say.

"Hmm." She squints at me again.

"I said *stop*."

The door opens, and Sokayawin appears. She enters the hall, the other healers behind her. The women settle themselves across from us. "We have spoken with Huritt," she says. "He will approach the Dominion camp in peace. He will attempt to negotiate time to procure the remedy from Emmeline's settlement."

Matisa and I share a relieved look.

"You, Emmeline, will go with him."

"Me?"

Sokayawin nods. "We believe your presence will help secure the Dominion's cooperation. You will be a familiar face."

"But I'm not . . ." But I realize what she's saying. My skin will be familiar, as will the fact that I speak English as a first tongue. I feel a rush of pride that they think I can help, but my heart beats fast. I'm a sixteen-year-old girl. In my settlement, this meant I was nothing but eligible, of binding age. Could the Dominion men truly take me serious?

"You have said yourself you can convince your settlement to cooperate with us," Meyoni says. "This means you have the gift of speaking with a level head and fair words. We believe your purpose here is to use that gift."

I hesitate. Not sure any of those things she says about me are true. I look at Matisa. Her eyes are shining with hope.

I raise my chin. "Course," I say.

Matisa and I walk back to our sleeping quarters arm in arm, the moon shining on us. Sweetgrass smoke hangs in the air, fragrant and familiar. Matisa's people waft it through the village so the children sleep peaceful. I smile. Tonight's the first night in a long while that Matisa will do just that.

She's stopped fussing around me; the time of the Bleed taking hold has passed, and the worry on her face is gone.

"We will leave the day after tomorrow," she says. "While you ride out with Huritt, we will make our preparations. And when we return with the remedy, the circle will finally tell our people the truth about it—the truth of our history." She squeezes my arm with hers. "Oh, Em," she says, her voice happy. "We figured it out."

"You figured it," I say. "I just made sure."

A tall shape waits for us at our sleeping quarters. Dark slice of hair, arms folded across his chest. Kane—and he's alone, thanks be.

Matisa's eyes get a glint in them. "What's this?"

I hide a smile and shrug.

"Did you ask him yet?" She keeps her voice low.

"Not yet," I say, but I'm feeling light-headed with relief, with excitement. I was scared to ask him why he came here, nervous to tell him about heading back to the settlement. But now . . . now I can't help the foolish grin on my face.

"I will be inside," Matisa says. Her smile is mischievous. "Do not rush."

I watch Kane approach, trying hard not to look like I'm watching him. He's wearing a mix of *osanaskisiwak* clothes and those from Genya's village: a shirt that hangs open at the neck, and those boots. He's handsome, so handsome, moving toward me in the moonlight. As he gets close, I see he looks fit to bust straight through Matisa to get to me. He gives her a distracted nod as she moves past, and he draws up a stride away from me.

"Been waiting for you," he says. For sure he's heard the news from Tom or Isi. He knows what I've done. But the way he's looking at me . . . he's not here to congratulate my Bravery.

"Oh," I say.

"Is it true? You ran off and drank infected water?"

"I . . ." I imagined having to feign being not as pleased with myself as I feel, but looking into his eyes now, dark with concern—fury?—any feeling of satisfaction is snuffed out. "Yes," I say. "I needed to prove we had the remedy before Huritt rode to war."

"So you knowingly drank the Bleed." It's like he can't believe what he's saying or hearing. Either that, or he doesn't want to.

"I had the remedy in me," I explain.

There's a heavy silence.

"You *thought* you had the remedy in you."

"I *knew* I had it."

"Because your dreams told you?"

"Well . . . yes. Not just that. But . . . but I knew."

"You knew. *That's* why you ran off in secret?"

"I . . . I couldn't tell Matisa. I didn't have much time, and I knew she'd try to talk me out of it, so—"

"And me? Did you not tell me because you knew I wouldn't want you to? Or did you even spare me a thought?" His words hit me like a slap.

I step back. "I w-w-wanted to help."

"Right," he says. "No matter the risk."

"There was no risk! I knew it was the answer."

"If you were so sure, why couldn't you tell me?" His voice is so hurt. My heart races, and my thoughts are muddy. This isn't how this was supposed to go.

"I didn't have time. I . . ." But he shakes his head and takes a step backward, his gaze dropping away from me. "Kane—"

He's not listening to me anymore. He brushes past.

I spin, wanting to call him back. The words don't come. I watch him disappear around the side of a building. I turn and stumble forward to our sleeping quarters.

Matisa catches me at the door. She either overheard us or can tell by the look on my face what's happened. She pulls me into the room, squeezing my shoulders. "He will not stay angry," she reassures me.

I nod, but for once, Matisa doesn't know my thoughts. It's not Kane's anger that turned me inside out as he walked away. It wasn't the hurt in his eyes.

It was the look written all over his face and body: defeat.

10

WE RIDE.

In a flurry of thundering hooves, the mountain air whipping at our clothes and hair, we race toward the east end of the valley. The creaking of oiled leather and jangle of our personal effects around me is deafening. Exhilaration and fear mix with the heady scent of horse sweat, washing over me in waves.

It's a fierce picture: a group of warriors streaming across the rocky shore in their battle leathers, eyes and cheeks darkened with pigment, shaved heads bent into the wind.

I'm in the middle of the group, near Nishwa. We ride so close together, a wrong move could be disastrous, a fall could mean being trampled to death, but the warriors aren't concerned; they don't ever make such mistakes.

I try to trust that Beast is taking cues I don't understand from the horses around him, that they're doing the same. But the ground beneath races past so fast, I tighten my grip on the reins and force myself to take a deep, slow breath.

Ahead, the sun's rays creep over the horizon, burning

away the blue of dawn. I'm too nervous to feel the weariness of last night; my pounding heart silences the fatigue that comes from a fitful sleep.

But the image of Kane's hurt face swims before me.

Surely he'll see that I had no choice but to act quick? Surely, when we return from this task, he'll see.

The lake disappears behind us and narrows to a rushing river. We slow our gallop but urge our horses quick across soft carpets of low evergreen and spongy swamp soil. Huritt leads, his back straight as an arrow, his head tilted forward in determination.

When the valley narrows and the sentry points become visible, we slow. On Huritt's command, the warriors break into three groups of thirty.

Nishwa and I are called forward to join Huritt. The groups head off into the hills and forest around us, disappearing silent like ghosts into the trees and cliffs.

And Nishwa, Huritt, and I are alone.

Huritt said this was the best way. Three riders approaching the Dominion looks like a negotiation; close to a hundred looks like a battle. The warriors will remain out of sight, watching, in case it comes to that.

We press on, heading for the mouth of the valley, where the Dominion camp was spotted by the scouts who patrol. The wind gusts down the mountains and against us, whipping loose strands of my hair into my face. I'm wearing a leather breastplate, wristlets, and my cloak, but I have no weapon. And now, without the barrier of armor and horses surrounding me, I feel exposed.

We pass through the high walls of rock, and the land

opens up into grassy, rolling knolls. Smoke rises from a cluster of gray tents at the base of the hills in the distance.

There are signs of life and movement, but the most important of these is the pealing of a bell.

Someone in the Dominion camp has seen us. It's what Huritt wanted, but even so, a pang of fear slices through me. Suppose these men can't be bargained with, after all?

They take what they want. Kane's words. But he wasn't speaking on land and resources; he meant Genya.

Three riders approach, small specks from this distance, and not in any particular hurry.

Huritt gestures for us to stop.

I glance behind. We're only moments' hard gallop from the mouth of the valley, moments from the protection of the hidden warriors.

Still, my heart speeds as we watch the riders approach.

They pull to a stop about twenty strides away: three pale men in coats the color of moss with shiny metal buttons. Their horses' effects are strange and bulky, and they have long guns in sheaths that hang near their knees.

The one in the middle, a bearded man wearing a strange hat with half a brim, raises a hand in greeting. I return his gesture.

There's a brief silence while he looks at me, at Huritt and Nishwa, and at me again.

"We extend the protection of the Dominion," the man calls, his accent strange to my ears, "to all who are peaceful."

"*Osanaskisiwak* welcome all who are peaceful on this land," Huritt replies in English, his voice booming across the empty space.

The Dominion soldiers exchange a glance.

The bearded man clears his throat and draws himself a little higher. "What is the nature of your visit?"

I look to Huritt for a cue. He nods.

"Got something important to speak on," I say. "And we'd like to speak to the man in charge."

The bearded man's eyebrows go up. The other two shift on their horses. It's clear they can't figure what I'm doing in the mix or why I'm speaking.

"I lead these men," the bearded man says. "How can I help you?"

"Think we can help you," I say, and look to Huritt.

As we ride toward the cluster of tents, I notice rows of shabby wooden crosses at the base of the hill nearby. They've been put up hasty, marking mounds of freshly dug earth.

The leader, who introduced himself as McKern, interrupted halfway into Huritt's explanation of our purpose and invited us to his camp to discuss the matter. Seemed he only needed mention of the Bleed to believe we had something valuable to say.

Huritt was wary but accepted the invitation. I'm guessing because it's the friendly thing to do and also because we might see the Dominion's weapons up close. Getting into their camp is a chance to find out what we're up against. When the Dominion men turn to lead the way, I see him signal to the hidden warriors to stay put.

I watch this McKern as we ride, unable to decide my impression of the man. Doesn't have Leon's dead eyes, that's certain, but there's a formality to him that unnerves me a mite.

Reminds me too much of Council.

We smell the camp before we reach it. The mingling odors of sweat and waste and cooking are familiar. Smells something like my settlement, I realize, but stronger. Worse.

We pass by dingy tents and men who look at us, curious. They're dressed in that green color with strange small caps and clunky boots. My gaze is drawn to two large crates piled high with ammunition—large orbs and cylindrical shells. We pass by the next tent, which is open, and I see rows of belts and jackets. And masks. The kind Nishwa was wearing when he arrived at my settlement; the kind I learned were to protect against a poison gas that could scramble your mind, tear apart your insides.

A chill lights on my skin.

The commander and his men dismount before a large tent. As we follow suit, I notice that Huritt's face is creased in disgust at the smell in the air.

Nishwa takes Beast's reins from my hand, looking amused. "At least we will know where they are at all times," he says, low.

McKern signals to his men to take his horse away. "Please," he says, sweeping his arm to open the door of the tent. "We can talk inside." He glances about the camp with a bit of disdain. "Away from this mess."

"My trainer will stay here with our horses," Huritt says.

"If you wish."

I duck past McKern, relieved to know Nishwa will be our

eyes outside. Inside, a hearth like the kind in Matisa's village sits in the middle of the tent, its chimney extending out the top. There are chairs and tables, one of which is cluttered with rolled parchments. Maps, no doubt.

"Coffee?" McKern walks past us and reaches for a shiny urn on top of the hearth.

Don't know what that is, but Huritt declines, so I do, too.

"Awful brew," McKern admits. He pours himself a cup, gesturing to the chairs.

"Please sit."

We settle ourselves across from him, Huritt's huge frame dwarfing the chair beneath him.

"So, you have information about the Bleed," McKern says, looking at each of us in turn. It's clear he's set aside his doubts about my authority.

Huritt nods.

"And you think it can help us?"

"Yes."

The man's face is serious. "Tell me."

"We have a few questions first," I break in. "If you don't mind."

McKern frowns, but his lips quirk. "Such as?"

"What's your purpose here?"

"Purpose?"

"Why have you come?"

He frowns, like I've asked something foolish. "The Dominion is expanding west," he says. "This wild land will be tamed under our rule."

"Tamed. How do you mean?"

"We'll bring law and order. At last."

"The only unlawful types I've seen came from the east," I say. "There are men in a Keep north of here killing and slaving people, keeping women—"

"The men you speak of are here without the sanction of the Dominion."

"Is this land yours to sanction?" I ask.

McKern measures me a long while. He tilts his head. "Young lady, we will deal with the troublemakers."

"Not dying at the rate you are."

A muscle moves in his jaw.

"Saw that burial ground," I say. "And we know you're occupying that village to the east because it's safe from the Bleed."

He sits back and takes a long drink from his cup, his eyes watching me over the rim. He pulls it away and turns his attention to Huritt. "You were saying you could help us?"

"You are looking for safe land," Huritt replies. "This is why you arrive at our valley."

"We've heard there are First People out here, thriving."

"We can help you do the same."

"How?"

"We have a remedy that protects us from the sickness you suffer."

The man holds Huritt's gaze, trying to keep his face neutral, like he's weighing the truth of the words. But his eyes are bright, and his breath seems shallow.

"Go on," he says. The look on his face is more than interest; it's desperation.

Just like Kane said.

"We are willing to share it with you."

The man tilts his head. "In exchange for what?"

"We wish to rule ourselves."

There's a long silence. McKern looks over at me. "Where did you say your family's settled?"

"I didn't," I say. "But I'm proof these people mean you no harm; they only want to be left to their land and ways."

He takes another long drink. He sets his cup down, careful. "If we agree to these terms, you will share this 'remedy'?"

"If you pledge to stay out of our valley," Huritt answers, "we will bring it to you."

"In three weeks' time," I amend.

McKern looks at me, surprised. "Why three weeks?"

"The remedy takes time to prepare."

"You're telling me you have none at your disposal?"

"None to share, no." None at all, but I don't want him to know that the valley's water source, the giant river, is still safe—that the people survive without the remedy so long as they stay away from the little waters in their valley.

He presses his lips together. Takes a drink from his cup. Swallows.

"You have two." He states it as a fact.

"Beg pardon?"

"You have two weeks."

I stare at him. Asked for three as a fail-safe, in case we are delayed on our journey, but this arrogant dismissal of our request . . .

Anger springs up in me. "You think you're in a position to make demands?"

"Are you?" he asks. "Surely you noticed our weapons cache when you arrived."

My skin flushes hot. "You're threatening us?"

"I'll do what it takes to protect my men."

"You even think about moving into our valley—"

"Enough!" Huritt's deep voice is like a roll of thunder in the tent. He puts a hand on my shoulder. I duck my head, cheeks flushed. He addresses McKern. "We desire the same thing: survival. What troubles you that you must speak of violence?"

"I wonder about this delay. I wonder if you're not bartering for time for another reason."

And all at once I'm angry with myself for losing control. We prepared for this. The healers' circle predicted that the Dominion would require an act of good faith, a guarantee that we're not feeding them a lie to get close and learn their weaknesses, give ourselves time to organize.

"You need to know that we speak the truth," Huritt guesses.

"I'd be more at ease with better assurances, yes."

I look to Huritt. He gives a slight nod.

My stomach clenches tight, but I force the words out. "Boil your water," I tell McKern. "The Bleed lives there. Boil the water you use, but especially what you drink."

He sets down his cup in surprise. "The water."

"It's a short-term solution," I explain.

He looks at Huritt and back to me. "None of it is safe?"

I avoid answering his question direct. "Can't tell until it's too late. I wouldn't take chances. Boil your water, and the deaths will stop."

There's a long, heavy silence.

He glances at the cup in his hand. "Suppose I should be

grateful this is always burnt," he mutters. He looks back to Huritt. "All right. We'll wait for your remedy. But I ask that you make haste."

"We will try our best to return in two weeks," Huritt says. "But I must know that you can make this promise of peace. Do you speak for all of your people?"

McKern smiles. "You have something everyone wants. It's safe to say yes, I most certainly do."

We race back to the village, like a dark cloud rumbling through the valley. The mountains are sharp lines etched against a cloudless blue sky, and I feel like an eagle, climbing high above them on the wind's currents. My heart soars, and my blood thrums in time with the pounding of Beast's hooves.

The valley will have to remain on guard, of course. Our act of good faith was necessary, but it leaves us more vulnerable. Now that McKern knows how to survive, *osanaskisiwak* need to remain vigilant in case he gets skittish waiting around and goes on the offensive.

Huritt didn't full trust the man, so he's unlikely to spare too many warriors for our journey back to my settlement. The task ahead of us looms giant like a mountain.

But I don't want to think about tomorrow right now.

I want to enjoy the rush of mountain air through my hair, my skin flushed with exhilaration. I want to stay in this feeling of being alive right down to my bones.

The warriors around me feel it, too, and as we reach the lake and clatter along the shore, a cry of victory rises up around me. We thunder onto the flats near the gardens, the riders' voices calling our safe arrival out to the village.

Within seconds, the call is answered. People appear at the outskirts, running out to greet us with cheers.

Huritt signals for us to slow and then stop, which lets the crowd stream around us, eyes bright and faces happy.

I search for Kane and Matisa in the crowd. For Tom and Isi.

The crush of people engulfs us. The people call out in their tongue, embrace the warriors, and offer us small gifts of food and water.

"Em!" Matisa is suddenly at my side, her face elated.

I swing down beside her, and she grabs me into a fierce hug.

She pulls back. "All is well?"

I nod, breathless. "It worked."

Again I scour the crowd for Kane. Tom's blond head is among a sea of dark; the warriors who've returned are jostling good-natured with the warriors who stayed behind.

Lea appears. "I'll take Beast and dress him down," she tells me. "You should rest up for tonight."

I frown. "Tonight?"

She nods. "There will be a ceremony that celebrates our victory and asks for bravery and strength for us in the journey ahead."

I don't reply, because I see him. Standing on the outskirts of the crowd, Genya at his side. She smiles and waves. Kane gazes at me, relief plain on his face.

I wave back, hoping he'll come forward, dreaming, for a

moment, of him pushing through the crowd and pulling me into his arms.

But he just nods, a small smile pulling up one side of his mouth. Like he's happy for me, mayhap? He doesn't move.

"Come." Matisa puts an arm around me and leads me through the crowd, joining the dozens of people who are chattering and smiling, escorting their family members back to their homes. It's everything Matisa and I have been hoping for. And being a part of the crush of people, the cheers of victory and relief, fills me with pride.

Only one thing's missing.

11

THE NIGHT AIR IS ALIVE WITH VICTORY. WE dress in the best clothes we have. I'm in a bright, beaded tunic Sokayawin gave me. It's heavier than anything I've ever worn, but the beads shimmer and catch the lamplight, and I know it looks real nice.

Matisa wears a dress beaded with dazzling silver and red. She braids her hair back from her face and ties it with a beaded band. She looks hopeful. Joyful.

I should be, too.

We're headed out tomorrow with a clear purpose. Matisa's people are safe for now. Huritt has even allowed Lea and two other hunters to accompany us, under the condition we find out whether or not the first group of scouts is alive. Eisu's request was also granted, on account of him finding Kane in the woods, helping to bring the news of the Dominion's presence nearby. There are eight of us: Matisa and Isi, Lea and her hunters—Amo and Bly—me, and Tom and Eisu. There might even be nine, if Kane decides to join us.

But right now that feels unlikely, and it's what keeps me from sharing Matisa's joy.

I trail after her toward the center of the village, toward the crowd of people gathering, humming with energy.

The space is aglow with a huge bonfire and everyone in fancy dress. Drums bang out a quick rhythm, and voices call out in song as dancers move in the circle. The air is thick with the familiar smell of burning sweetgrass.

Straightaway I lose Matisa in the crowd and, after a few minutes, give up looking for her. I wedge myself in closer to the fire to watch. Several men are singing and drumming on the far side of the circle, and women dance in the middle. Across the circle, I see Genya and Tom with Eisu. No Kane.

I force my gaze back to the center of the circle—to the dancers, turning and stamping. Dozens of little bells on the women's dresses jingle in time with their quick steps. Matisa tells me that only certain women can dance in those dresses, that the dance is a sacred act. The woman nearest to me closes her eyes as she lets the music wash over her.

This is a celebration of bravery and hope. But my courage from before—that bravery I felt heading off to the creek alone—I can't find it.

Others feel courageous; I can see it on the faces around me. It's in the air, in their bodies. I study the women before me. One in a bright silver dress turns in a circle, and the other women twirl and stamp around her, a mesmerizing blur of color and movement and heat and skin. They're losing themselves, opening their hearts and letting the music fill them.

The drums are dwindling, and the dancers are changing

out when I feel him beside me. I take a deep breath and look over.

He's changed into a new shirt—the blue favored by Matisa's people—and someone has gifted him a necklace of leather and bone. It hangs against the hollow of his throat. I look down. He's changed out his boots for moccasins, like the rest of us. Like he used to wear.

For a moment I'm back at the Harvest Dance last fall. I'm back inside the stuffy walls of the ceremonial hall, the tin flutes and fiddles playing loud, people laughing and talking. Standing in my ma's dress, feeling light-headed. Hoping Kane will ask me to dance.

I see Genya gazing at Kane from across the circle. He smiles at her, raising a hand. She flashes a relieved smile back.

My heart drops.

"It's not what you think," he says.

"I think nothing," I say, watching the new dancers take their place at the center of the circle.

"That's not true." He's willing me to look at him.

I drag my gaze to his handsome face. "You think you know my thoughts?"

"I did once."

I swallow hard.

"Can we . . ." He gestures to the back of the crowd.

Is he coming to make amends? He doesn't look angry. I thread my way through the crowd, my heart beating fast.

Outside the circle of the dancers, away from the glare of the bonfire, the night is still. The stars are brilliant above. We turn so that we can see the gathering—hundreds of dark shadows reaching toward the glaring light of dance and song. Hunger appears from the shadows of the nearest building and pads over to me. Kane takes a quick step back.

"Still getting used to these animals," he says.

I reach out a hand to touch her head.

"Is she yours?"

I keep my gaze on Hunger. "As much as anything is mine." I straighten up and look back at the festivities.

From here, I can see Tom's blond hair standing out like a beacon. I catch a glimpse of Genya, craning her neck to see our side of the circle.

"She'll wonder where you've disappeared to," I remark.

He doesn't respond, and I regret bringing it up again.

The silence stretches between us, not full comfortable. But the fact that he's here, wanting to talk, makes me bold. I'm running out of time to do what I should've done straight-away.

"We leave at first light," I say.

"Yes."

I force my voice steady. "Yes, *we* leave?" I ask, gesturing between us.

He's quiet. My heart beats fast.

"Huritt won't spare many warriors to our journey," I say, "in case the Dominion goes back on their word. We—" I press on while I still have the courage. "We could use you."

"Use me," he repeats.

I stumble on my words. "Y-y-you still have family at the settlement—they're respected. You could help me convince them to help *osanaskisiwak*."

"That's why you want me along?"

No, I want you along because I can't bear to be without you.

But the look of defeat on his face when he knew what I'd done, and the uncertain furrow on his brow right now . . . I can't say it.

"I know I'm asking a lot," I say. "And if you can't, it's all right. It's just . . ."

"It's just what?"

"I know you want to make sure Genya's village and your brothers are all right. You risked a lot to come here."

"I came here because I was sure you'd want me here," he says, frowning. He clears his throat. "But mayhap I made a mistake."

My heart stutters. "Why would you say that?"

He sighs. "Because I can't figure what you did, Em. And you know I don't understand it. But I'm wondering if that matters to you."

"What do you mean?"

"Just that certain things seem more important to you than . . ." His eyes are black in the shadows. "Us understanding one another."

"Course I want us to understand each other!"

"You sure about that? I left our settlement for you. I would've followed you anywhere if not for my brothers. And you run off to risk your life for Matisa's people and don't give me the courtesy of a thought?"

"That wasn't—"

"Or am I supposed to be glad you didn't outright lie to my face?"

A rush of anger fills me. "You want honesty? You want to understand one another? How about telling me why Genya's here? How about explaining why you needed to take her away from the Dominion men?"

His face is dark. "It's not what you think." It's the second time he's told me that.

"No? You're telling me you didn't care that she might've chosen one of them?"

"I didn't want one of *them* to choose *her*."

"It's the same thing."

"It's not the same thing at all. You of all people should know that."

What does he mean? Tears well. My head feels stuffed with wool. "You wanted her to be able to choose you?"

"Em. Not *me*." He shakes his head. "I wanted her to *have* a choice."

"What are you speaking on?"

"Exactly what I told you: they take what they want. Didn't want her to have to be part of that."

I draw back. I thought he meant the men were a threat to *him*, to what *he* wanted. But it sounds like what Elizabeth Sharapay—that mapmaker we came upon months back— had said about what was happening at the Keep: the women not having a choice to have families with the men. It gave me shivers then, thinking on that. So if Kane was trying to keep Genya from being forced into something she didn't want, can I fault him for it?

"Does *she* know that?" I ask.

"If you're asking if I ever gave her the notion we were anything more than friends, no, I didn't." He pauses. "Is this why you didn't tell me what you were doing? Because you thought I'd changed my mind about us?"

"Have you?" The words come out in a rush. Finally.

He's quiet a moment, looking at me. "Is this why you didn't tell me?" he asks again.

His non-answer makes my stomach clench. Is he hoping I say yes? Would it explain what I did in a way he'd understand—a way he could forgive?

It's not the whole truth. Even if I'd known his true heart in that moment, I would've done it anyway.

And I'm done with lying to people I love.

"No," I say simple. "I did it because I had to."

He is quiet. When he speaks, his voice is so soft, I near miss the words. "I see," he says.

A rush of blood fills my ears. No use trying to explain. "Kane . . ." *Say it.* "I want you there tomorrow. With us."

"You sure about that?"

"Yes."

He's quiet, his dark eyes searching my face. "I don't know, Em," he says, and my heart falls through my feet.

And now I'm angry. I'm angry he can't see how important this is to me, angry he can't accept that what I did wasn't about me and him.

"Kane?" The voice comes from behind me. *Kahn.* "You were gone," Genya says, coming up alongside me. Her face is uncertain.

Can't bear this. Can't bear the look on his face. "You should take Kane back to the dancing," I say.

"Yes?" She looks at him, shy.

"Yes." *Take him. Comfort him. Be someone he can understand.* The voice in my head is caustic, biting. Tears threaten to spill. I turn away before Kane can see them, and I call for

Hunger. She and I retreat, back behind the first row of buildings, away from Kane and Genya. Away from the merriment and color.

I need shadows right now.

I sit with my back to a lodge and pull Hunger toward me, burying my face in her soft fur.

Don't cry.

It's foolish to cry.

I run my hand along Hunger's rib cage—once protruding something awful but now hidden by a layer of healthy fat. Matisa always rolls her eyes at me, saving bits of my dinner for Hunger, since we feed her every morning regardless. It's foolish and unnecessary, but isn't that just the way when you're thinking with your heart?

I've changed, I know, since leaving the settlement's fortification walls. We both have. Kane is not the carefree boy I fell for in the settlement, the boy who followed me out into the woods and kept my secrets from Council without even knowing full why. We parted after the Thaw because he had a new responsibility—his brothers—and I was on a path he couldn't walk. Still, I always believed we'd find our way back to each other because we both wanted to.

But mayhap he's right: mayhap understanding each other isn't possible anymore.

I push to my feet and stumble back to the drums and voices. I press through the crowd, mumbling apologies, aiming to be right in the middle of the song. Aiming to let it fill my hollow insides. When I get close to the center of the circle, I stop.

The drums and voices flow over me.

I push every thought from my mind, asking for strength for tomorrow. Whatever Kane decides, I need to see this through for something bigger than us. Bigger than me.

The firelight flickers, casting long shadows against the dancers who are spinning, spinning. The drums pound and echo through my heart, my blood. And now, though I can't understand the words, I feel the meaning in the song. It's about strong hearts and minds. About bravery.

The sound fills the space around me, settling on my skin, like armor, sinking into my heart. Covering me. Filling me. Protecting me. Telling me I am brave.

I let it pierce me through and hit something way down deep in my core.

The voices blend together like one, and the melody rises like the flames of the fire.

My heartfire burns bright, answering the song.

12

WE SET OUT FOR THE NORTH END OF THE VALLEY.
Isi leads. We are laden with supplies—not so much that
we're weighed down, but surely prepared for anything we
might encounter. When we reach the river that runs past the
Keep, Isi and Bly will leave us; they'll find out what's happened with the imprisoned scouts while we continue to my
settlement. I lift my chin to the wind as we climb high into
the peaks, fix my gaze on the pass Matisa was just speaking
on.

But my thoughts race back to leaving the village, to our
departure. To the crush of people wishing us well. To me
searching the crowd for Kane. To him, finally, appearing on
one of Lea's horses, outfitted in *osanaskisiwak* leathers. Ready
for the journey.

My heart wanted to leap from my chest. I waited for him
to look at me, waited for him to see my relieved smile. But he
didn't meet my eyes.

Genya did, of course, offering me a sincere goodbye, her
face full of heartbreak.

Sokayawin has offered to take her in. Genya will be our go-between with her village when we return with the remedy. That idea pleased her, but our departure—Kane's departure—didn't.

She stood at the edge of the crowd beside Sokayawin, watching us mount up, her face stricken. And then, as we bid our final farewells, she hurried forward and pressed a little white cloth into Kane's hand, a handkerchief with colorful threads sewn on it. I watched Kane, looking so fierce in his leathers, reach down from his horse and take it from her. He tucked the kerchief into his saddlebag and smiled at Genya, and I wondered what Genya thought she was imparting with that token. She put a hand to his knee in farewell.

And I looked away, wishing I knew what it meant that he was coming.

I glance at Hunger slinking along the path, far out of reach of the horses' hooves. There was no dissuading her, and I didn't feel right about leaving her back in the village, with no one looking after her. But I'm glad she's here. I'm glad for her ears that prick up and her tail that wags when I call her name. Glad for her kindness.

Wouldn't want to be feeling what Genya's feeling right now. And mayhap I should just give up wondering about Kane, so I never have to feel that way.

Matisa turns in her saddle, breaking into my thoughts. She points at two peaks before us. "The pass," she says again.

I look to the wall of rock ahead. From here, the mountains look impassable. And yet, just over them to the northeast, lies a humble place I once was sure would be my whole world forever. The world is so much bigger now, and when it opened up, I never thought I'd go back to the settlement. Being truthful, I never thought I'd see it again. Or mayhap I hoped that I never would.

One thing's for sure: I never thought I'd be headed back to it feeling this alone.

Hours pass, and I still can't see how we'll manage our way around the wall of rock before us. The closer we get, the more impossible it seems. Just when I'm sure Isi is leading us into a dead end, I notice a crack in the mountainside.

And, as I'm eyeing it, he disappears.

Matisa turns back and smiles at my stunned face. "There is a reason we do not guard our boundaries to the north like we do to the east," she says. "Finding the passage is almost impossible unless you know where to look."

And, sure enough, the riders ahead of us seem to walk straight into the rock as they approach the fissure. When Beast is twenty strides away, I see it's a trick for your eyes; the walls of rock overlap, looking as one, but a path winds between them, a narrow space just wide enough for a single horse to traverse. We cross between shoulders of tall rock, and the path begins to climb upward.

As we get higher into the pass, up onto the spine of the mountain, the foliage gets sparse, dwindling into carpets of fragrant, low-growing greens. Brilliant orange lichen coats the rocks. The wind blows fierce, chilling us straight through, though the sun beats on our heads without mercy.

"Protect yourself," Matisa calls to me. "The sun is far stronger than it feels here."

I pull my hood up, feeling cold metal dig into my skin as I fasten my cloak at my neck. Lea gave me a whistle before we headed out—one to Tom, too. Said it was to call our horses if they ever broke tether and wandered too far overnight. Nobody else has whistles, but they can all whistle shrill and in various tones—it's how Matisa and the boys talked to one another when they found our settlement last fall.

I can't whistle to save my life. Tom can, but Lea must've assumed he was like me: not as equipped as the others and needing a bit of help. He didn't say anything, just accepted the whistle gracious-like, though I'm not sure he brought it along. He won't need it the way I might.

I press the cold metal against my skin. I wonder if I could train Hunger to come to it, too. She's still keeping pace with Beast, but, looking at her small form, I have to wonder if she'll truly be up for this journey.

We traverse the pass, hoods up, scarves of soft leather covering our noses and mouths. The wind blows strong, and dust kicks up, coating our arms and hands. The mountains here are menacing creatures—sheer cliffs with deadly drops. Up ahead, I see one of Lea's two hunters, Amo, struggling with his horse, who's shying and dancing, tossing its head.

"Lea said that mare would be trouble," Eisu remarks from behind me.

I nod. Lea wanted Amo to bring a different horse. She said that the beast was too skittish, but Amo insisted. My pulse races as I watch the horse rear and slip on the shale. Amo tightens the reins and barks a command. The mare dances another few steps, then drops her head and rejoins the line of animals. Amo doesn't look rattled, but I'm suddenly glad for Beast's calm manner. I'm adept at riding now, but I'm not sure I could handle a horse like that.

High on a shelf to my right, I spot white dots moving along a steep incline.

"Goats?" I call to Matisa, gesturing to the creatures. They are also new to me, but they're similar to the sheep we had in the settlement, and sheep are dumb as sticks: forever wandering off cliffs and stumbling down ravines and breaking their legs in the river. It's why they need someone to tend them.

Matisa cranes her neck and nods.

"How do they survive up here?" My eyes trace the unforgiving wall of rock. They're perched in the most impossible of places.

She smiles back at me. "Remember what I told you about the deer? The goats have changed to suit the landscape. They are happy on these dangerous cliffs."

"Happy or addled," I mutter, turning my head against a gust of grit-laden wind.

Behind me, Eisu laughs.

I turn back to him and peer at the gun strapped at his belt. Can tell from the ornate handle, it's the one Tom gave him.

"That's a prized possession," I say, nodding at it.

"So he said." Eisu says it easy-like, but I can tell he's pleased.

"You be careful with that, you hear me?" I'm not speaking on the gun, and we both know it.

Eisu's face gets serious. "I'll guard it with my life," he replies. And I can see he means it.

Almighty.

He's head over heels, just like Tom.

I turn to the front to hide my smile.

We traverse the windy pass for most of the afternoon before the path descends. The walls of the mountains slope more gentle here, and the wind stops gusting, dwindling to a soft breeze. It's warmer, but sitting in the wind for the entire afternoon has chilled me through to the bone. I shiver as we pass into the shade of some tall pines and descend into a forest. The path is well worn, like it's been used over years and years. We traverse the woods quiet, the horses' plodding footsteps interrupted by the odd bird call from the trees. It's getting on evening when I notice that the air has changed, and not in the usual way it does as dusk descends. It's thicker here and has a peculiar smell.

Matisa looks back at me again, but she's happy, not wary. "You remember the springs I told you about?"

I remember them as she described them. She talked about a secret place, up in the mountains, where warm water came from the rock. She told me that she and her friends would sneak off there to be alone, away from watchful eyes. I was desperate to see it, but these past weeks never afforded us the time.

"Yes."

She gestures to the path ahead of us.

"They're here?" I ask, frowning. I didn't imagine them so far from the village boundaries.

"The same waters," she says.

"Is it safe?"

"It passes through many layers of rock, like the spring in Genya's village," she says. "And it is hot already—too hot for the sickness to survive."

The smell gets more caustic, and the path winds into a rockier part of the hillside.

Soon we reach a stream, about a stride across or more, burbling merrily along. It disappears into the ground under some deadfall. I scan ahead and see it appearing and disappearing as it rushes, bursting forth from the rock in a hurry to disappear again. Where the rocks have caught the river and held it, large, teardrop-shaped pools have formed.

We approach the pools, which are steaming in the late-evening sun.

"Is the water too hot to touch?" I ask.

"Not at all," Matisa says. "It is the most lovely heat . . ." She trails off and looks ahead, because Isi has stopped our procession.

"We will camp here tonight," he calls.

Matisa's face breaks into a grin. She nods at my dust-coated hands and cloak. "Last chance for a hot wash in a long while," she says.

"But . . ." I look around, but Lea and the rest are not hesitating. They are securing their horses and stripping off their armor and shucking off their outer layers of clothing, too. My face flames as I watch them strip down to next to nothing.

"Now is the time," Matisa says. "Before the sun goes down and we are vulnerable."

"But . . . *with* everyone?" I ask, my face still hot. I look at my leathers. Can't truly picture myself getting bare . . .

"Why?" Matisa frowns, teasing. "You wished to be alone?" She throws a pointed look at Kane, who is standing with Tom, his eyes as wide as mine feel.

"Course not!" I protest, but it's drowned out by shouts of glee.

Lea and her hunters have entered the pools, and there are raucous shouts of laughter and splashing. I look at the warm water, imagining how good the heat would feel on my skin . . .

"You can do what you wish." Matisa shrugs, pulling her leather breastplate over her head and setting it on the rock next to her horse. She wriggles out of her shirt and breeches and turns away from me. "I am going in."

I glance around at the darkening treetops, the looming shapes of the mountains behind. Dusk is upon us. If I want to try these waters, it's now or never. I dismount as Tom and Kane approach. I throw a helpless look at them.

Tom grins and heads off in the direction of the pools.

Kane stops beside me. He smells of leather and horses, and it sets cabbage moths to flitting around my stomach. I risk a glance at him, but the way he stands, so casual and so strong, that necklace of bone standing out against his throat—I feel my cheeks heat.

Foolish.

I force my voice steady and speak my first words to him today. "You going in?"

He shrugs. Pauses. "Are you?"

"Not real comfortable in water," I say, "You know I can't

swim." But as soon as the words are out, I remember him pretending to teach me at the waterfall we found on our way to Matisa's people, months back. The water was so cold, but our skin was searing one another like we were on fire . . .

"Don't think swimming's necessary." Kane nods at the shallow pools.

Everyone is talking loud, laughing, relaxing in the steaming water.

"I know that," I say. "It's just . . ."

It's just what? I'm still stuck inside the settlement? My thoughts are still so caught there, I can't see that this is exactly what people should do when they see hot water in the wild?

I raise my chin. "Yes," I say, "I'm going in." I walk forward, fiddling with my leather wristlets and unfastening the ties of my breastplate.

I keep my gaze on the treetops. I don't let myself look on Kane again until we're both safe under the water.

We sit in the steaming pools until it's too dark to see clear. Isi and Lea and her hunters leave to set up camp. Tom, Eisu, Matisa, and Kane remain with me. Along my side of the pool, Kane leans his head back against the rocks and closes his eyes to the twilight.

I try not to, but I can't help but study his profile. His slice of dark hair, strong nose, collarbone, and the top of his chest just visible above the black water. Behind him the rock rises steep into craggy cliffs. I force my eyes up to the sky, where the stars are coming out.

Right now, I just want to be grateful for the things I have. The dark sky is bright with stars, and the water is warm, and everyone is at peace. We sit, watching the steam rise up around us in great plumes of white. My friends appear and disappear in the clouds.

"We could live here," Tom says, breaking the silence. "We *should* live here."

Kane turns his head and cracks an eye open. "Who should?"

"All of us," Tom says. He looks at Eisu next to him.

"Why not?" Eisu says with a shrug.

"Why not is the Bleed," I remind him, but I'm feeling so warm and relaxed that it sounds like I'm reminding him of some pesky biting bug.

Tom waves a hand. "I meant after all that."

"You mean after we have secured peace?" Matisa says. But her voice, too, is languid, like we're discussing something trivial. She tilts her head. "It is not a bad idea."

"It's a real good idea," Tom corrects her. "Out here we don't have to worry about anyone thinking we're outsiders. Not at your village and not at our settlement. Anyone who joins us will *want* to be here." He looks at Eisu. "We could build our own home out here." And his voice is so full of hope.

I sit up. "You're serious."

Tom frowns at me. "Course I'm serious."

"Tom—"

"It makes sense," he insists. "Think about it, Em. We could start new up here. Isn't that what you always wanted?"

I nod, my eyes fixed on his face. Can't bear to look at Kane in this moment. Because of course it's what I always wanted. It's just that I used to be sure that Kane wanted it, too.

"It's protected here," Tom continues. "We'd have these springs. We could hunt. Matisa could plant a garden—"

"Isi can do the garden," Matisa cuts him off. "I would like to fish." She smiles at me. "And finally teach Em to swim."

"Your little brothers could learn to ride," Tom says to Kane. I don't look at Kane to see how he receives this. "Em could teach them."

There's a silence.

I rush to fill it. "Think I'd be too busy mending your hunting wounds," I say.

"Who says I'd have wounds?" Tom frowns and splashes me.

Eisu watches him with a soft smile.

"So, we're agreed?" Tom asks.

And I can't help it. I look to Kane.

His eyes are dark. He says nothing. Not yes. Not no. Nothing. He looks away.

Matisa speaks up. "It could happen." Her voice is light and all at odds with the feeling in my chest—with my heart sinking deep and deeper into my stomach.

"It should," Tom says. "When all of this is over." He speaks with such conviction. Like he already knows that we'll succeed.

And the truth is, I'm not letting myself think on what will happen if we fail. Right now, there's nothing to say we won't succeed. But I'm not letting myself think on what happens after. Can't think on what happens if we secure the remedy and return to Matisa's people. If we return to Genya's village to help them.

Won't let myself think on what Kane might decide then.

I drop my head back and shut my eyes tight, willing the tears away.

13

BY LATE AFTERNOON THE NEXT DAY, WE'VE descended into the foothills. The mountains loom in the background, seeming close enough to touch, but the air is warmer and the trees more dense. For hours we pass through forest where spruce needles litter the ground and moss covers the deadfall, creeping wispy fingers up the trunks of the spruce.

Last night, the warmth of the springs stayed in my body and lulled me into a dreamless sleep, next to Matisa. I was grateful I didn't lie awake, turning the same things over and over in my mind. It occurs to me I haven't dreamt since figuring out the remedy, and I wonder if that's a good sign. I wonder if it means I don't need to be afraid of what's coming.

I chew on the inside of my cheek as Kane creeps into my thoughts again. I avoided him when we ate this morning and chose a place in line far away from him when we set out. It's coward-like, I know, but I'm saving my bravery for something else.

Least, that's what I tell myself.

I spot Hunger slinking along in the shadows and smile. Just like she would at Matisa's village, she disappeared to find a place to sleep last night. Doesn't seem to feel any desire to stay close in the dark, but as always, she's back by daylight, looking for breakfast. I named her perfect.

Ahead of us, the sun shines bright on the front of the group. The trees have parted, creating a wider path. As we move forward, I hear the rush of a river.

Bly is on the banks, in conversation with Isi. We nudge our horses through the trees and crowd onto the shore.

"This is the river that leads to the Keep," Isi says as we approach.

"You're sure?" I ask him.

He nods. "This is the Flashing River."

"This is where we will part, then," Matisa says. She looks at Isi, and a flicker of worry crosses her face. "You'll be careful?"

"Always," Isi replies, flashing a rare smile.

"How far is it?"

"A day's journey," Isi says. "No more."

Bly points to the river's fast currents. "This crossing is troublesome. We will find something better to the east."

I look at the river and wonder how we plan to get across without following them and journeying out of our way.

"Troublesome but not impossible," Isi says, like he's reading my thoughts. "It is better for you to cross here and avoid the Keep. You will continue the quickest way back to the settlement."

Kane pulls his horse next to Beast and looks up and down the river, searching the banks on the far side.

"We will need to do it quickly," Matisa says. "I do not wish to be near the river for too long. In these hot days, the snow from the mountains can melt quickly and cause a flood we cannot predict."

A sliver of fear spikes in my chest. I've been caught in a river before—got no desire to feel that icy death again.

I look to Isi. "You'll come to my settlement?" I ask him. "After?"

Isi nods. "Bly will take what information we learn back to Huritt. I will meet you at the forbidden woods in three days."

A lump rises in my throat as Matisa moves forward to say goodbye. Isi pulls his horse close. She speaks words in their tongue. Sounds like a blessing.

"Âmopiyesîs," he says, reaching out and touching her face.

I look away.

When Matisa and Isi move apart, Bly says, "We will stay to see you cross."

"There is no need," Matisa replies. "You should make the most of the daylight."

They set out. Isi raises his hand by way of parting, and soon they are swallowed by the trees downstream.

I clear my throat when they have disappeared. "So, about this river," I say. "I . . . I don't swim."

"You will not need to," Matisa says, eyeing the rushing torrent. "Beast will swim it for you."

My hands are slick with sweat as Beast takes his first steps into the water.

"It is all right, Em," Matisa calls.

I look upriver. Matisa led us past a shelf of logs that spans the width of the water, saying it was safer to cross down-stream. The currents run strong here, and Matisa said that if we tried to cross above the shelf, the force of the water might pull us under the logs and drown us.

Tom and Lea are leading the way, with Eisu on Kane's horse, and behind them the horses that Eisu and Matisa were riding, both proving too skittish of the water to carry a person. The horses would follow the lead of the others, but Matisa said they should be left on their own to do it. Amo is last, on his fiery-tempered mare.

Kane and Matisa will go it alone, since they're the best swimmers of us all.

"What if Hunger can't swim?" I ask for the third time.

The little dog is on the shore, her ears pricked forward, eyes trained on me.

"Well, she can't very well ride one of the horses," Tom quips, looking back at me. "Don't worry; Amo says all dogs can swim."

I run my hand along Beast's neck. He dips his head and snorts at the water.

"Give him time, Em," Lea says, looking back at me from her horse, which is well into the fast-flowing stream. "Let him take the lead."

I cluck my tongue. Beast takes another step forward and stumbles, throwing his head forward, and I have to grab at his mane to keep from pitching off. Panic spikes through me, hot and bright. I lose my nerve and rein him to a stop.

"I can't do this!" I call, my heart pounding as the waters swirl past.

"You can," Matisa calls.

"No. Not alone." Fear is shooting through me like ice shards. I'm too desperate to be proud. I risk a glance behind at the three of them on the bank. Kane stands with his arms crossed over his bare chest, watching me with concern. His knitted brow softens.

"Need someone beside me." Can't come outright and say his name, but my gaze goes to him, betraying my thoughts.

Matisa's eyebrows rise. Kane just steps down off the bank into the water.

"Kane can't stay with you the whole way," Matisa cautions as he wades in beside me.

"I know," I say. Kane can't risk being close to Beast when he swims, can't risk getting kicked or knocked under. "Just need him here for this first part."

Kane puts a hand on my leg. "You'll be fine, Em," he says. He's knee-deep, same as Beast. He reaches forward to tug at Beast's bridle, clucking his tongue.

"Easy, boy," I murmur as Beast moves forward. He keeps his head down, eyeing the water, and paws with his hooves, searching for the river bottom. He wades in slow.

Ahead of me, Lea's horse takes another two steps and lunges forward into the deep water. And now it's struggling, getting pulled by the current and pushing hard for the far bank. To lighten the weight, Lea swings off the saddle into the water. She dangles beside her horse as it strains.

Tom's horse is next, plunging into the cold torrent. I watch as Tom pulls his leg up and over and clings to one side the way Lea did. The riderless horses follow. Eisu goes after them.

And my attention is pulled away, because Beast is belly-deep and Kane has fallen behind. I throw a quick glance back, alarm spiking through me, but Kane gives me a reassuring smile.

Beast wades a few steps farther, until the water is over my moccasins. My heart is beating fast as he stumbles a mite, trying to find footing on the rocky bottom. He snorts loud, tossing his head back away from the water.

"You're all right, Em," Kane calls.

I nod, fixing my gaze on the opposite shore. Beast gathers his strength, and I force myself to relax. And we're plunging into the icy water. The shock steals my breath, my thoughts, for an instant. But I force myself to move, dismounting to one side and clutching at the saddle with my hands. I pray my legs stay out of the way of Beast's mighty ones, and close my eyes as he struggles in the current.

The sensation is odd; both weightless and full of force at once. I can feel Beast straining, his head high, his muscles churning against the waters, and I know we're being pulled downstream.

I turn my head and risk a look behind but can only see Amo's skittish mare dancing about on the shore, whinnying. He puts heels to the horse hard, calling a command, and she leaps ahead and into the water, eyes rolling.

I cling to Beast, soaked through and frozen, clenching my jaw against the cold and praying for it all to be over quick. As I watch the shore pass us with alarming speed, I'm sure we're getting swept away, that Beast has lost the fight with the river and we'll be dashed to bits on rocks . . .

Beast stumbles, his front hooves finding purchase on solid ground again, and as he straightens up with a heave, I remember to pull myself up and throw my leg over his back.

I cling to his mane for balance as he wades ashore.

"You beauty!" I exclaim, feeling out of breath, though I've done no work at all. Beast labors up the bank, stopping once we're among the trees. I slip off and hug him around his neck. "You beauty," I say again. "Good boy." He blows out his breath, like it was nothing, but I can feel him trembling a mite.

I duck under his neck, searching the waters. Amo comes ashore upstream of us; Tom and his horse are farther downstream. Tom lifts a hand to let me know he's fine. He's grinning.

Course he enjoyed that.

Kane is still standing thigh-deep in the water. Matisa joins him, speaks a few words of instruction, and dives under.

Kane hesitates. He looks back. Hunger hasn't moved. She stands on the shore, whining. Matisa pops back up halfway into the river and pulls hard for the shore; the current doesn't take her the way it took our horses.

Kane calls to Hunger and claps his hands, trying to coax her toward him.

On our side, Matisa emerges, leggings and shirt soaked and clinging to her, breathing hard with the effort of the swim.

On the opposite bank, Hunger wags her tail and paces the shore.

Kane calls again.

"He will have to leave her," Lea remarks beside me.

"Hunger!" I call. "Come, girl!"

She whines again and backs away from the river. I watch in exasperation as she runs upstream, away from Kane.

"Kane!" Matisa beckons. She draws a line with her finger, indicating the path Kane should take across the current. "Try to stay under for as long as you can!" she calls.

Hunger has moved farther upshore, to a place where the bank is high. Kane sighs and turns to wade back, but my eyes are drawn to Hunger again. She noses the earth, looking at the river. She looks up at me. And she leaps.

Her lithe body plunges into the water with an enormous splash. She surfaces, bobbing back up like a piece of driftwood. She's paddling hard, but I can see she's not strong enough; she's getting swept up in the current. I shout in alarm.

Kane sees. He leaps ahead and dives under the surface. For a heartbeat he's gone, and it's just Hunger struggling in the waters, getting pulled downstream.

Kane surfaces in the middle of the river as Hunger sweeps past. He takes two giant strokes toward her and catches her by the scruff of the neck. He flips onto his back and starts kicking hard for the shore, using his one free arm to propel himself and the dog.

He's close to shore when a large tree branch barrels toward him.

My blood flushes ice cold. It's going to crash into him, knock him under, send him, broken, down the river. My voice leaves me in a panicked cry. But he pulls hard, and the debris swirls past, only grazing him. And then he's found his footing on the rocky riverbed, and he's clambering upright.

He shoves Hunger ahead, and she scrambles through the shallows and up onto the shore. I drop Beast's reins and run to the riverbank.

Hunger stops and shakes, covering me in a great shower of river water as I kneel and put my arms around her. I jump up as Kane wades ashore. He stops and puts his hands on his knees, breathing hard.

I march over to him, Hunger at my heels. "That was foolish!" I scold. My hands flutter up. I'm unsure if I want to shove him or throw myself into his arms.

He turns his head and looks up, one eye squinting against the water that streams off his brow. "Guess not *all* dogs can swim," he says. He blows out his breath. "But she wanted to try." Another breath. "For you." River water runs off him, down his bare chest to his soaked leggings.

"You shouldn't have done that."

He straightens and runs his hands through his short hair, wicking the water away. He looks at me, his chest heaving.

A ruckus behind me interrupts us. I spin.

Amo has dismounted, shouting as his horse drops to her knees.

I step back in surprise as I watch the big gray mare flop onto her side.

Matisa shouts in her tongue at Amo, who grabs his knife from his belt. The horse flings herself like she wants to roll over, legs flailing. Amo darts in, quick as a breath, and cuts through the leather strap on the saddle, yanking at it and pulling it free as his horse goes right over onto her back and other side. The mare does it again. And again.

Finally she seems satisfied and labors to her feet. She shakes, her whole body shuddering, shedding soil and twigs.

"What on earth?"

"She wanted to roll the river off her skin."

"I knew that hotblood would give us trouble," Lea mutters, coming to stand beside us. "How badly damaged is your saddle?" she calls to Amo.

He holds it up by the broken strap.

"He had to pull it off or the horse would have hurt herself," Matisa explains to me. She looks around at the lot of us, drenched.

"Well, then," she says. "That is enough adventure for today. We will camp here."

14

WE MOVE UP INTO THE WOODS UNTIL MATISA tells us we're far enough away from the shore to be safe from a flash flood. We build a fire and set to drying our soaked clothes. The bag Matisa stocked with extra clothing has remained dry, so we change quick. In my pack, my *ceinture* also stayed dry. I wind it around my middle, feeling comforted by its warmth.

It's near dinnertime, so we make a hot mush over the fire with some root vegetables and meat—once dried, now soggy from the river. Some of our food stayed dry, but better to use the damaged supplies first.

I avoid looking at Kane but can't help reliving his rescuing Hunger over and over in my mind. Now that my fear has melted away, I'm not angry. I'm nowhere close. Now I want to march over to him, press him backward, and kiss him as hard as I can. Can't get the idea out of my mind. And I know if I look him in the eye, it'll be all over my face.

I stick close to Amo as he examines his cut saddle strap.

He says it'll need to dry before he tries to mend it—the leather stretches too much when it's wet. I pretend to be interested in this because Kane is gazing this way, and I don't know where else to look.

Matisa goes to rinse our pots in the stream and returns with a grave face. "The river is much higher than it was this afternoon," she says. "It is rising quickly."

"One of those sudden floods?" I ask.

She shakes her head. "No, but the snow must be melting in the mountains."

"Are we safe here?" Tom asks.

"Probably," she says. "But we could move higher, to put our minds at ease so we can sleep well. I worry about that cluster of logs we crossed below. If it lets go, the water might come too fast to avoid."

It takes some time to dismantle the drying lines that hold our leathers, as well as our cooking tripod. We shuttle all of it and lead our horses to higher ground. Once we've set up our new camp, with our sleeping lean-tos placed under sheltering low branches, Lea puts herself and Amo on first watch. It's early evening, with hours of daylight still, but everyone is tired from the river crossing, and Matisa wants to get an early start in the morning.

I pass by Kane on my way to wash my hands and face.

"She's disappeared again," he remarks, his eyes scanning the camp.

I stop. "Hunger?" I scan the camp, too, more for somewhere to look. My insides flutter as I stand this close to him.

"Would've thought she'd want to stay near and guard us

all night. Return the favor of me saving her scruffy neck." He's pretending to take offense.

Overhearing from nearer the fire, Matisa turns. "Perhaps she prefers wild squirrel to our root mush? Strange." She says it with a smile.

I smile, too, glad for her intervention, but Kane's words have ignited a small worry in me. "What if she sleeps too close to the river tonight?"

"She will be fine," Matisa says. "Animals have good sense about these things."

I bite my lip. "I'll go call her. See if I can coax her near."

"I'll come with you," Kane offers.

I glance at him, wondering if he's truly worried about Hunger or if he's trying to talk to me alone . . .

"Good idea," Matisa says quick. "Yes, go with Em."

I squint at her. "Thought you just said she'd be fine?"

She waves her hands. "Just go," she says in exasperation. But her eyes sparkle. "You may as well be *certain* that she is not near the river."

Almighty.

We head off into the trees, back to the swollen waters, where I crouch and wash my face and hands. Kane stands nearby, looking off into the woods and chewing on some kind of root, like he's trying to appear casual.

I dry my hands and face on the tail of my *ceinture* and stand, looking up and down the riverbank. Now *I'm* trying to look casual. "You think she's out here?"

"If I were a dog who couldn't swim," Kane remarks, "I wouldn't go anywhere near the river."

"Let alone sleep there?"

"Exactly."

So he's not out here to look for Hunger. Not truly. I wrap my arms around myself and turn to wander the bank. He falls in step with me, that piece of root moving in the corner of his mouth. The silence stretches between us. "Did you sleep better last night?" I ask to fill it.

He nods. "Best sleep I've had in months."

"Months?" I squint over at him. "That can't be true."

"It is."

"Why?" I ask. "I mean, where . . ." I think about discarding the question but decide it doesn't matter. "Where did you sleep when you were in Genya's village?"

"In a room with my brothers."

I feel a childish pang of relief at his answer.

"But I never slept that well," he says.

"Were they noisy sleepers?"

"Not particular noisy. Just at night everything is so quiet, and you remember what you're missing."

"It's even quieter out here," I point out.

"Right." He pulls the root from his mouth and throws it at the river. "But it's not *missing* out here."

I suck in a breath. Does he mean me? I want to turn to him and see the answer on his face. Instead, I clear my throat and press on. "Hunger!" I call. "Come, girl!"

Kane follows, sending a halfhearted whistle out into the trees.

After several strides I stop and look up and down the bank.

"Doesn't seem she's around here," Kane says, though we both know this by now.

I turn to him. "Never thanked you," I say. "For saving her life."

"It's all right."

"No, Kane. It was real good of you. I'm—I'm real fond of that dog." Sounds foolish, leaving my mouth. My cheeks pink.

But he's not looking on me like I'm foolish. "I know," he says. "I know you are. And it's clear she's fond of you, too. She'd follow you anywhere." His mouth pulls into that funny smile.

"You're not fond of dogs, though." The river rushes in my ears. My heart pounds along with it. I take a deep breath. "Why'd you do it?"

"Because I know how she feels," he says.

The relief that floods through me is so immediate, so strong, that I can't move. He's forgiven me, somehow. I want to tell him how glad I am he's here. I want to tell him that the idea of us being together at the end of this matters as much as our being alive. But there's a lump in my throat I can't speak around.

A shout comes through the trees.

Kane's head snaps in the direction of our camp. "What was that?"

"Should we go see?" I whisper the words like I'm suddenly short for air.

Say no.

We listen. It comes again.

"Yes," he sighs. "Come on." And he offers me his hand.

I take it, and as we hurry through the woods back to our

camp, the cabbage moths in my stomach are flittering around furious. The feeling of his hand grasping mine, so fierce and protective . . . I want to pull him up short, press him against the nearest tree . . .

But we're already at the camp, and I can see Matisa through the trees. Two more steps and I see she's standing with her knife out. We hasten into the grove. Tom and Eisu have their guns drawn. Lea and Amo, too. They all have their weapons trained on two men standing at the edge of our camp.

One is tall and stocky, the other tall and lean. They've got nothing with them: no packs or weapons. Their clothes are travel-worn.

"We want no trouble," the tall man says, his hands up in surrender. He doesn't look menacing. Looks contrite, even. But he's familiar. Blond hair, unnerving handsome face . . .

My blood runs cold. I tell myself to stay calm, to make sure I'm seeing what I think I'm seeing.

I look close at the blond man. Didn't get a real good look at him that day at the Keep, the day Isi and I rescued Nico, but . . .

Sure looks like Leon.

Lea nods at Amo beside her. They sheath their weapons and approach the men. Skimming their hands over the men's bodies and patting their clothes, they check for concealed weapons. Amo shakes his head at Lea when he finds nothing, but Lea's hand stops at the blond man's left side. She pulls his shirt up, none too gentle, and exposes a crude bandage, dark brown with matted blood.

"Like I said," the blond man says, "we don't want trouble."

"What *do* you want?" Matisa demands.

Eisu speaks some words in their tongue to her. Sounds like a warning. She holds up a hand and waits for an answer.

"Truth is, we need your help," the blond man answers. "And I'm happy to trade help in return."

"We do not need help," Matisa says.

"Well, that's not entirely true." He nods at Amo's broken gear. "Malachi here is a leatherworker by trade. Could fix that gear for you in no time."

"In exchange for what?"

The man smiles, apologetic-like, and his hand goes to his side. To that bloody bandage.

"What's your name?" Matisa demands.

"Apologies," the blond says, dipping his head. He moves his hand to his chest. "Name's Merritt. Merritt Leon. But most people call me by my last name."

A hot flush courses through me.

"Matisa," Eisu hisses.

She looks at us. Back at Leon. She speaks words in her tongue to Lea and Amo. In answer they take wider stances and draw their weapons again. Matisa gestures for the rest of us to step away from the men with her.

"What are you doing?" Tom asks her when we are out of earshot. "This is the man Em told us about. The brother of the man who held you captive."

Matisa looks at me to confirm.

I nod. "People called him Leon," I say, keeping my voice low. "I'm sure that's him—he looks just like his brother . . . did. But I don't think it's wise to let him know we recognize him."

"He's dangerous," Eisu says.

"Of course he's dangerous," Matisa says. "But . . ."

"But?"

"But it will be night soon, and I would rather know where these two men are in the dark."

Tom nods. "Matisa's right. Better to keep a close eye."

"And we could get some answers," she adds.

"What kind of answers do you need from him?" Eisu asks.

"I would like to know why he is out here away from the Keep, without protection."

We look at one another. Again, she has a point. Knowing that would give us an idea of what Isi and Bly are headed into.

"Why would he approach us like that? Unarmed?" Kane asks, throwing a glance back to where Lea and the boys are watching the men. "I don't trust it."

"Neither do I," Matisa agrees. "But we can be careful." She nods at Amo's horse. "And we do need that saddle repaired."

"Amo can mend it himself," Eisu replies.

"Yes," Matisa says. "But Leon does not know that."

Again, we exchange a glance.

"Even if we look vulnerable," Tom says, "even if it looks like we're trading with him, what's to say he'll tell us the truth?"

"Nothing," Matisa says. "But there are ways of getting to the truth without asking for it directly." She looks at me. "Will you see to his wound?"

My heart stutters, thinking on being that near Merritt Leon: the man who sent his followers to burn that homestead, to take little boys—Kane's brother. To the man who's keeping women . . .

I swallow hard and nod.

"If Em's tending to him, I'm going to be right beside her," Kane says, his hand on his knife handle.

Matisa shakes her head. "It is important to give him the sense that we might be willing to trust him."

"Meaning what?"

"Meaning that we cannot look like we will harm him at the slightest provocation," Matisa says, looking at his knife.

Kane blows out his breath. He lets go of the knife handle with effort.

"From now on," Matisa says, "our story is that we have just met." She looks at me. "We are helping you and Kane and Tom find your families." I look at us, over at Lea and Amo. Without our battle leathers, we don't look so unified. It could seem that we've only just met.

"And tomorrow morning?" Tom asks. "What do we do then?"

We look at one another. We know what he's truly asking: whether or not we get answers, what happens after?

"We will decide once we get some information," Matisa says.

"But if he's who Em thinks, can we risk leaving him alive?"

My stomach drops at Tom's question. Matisa's eyes meet mine. I've never killed anyone. Not on purpose, anyhow. But this man . . . he's a monster. If he's anything like his brother Julian was . . .

My thoughts fly to the travelers Isi and I found—Elizabeth and Ulysses Sharapay. Leon cut off Ulysses's finger as a warning. He wanted to keep Elizabeth, too. And he killed people, shackled people . . .

But something in Tom's question stalls my thoughts.

If he's who Em thinks . . .

Truly, what I think I know, I've heard from others. The things I've seen . . . well, I never actually saw him do anything but take to his weapons under attack.

All I truly know about him is that he approached us unarmed, asking for help.

He doesn't know Isi and I are the ones who rescued Nico from his Keep. And he surely doesn't know we're the ones his brother, Julian, held captive for that short time. Not even sure he knows Julian is dead—that Tom shot him. But as to what he's doing out here . . .

"I'll find out," I blurt, my heart pounding loud in my ears. "I'll find out who he really is."

"Em," Kane frowns. "You know who—"

"I said, *I'll find out*," I say, fear sharpening my tongue. I sigh and soften my tone. "I'll be mending his wound, so I'm in the best position to gain his confidence. I'll figure what's going on."

Kane crosses his arms, his dark eyes unhappy.

"You can stay close by," Matisa says to Kane. "We won't let down our guard for a minute. We will sleep in shifts."

A muscle works in his jaw.

Matisa looks at me. "Are you ready, Em?"

I nod. "I'm ready."

15

MY FOOLISH HANDS SHAKE AS I PULL THE CLOTH
away from the skin on Merritt Leon's stomach. He's stretched
out on the ground, cradling his neck in his hands, his head
raised to watch me. His shirt is off, and I'm using the help of
a lantern, since the sun is low in the sky now, dipping below
the trees.

Kane is a few strides away, pretending to see to Beast. I
can tell by the way he's standing that all his attention is on
Leon and me. He can't hear what we're saying from where he
is, but he's watching it all real careful.

Lea and Amo stand a few strides away, weapons in hand.
Eisu and Tom keep an eye on the other man, who's looking
over the saddle. Matisa sits across the camp.

"You're a strange mix," Leon remarks, throwing a glance at
the others. "What're you all doing out here?"

I still my hands and look at him. "Could ask you the same
thing," I say.

"Just making conversation."

I continue, my hands moving slow, but the cloth catches

on one corner, stuck with matted blood, and I need to tug just slight. Leon sucks in a breath. My eyes fly to his face, sure he's angry, but he winces, apologetic-like.

"You must think me weak," he says. He's more handsome, close up. Strong chin, perfect straight nose. His blond hair curls against his neck. He holds my gaze. "I saw how you move on that foot of yours. Living with something like that has to be painful. If not there"—he nods at my foot—"then here." He pulls one hand from behind his neck and touches his temple.

Heat rises in my cheeks. "Doesn't bother me," I say. And it doesn't. I've had a tincture for the pain ever since I've known Matisa.

"You're stronger than you look, then," he says.

I clear my throat against the fluttering of nerves in my belly and focus on the wound. It's a gaping hole in his side, and without the cloth, it'll gush blood when he moves. I peer closer and am relieved when I smell fresh blood—no putrid stink of decaying flesh. Somehow, the wound is clean. "I'll need to sew it," I say, like I do this sort of thing every day. In truth, I've only ever had to sew one wound: Isi's. But I want to give Leon the sense that he's in good hands, that he can trust me. If only I could get my hands to stop trembling . . .

"Don't suppose you have any hooch?"

"Any what?"

"Hooch." He grins. "To numb the pain." He squints at my confused face. "Liquor? You know, brandy or wine or something of the kind?"

I tuck my hair behind my ear and rummage in my satchel for a clean cloth. "No," I say, though I've never heard that word. I dip the cloth in a pot of boiled water sitting beside me on the ground and wash the skin around the wound. His skin is pale, but it's healthy-looking. And he's strong. My eyes are pulled upward to the curve of his chest, his broad shoulders.

He tilts his head, smiling again. If he's trying to unnerve me, it's working.

Don't let him see that.

With effort, I hold his gaze. "How'd you get this?"

"My horse bolted. I fell off directly onto a tree branch. Nearly pierced me through."

It *is* what the wound looks like. I remember a dog back at Matisa's settlement had pulled free of its tether and tried to sneak into the rabbit hutches. A wooden fence pike had pierced its neck just like this.

"And your friend?" I ask, going back to my task. "His horse bolt, too?"

"It did. But he's more fortunate than I. Nothing but scrapes."

I pull a jar of yarrow paste from my satchel. "This will hurt at first," I tell him, and I begin smoothing it around the gaping hole. He takes a deep breath again. "In a few moments you won't be able to feel much. The paste numbs pain."

He looks impressed. "Where'd you learn that?"

I fish around in my satchel again. "I was taught by a healer woman." I clink some jars together. "Why'd your horses bolt?" I ask, casual-like. My heart is beating so fast in my chest, I'm sure he can hear it.

"We were running away from a skirmish," he says. I raise my eyes to his. Those eyes—when I saw him the first time, they seemed hollow. His brother, Julian, had the same eyes—it's how I figured who Julian was—but right now they're . . . vulnerable. But are they truthful?

"What kind of skirmish?" I try to keep my voice even, but my insides are all upside down that he's speaking this easy with me already.

"Well, I have a place just downriver of here. And some people aim to take it from me."

"What people? What kind of place?"

"You ask for a lot of information for someone not willing to part with any."

My stomach swoops as I scramble for an answer. "I've just learned not to trust too many people out here, is all. And talking's a good distraction."

"That's the truth." Leon leans his head back and closes his eyes.

I take a quick sip of air and grip my hands into fists to steady them. I open one and touch his stomach. "Does that hurt?" I press with two fingers near the open part of the wound.

He turns an incredulous look on me. "Goddamn," he says, "I can't feel a thing."

I take out my needle. I planned to take my time getting it threaded, but I won't have to feign anything: my foolish hands are still shaking. I turn away from him, pretending to rummage in my satchel again.

Get ahold of yourself.

"So you were running from them—those people?" I ask, still turned from him and trying like anything to get the needle threaded.

"Yes," he says. "Malachi and I escaped."

"Who were they?"

"Dominion," he says. "Fools."

"How's that?" I turn back around, knotting and snipping the thread with my teeth.

"They're fighting us free people so the same bastards who rule everything in the east can have this land, too. Bunch of sheep who can't think for themselves, coming to fight the bluebloods' war. It's why I left the east. Why I came out here and made myself a place. They have no right trying to take it from me."

I want to ask him what right he had to burn that homestead along the great river. What right he had to take a small child, keep women. I swallow the impulse, remembering how I lost my temper when I was talking to that Dominion commander. Can't make a mistake like that again. I set to sewing the wound. "So, your place," I say, keeping my eyes on the needle as it pierces his flesh. With effort, I pull it gentle through the skin. "It's gone now?"

"Not sure." He winces as I hit a part of his skin that's obviously not full numb. I pull the thread through quick.

"And you and Malachi—you're the only two left?"

He raises his head and looks at me again. I'm asking too many questions.

"We met some people weeks back," I say. "A man and a woman. Mapmakers." I pierce and pull. "Were they . . . your people?"

There's a silence.

I risk a glance at him.

"Now, why would you be asking if they were my people?" His voice is quiet, but there's an undercurrent in it. Anger.

I shrug one shoulder. Need to offer him something—anything—that'll make it seem I don't know much, that I'm as vulnerable as he is. "These aren't our people." I toss my head at Lea and Amo. "We met a day ago. We got split up from our families. Was just wondering if it was the same for you. If that man and woman—"

"If they're the mapmakers I'm thinking of, they came to my Keep, all right. Pretending to need help. We fed them. Then they tried to steal my horses." His eyes are cold. "I let them go, but I gave the man something to remember me by."

I study the thread as I pull and tug. Tried to steal his horses? Elizabeth and Ulysses told me Leon took theirs—that he tried to take Elizabeth, too, and cut off Ulysses's finger when they refused—giving them a reminder to return with maps of the north. "They didn't say much," I say. "Just that they were drawing up maps." I'm finished with the stitching. Too soon. "And they were headed up north."

He tilts his head up to examine me. "My brother was headed up north," he says. "But he left our Keep over two months ago, and I haven't seen him since."

I will my hands to stop shaking as I tie off the thread. I'll have to bring my face right to his newly stitched skin to bite through the thread. I look to Kane again, dip my head, and take the thread in my teeth. Kane's eyes are dark.

"Easy, now," Leon says.

I hold the thread taut and bite through it. Hard, but making sure to hold the thread in a way that he doesn't feel any tug. "I'll bandage it now," I say. "Sit up." I get a fresh bit of cloth and put it to the wound, then grab a long bandage. He raises his arms as I wind it around his middle.

"You're awfully interested in these mapmakers," he remarks as I tie off the end.

"Just trying to figure things. Haven't been out here long."

"Well, I can see that," Leon says, and he laughs. He catches himself with a wince. "You look fresh off the wagons."

I try a sad smile. "We got split up from our people. These folks"—I gesture again to Lea and Amo—"took us in. They're helping us get back."

"Is that so?" Leon says. He looks Lea over. "Just helping out of the goodness of their hearts?"

I bend my head near him, like I want my words to be for his ears only. "I hope so," I say.

He smiles, like we're sharing something. "Had a few working with me at my Keep."

"Oh?"

"They'd left a big group of them who were traveling around out this way. Said there are more socked away somewhere in the mountains."

I keep my face blank. "Mayhap that's where these three are from," I suggest. "They never said." But my thoughts race. The First People we saw working with Leon must've been defectors from *sohkâtisiwak*. Abandoners from the abandoners.

I draw back and nod at his bandage. "That'll be all right now."

"Obliged," he says, and he reaches for his shirt. "What did you say your name was?"

All at once my throat is tight—I have to force the word out. "Emmeline."

"Well, Emmeline," he says, "that was very good work." He shrugs into his shirt careful and nods at Lea and the rest. "Wish they'd understand we're not here to harm you."

"They'll stay on guard," I say. "It's their way. They were like that with us the first few days, too. They'll come around." Too late I realize I've contradicted my earlier statement about just meeting them. I stumble on my words, trying to distract him, and come out with the only thing I can think of: "They—they say there's a bad man around here. Slaving their kind. Keeping women."

Leon tilts his head. "They give this man a name?"

"No," I say. "But they said he's got a fort somewhere nearby." And then, because I'm feeling reckless and nervous, I ask, "You know anything about that?"

There's a silence.

"Let me ask you something, Emmeline," he says, dropping his gaze to his fingers, which begin to button up his shirt. "Say you found a pretty little piece of land—near heaven on Earth in your estimation—and you had a little community there. Say you were planning on a fresh start, right there in that little community, and then someone showed up and tried to take it away from you." He squints up at me. "What would you do?"

I hesitate. The way he's describing his Keep . . . it's uncanny. He could be talking about me in Matisa's village. He could be talking about Genya in hers.

I shake my head. "I don't know."

"I think you do know," he says. "Because you're tougher

than you look." He looks over at Kane. "I'm willing to bet you'd fight tooth and nail to protect what you felt was yours."

The back of my neck prickles. He's not a simpleton, that's clear, but picking out my feelings for Kane like this . . . how can he have seen so much in this short time?

I clear my throat. "Who's to say it's yours to begin with?"

He spreads his hands. "I was there first. Why shouldn't I lay claim?"

It's true that Matisa's people no longer roam these lands. But they left because they knew what had happened in the east, and they knew it would happen again. And, true to their predictions, the Dominion is out here, parceling up the land. They've done it before, and they cared nothing for the First People when they did it. Leon . . . well, Leon just got here before the Dominion.

But the kind of person he is, the kind of community he aims to build and how he plans to keep it . . .

My voice is barely a whisper. "Are you keeping women against their will?"

He tilts his head. "You make it sound like they didn't choose to come out this way," he says. "They did. They made that choice. That they didn't like it so much once they got here isn't my fault. I don't think I should be expected to risk my life escorting them back east." He holds my gaze. "There are bad people about."

I resist the urge to touch my knife, wedged under my *ceinture.* "So you're not keeping them." I choose my words careful, trying to make it seem I think he's reasonable. "They just won't leave by themselves, and you won't take them."

He nods.

I try my best to look relieved.

"It's not an easy life out here," he answers. "People need a leader, and a leader needs to make decisions." He sits up straighter. "I'm helping people survive. Are you going to fault me for that?"

I shove my implements into my satchel, straightening and slinging it across my body. "Course not," I answer. I nod at his bandage. "Be careful with that while the stitches set."

Leon and Malachi are asleep, with Lea and Amo standing guard. The rest of us tuck back into the spruce, out of the men's sight and earshot.

Once we're assembled in a tight circle, I start. "I told him we met those travelers—those mapmakers from the east. And I told him you were helping us find our people. But nothing else. He didn't ask, neither."

Kane frowns. "You think he believed you?"

"Seemed like it."

"Why is he out here?" Matisa asks.

"He said his Keep was under attack. He said he and the other man—Malachi—were the only ones to escape."

"From the Dominion?"

I nod.

"And you believe him?" Tom asks.

I hesitate. "Don't know what I think. Can't figure why he'd approach us the way he did. He needed help—that was plain. That wound wasn't dirty, but it wouldn't have healed proper left like that."

Eisu looks over at the men, his face troubled.

"He talked a bit about the north," I say.

"Does he know about your settlement?" Matisa asks.

"Don't think so. He just mentioned Julian being interested in it." I share a look with Tom. "He . . ." I try to think of the right words without sounding addled, like I'm siding with Leon. "He said some things about being out here. How he's just been trying to defend against people who try to take what's his."

Tom snorts. Matisa watches me, calm.

"I . . . I don't think he's a good person," I say. "But he's doing what all the rest are doing—any of the newcomers that come out this way. The Dominion—"

"The Dominion had to rescue Genya's village from *Leon's* men," Tom reminds me.

"We *assumed* they were Leon's men," I say. "But we don't know for sure."

Kane shifts. "I never did see any of them. The battle was outside the boundaries—what I know about who attacked was hearsay, truly." He frowns. "But that doesn't mean we can trust him."

I hold up my hands. "I'm not saying we should trust him. He's not giving me the whole story—that's certain. But he's not much of a threat to us right now. And if his Keep has been taken, he's not much of a threat to us in general. Our concern is getting to the settlement."

"Okay," Kane agrees. "But what do we do with them?"

There's a silence. Tom's face is grim. I know what he thinks. And I know what he'd do if we asked him.

I spread my hands. Kane's eyes are fixed on my face. "I can't . . ." I take a breath. "I can't harm two men I don't even know." I clench my jaw against my trembling lip and look up.

Kane uncrosses his arms, like he's relieved. "Me neither," he says.

I look to Matisa.

"I am also not interested in being violent, unless we are defending our lives," she says.

"So what *do* we do?" Tom asks.

"We could tie them up so they can't follow us," Kane suggests.

We look at one another in grim silence. It's the best plan we have right now. Can't risk leaving them free, but I can't punish two men who've never wronged me in any way that I can prove.

Done enough things I regret out here already.

Our circle breaks up as we move back for the camp, but I can't help but feel a specter ghosting alongside me as we go. His thin shoulders, dirty teeth, scraggly beard starting up around his chin—I can feel him heavy at my back.

I will Charlie away.

16

IN MY DREAM, I AM RUSHING THROUGH DARK woods. A building—once a settler's cabin, now a ruined, mossy heap—is ahead, lying like a slumbering giant among *les trembles*. The trees rush past on either side as I scan the brush. The Watch flats loom near. I am flying along, quick, so quick.

Searching.

Following.

Chasing.

Hurry.

A cry cuts through my dream. My eyes fly open to the spruce-needle-covered ground. Kane's arm is over my shoulders, his body wrapped around me from behind, but he's awake—I can tell by the way his body tenses.

That cry. Sounded like Matisa.

An icy shock blasts my face, drenching me. Cold water.

I scramble up and trip backward into Kane, who's already

on his feet. He grabs my arm to steady me, and I scrub my other sleeve across my face, blinking hard.

A man stands before us with an empty bucket.

He grins. "Rise and shine." When he drops the bucket, I see he's holding a gun.

Kane draws me to him, knife already in his hand. I scan our camp.

There are six men surrounding our group, guns drawn. Lea has a wide stance, her arms at the ready. She doesn't have a weapon in hand, but it's clear she's prepared to fight.

Tom is frozen, watching Eisu. He's clutching that gun Tom gave him. And it's raised.

Two more men hover to my left. Someone is missing . . . Amo.

Amo's missing. He was on watch last, with Lea.

We're outnumbered, and we're surely outgunned—and that's just the men and weapons I can see. Are there more in the woods? How did they sneak up on us like this? How . . . and all at once I realize the air is filled with the sound of rushing water.

The river's come up farther still. It's clamoring loud. Must've hidden the sound of the men's approach, even from Lea and Amo.

I turn my head and realize the two men to my left are Leon and Malachi. They're standing casual, looking on.

The men surrounding us aren't pointing their guns at them.

Someone emerges from the trees across the clearing, drawing everyone's eyes. It's Amo, hands behind his back, being inched forward by another man who's got a knife to his throat.

"Put that down real slow," Leon says to Eisu. "Or I'll have Janz slit his throat." The man presses the flat of the blade against Amo's neck. Amo raises his chin, his eyes flickering with anger. Leon nods his head at Kane. "You, too."

Eisu lowers Tom's gun slow, then lets it fall from his hands to the earth. Kane drops his knife, his jaw clenched.

"Get over with the rest," orders the man before us. Kane and I cross the space, and soon we're all circled by the men, their guns trained on our chests.

Leon strides forward and puts a foot on Eisu's gun, dragging it backward with his toe. He picks up the gun, his eyes roaming over us as he tilts his head, like he's deciding.

"Merritt—" I begin.

"Shut up," he says in a mild voice. He strolls toward us. "Now it's my turn to ask questions." He's speaking like we're friends having a conversation, but there's all kinds of violence in his face, in the way he moves. "So. What are you all doing out here? Where could you be headed?"

No one says anything. I risk a glance at Matisa. Her face is a mask of calm and control.

"What do you want with us?" she asks.

"No." Leon shakes his head. "No, see—*I* ask the questions. You're on my land, after all. And I want to know what you're doing here."

"This isn't your land," Tom says.

Leon looks at Tom, amused. "It is if I say it is," he says. His tone turns deadly. "And I'm not going to ask again. What are you doing on my land?"

"I told you, we're lost," I blurt out. "We're trying to find our families. And they"—I nod to Matisa and Isi—"were helping us."

"You said that," Leon says. "The thing is, I didn't believe you then." He turns dead eyes on me. "And I don't believe you now."

I swallow.

He smiles. "It's all right. I know you weren't sure about me, either. We're not the trusting kind." He shifts his stance. "But I'd like to believe you. You can help me by answering straight."

My eyes flick to Matisa.

"See? Right there," Leon says. "You're looking to a girl you barely know for your cue? I don't think so." He hefts the gun in his hand. "So tell me who you are and what you're doing out here."

There's a silence.

A flicker of impatience crosses Leon's face. "You can tell me, or you can watch me hurt people." He nods at the man holding Amo. The man turns the knife so that the point is at Amo's neck. A thin trickle of blood starts down his throat. The defiance in his eyes turns to fear.

My thoughts spin. Think of something. Anything . . .

"We're trying to go back to my people," I say. "Up north. It's why I was interested in those mapmakers. It's why I wanted to know if you were headed there."

Leon nods at the man, who relaxes the knife a mite.

He tilts his head, studying me. "You're from up north." He runs his free hand over his jaw. "Now, that's hard to believe. Haven't seen any large groups of people heading that way since we arrived. And believe me, we've been watching."

"My people have been living there a long while. Far longer than you'd imagine."

He raises his eyebrows.

"Decades," I say, my voice growing in strength with the truth of my words. "We heard people from the east were finally moving out this way. We"—I gesture to Tom and Kane—"came out to see. Came for the adventure. But we got lost, and . . . and Matisa found us." It sounds lame, even to my ears.

Leon's gaze traces the ground like he's thinking hard. His face splits into a grin. "Well, how about that?" he says, looking up at me. "I was right." He shakes his head. "You know, when I saw you all out here, I knew it couldn't be coincidence." He smiles. "It's fortunate you came along, more fortunate you stuck around. Malachi and I couldn't take you all on our own. We needed the boys."

Matisa mutters a curse. *The boys.* His men. He pretended to be harmless, weaponless. She thought I was getting us information, but truly, all we did was give Leon the time he needed to get the upper hand.

"What do you want with us?" I demand.

"Been looking for you all for a while," he says.

Us?

Can't be.

"Ever since one of my men returned with some skinny pregnant girl a couple months back."

Rebecca.

"She was part of a real strange group: a mix of skins, you'd

160

say. Pales, reds, half-bloods. Those fools stumbled into my men teaching a newcomer to these parts what's what." The raid at the river—the burning homestead. "My men caught some of them: two pales and a red. But they couldn't agree what to do with them. See, my brother was sure he needed to use them to barter for some information, but my man wasn't inclined. They split up, my man took the pregnant girl back to my Keep, and Julian took a red girl and a white boy, planning to trade the girl for that information." His gaze skims over us. "Information I'm guessing you have."

"And what is that?"

He smiles a terrible smile. "About a place up north that cures the Bleed."

I keep my voice steady. "We don't know what you're speaking on."

"No? Well, that's unfortunate. You see, we were in a bit of a skirmish recently with the Dominion—fighting over a village to the south."

Kane stiffens. He was right: Leon's men attacked Genya's village.

"And when I realized these bastards weren't going to just roll over and let me have the land that's rightfully mine, I figured I needed to offer them something. I sent word with a captive, turned him loose as a show of good faith: I'll bring them a cure if they leave me in peace. Only problem is, I can't find the place that has it, so I figured I'd find the people who know something about that." He feigns disappointment. "I was so sure you were those people. So sure you'd know the place."

We're silent.

Leon looks at the man holding Amo. "But maybe you just need the right incentive to share?" The man presses the tip of his knife into Amo's neck again. Fear shoots through my body, ice-cold.

It's snuffed out by a ruckus. A growl. A savage bark. And the man holding Amo releases him and scrambles back, holding his leg. "Hey!"

Amo's alone for a heartbeat. Malachi, quick as a blink, shoots a warning shot into the tree behind him, telling him to stay put.

The man who was holding him is scrambling away from a blur of black and brown, all scruffy and growling something fierce . . .

Hunger.

The man with the knife darts behind the men who've got their weapons trained on us. Hunger skids to a stop, barking like mad at him. "It goddamn bit me!" he hollers.

She stands her ground, swiveling her head, barking at all the intruders in turn.

I think for a moment that now's our chance; she's giving us the diversion we need to get out . . .

But the men before us barely move a muscle; they're not bothered by her presence one bit.

"Goddamn it!" the man yells, still holding his leg. Hunger barks and barks.

"Shut that thing up," Leon says to Malachi.

Malachi nods and turns his gun around, wielding it like a club, and approaches Hunger from the side.

"No!" I yell as Hunger dodges the first swing. She darts

back, far faster than Malachi, who grunts in frustration. He swings his gun around and raises it, training it on her.

"Go!" I yell at Hunger. Malachi fires, and the earth at her back leg explodes.

And she's gone, scampering into the trees.

Leon narrows his eyes at me. "Is that your dog?"

I say nothing, but I can't help it: my eyes search the trees.

"Unfortunate." He looks at the young man still holding his leg. "Janz, when it comes back, shoot it." His voice is mild. He jerks his chin at the young man standing nearest us. Looks a lot like Leon—could be his son. "Move them back to the river." The man waves his gun at Lea. "Remy, deal with the packs and supplies. Bring all the weapons to me."

Under the watchful eye of seven men, one man walking backward with his gun up, two flanking us, and two at the back, we make our way through the trees toward the river. Kane sticks close to me, and I see Tom doing the same to Eisu. Leon follows, barking orders to the men who've been left with our things.

We leave the trees and step out onto the shelves of rock beside the swollen river. There are two more men here; one holds Eisu's smoke-white horse, and the other has Matisa's. I don't see Beast anywhere.

Leon strides to the front of our group. "Move them next to that drop there," he instructs, passing Eisu's gun from one hand to the other. "That way we only have to watch this side."

There's a patch of smooth rock where the river drops in a small shelf. The water rushes by in a torrent, and the far side is more than a stone's throw away. And I see what he means.

None of us would be foolish enough to try the river as an escape. We'd be dashed to bits in a heartbeat.

"It's not safe to stay near the river," Matisa says.

Leon silences her by cocking the gun.

The young man, the one who looks like Leon, jerks his head, telling me to move. I do, but not fast enough; he shoves me from behind with the butt of his weapon, and though I don't want to, I cry out.

Kane spins and grabs on to the rifle, shoving the boy back two steps. Before the boy can straighten, three rifles are pointed at Kane's head. He raises his hands and steps back. Malachi looks over at the young man Kane shoved and grins, like he's amused that he was manhandled by Kane.

The boy's face contorts with anger. He steps forward quick and jabs the barrel of his rifle into Kane's gut. Kane doubles over with the blow.

I cry out as the young man brings the rifle end down on the back of Kane's neck, dropping him to the earth. I dart forward, but a gun clicks in my ear, freezing me in place. Malachi puts the gun square to my temple.

"That's enough!" Leon barks. "I don't have time for theatrics."

"Get with the rest," Malachi says, pushing the barrel against my head once and withdrawing his arm. I stumble away from Kane.

Matisa grabs my hand as they crowd us onto the rocks.

"Sit," orders Leon. We do. Leon nods to Kane, who is still several paces back, in the trees. "You join us when you're ready," he says. Rage burns inside me.

"Should we check the woods for stragglers?" a man with dirty hair and teeth asks.

Leon shakes his head. "This is all of them. But keep sights on them. They look like kids, but they know what they're doing."

The three men position themselves in a semicircle with their guns trained on us, hemming us in against the violent river.

Leon smiles at us. "Now, some of you will come with me, and some of you will be taken to the Keep. You see, it was damaged recently by your kind"—he directs this at Matisa—"so I will need some help rebuilding. It seems only fair you provide the labor."

"You said the Dominion attacked your place," I say.

"Did I?" Leon says. "Well, you looked so cozy with these reds, I hated to cast aspersions. Would've made for a rather uncomfortable evening, don't you think?"

The river roars behind us.

"It is not safe here," Matisa tries again, raising her voice over the clamor. "For you or us. We must move to higher ground."

"Shut up," barks one of the men. "Or I'll shut you up."

Leon ignores them both. He's running his hand over Tom's gun, the one he took off Eisu. He peers at it. He's noticed the handle. *Almighty.* The initials. Tom had scratched a line through them, but they're still there if you look close enough.

He turns around, fixing his gaze on Eisu. "Where did you get this?" he asks. His voice is mild, like he's just curious, but there's danger in his eyes.

Tom stands straighter. Eisu says nothing.

Leon cocks his head. "The thing is," he says, "my brother used to have a gun just like this. Put his initials on the handle." He walks forward two steps.

I'm trying to keep my face blank, but my heart is beating fast.

"This looks an awful lot like his piece," Leon says, like he's thinking hard. He raises his voice. "And he'd never part with it voluntarily." He looks at the gun again, tracing his fingers over the inscription. "His body was found a few days' ride from our Keep. Shot dead." He pulls his head up and looks at Eisu. "Of course, you already knew that." He pulls the gun up and looks down the barrel. "And I've been wanting to find whoever—"

"He didn't do it!" Tom cries, scrambling in front of Eisu.

Leon lowers the gun, his face dead calm. "Well, now," he says. "You sound pretty sure of that. You sound like you know that for certain." His eyes are two hot coals. He jerks his head. "Malachi," he says, "bring those two here."

I make a sound of protest. Matisa silences me by squeezing my arm.

Malachi waves his gun at Tom and Eisu. Eisu climbs to his feet and follows.

My heart is in my throat, watching them leave the safety of our huddle.

"Over there," Leon says, waving the gun at the trees. Tom and Eisu stand beside one another, several paces away from Kane.

"You're certain?" Leon squints at Tom. "Certain this boy didn't shoot my brother?"

Tom says nothing. He nods his head. Once.

"But yet you have his piece," Leon says. "So I'm finding that hard to believe. And if this boy didn't shoot him"—he fixes Tom with his dead stare—"who did?"

Tom raises his chin.

No. Don't tell.

He takes a breath and opens his mouth—

"I'll show it to you!" I blurt out. "The place that cures the Bleed. I'll show it to you."

I hear Matisa suck in a breath.

Leon turns to me. "I knew there was more to you than met the eye. You're a pretty good liar—I'll give you that." He pauses. "Of course, you could be lying to me now."

"I'm not. My settlement's been living there for generations."

"Your settlement."

"And I'll take you there. But you need to set my friends free first."

"How about I don't, and you show me, anyway?"

"I'm no good to you dead."

He studies me a long while. A lifetime. "This cure," he says. "What is it?"

"I said I'll take you to it."

"You'll have to give me more than that to prove you're not lying."

My thoughts race. He and Julian must've learned about the place up north from his workers, the abandoners from *sohkâtisiwak*. His workers aren't looking for the place, so either they don't believe in a cure, or . . . or they're still afraid of those woods. They abandoned Matisa's valley before we arrived, before we brought news about what truly happened to their scouts there . . .

My head snaps up. "Your workers are scared of the place, aren't they?"

He raises his eyebrows, giving me my answer.

"Their people disappeared there, years ago."

He measures me.

"That was our doing."

"You killed them?"

The lie comes easy because it's so close to the truth. "We were protecting our cure."

His eyes flicker.

"And that's why you need me along," I say. "You have to know the woods to survive them."

He sucks his teeth, his cold gaze raking over my face. "All right," he says. He nods his head and tucks the gun into his waistband. "All right. I'll let them go."

Relief floods through me.

"*Em.*" The whisper comes from Matisa.

Leon turns his attention back to Tom and Eisu. "But, of course, there's still the matter of my brother," he says. He takes a step toward Eisu, touching the gun at his waistband again.

Again, Tom steps in front of Eisu. "He wasn't there!" he says.

Leon's eyes narrow in satisfaction at Tom's confession.

Tom knows he's said too much, but he presses on, "He had nothing to do with it." He raises his chin. "If you're looking to punish someone for it, punish me."

A hot wind rushes through my head.

Leon squints. "Punish? Oh, no. No." He relaxes his stance. "There's no need for that."

"Em."

I turn my head. Matisa's looking up the river, her face troubled.

And I hear it.

A deep rumbling, like the earth is mounting a protest, like the mountains are answering. It's faint, far away. But it's there.

Kane hears it, too. And Lea. Leon's men don't seem to; they're watching Leon with interest. I glance at Tom, who's standing in front of Eisu, an uncertain look creasing his features.

"No need," Leon repeats, rubbing a hand over his jaw. "There's only need for compensation."

"Compensation?" Tom's eyes flick to the men behind Leon. Eisu reaches out a hand and touches Tom's back. The rumbling is louder now. Closer.

"Yes," Leon says, pulling the gun from his waistband. "Eye for an eye." He raises the gun and shoots.

NO!

Tom jerks backward and sideways, hand grabbing for his chest. He staggers a step and turns, his wide eyes finding mine. His legs wobble. He stumbles and falls back.

Into Eisu's arms.

A scream echoes around my head, shrill like the winter wind.

Eisu's hands grasp at Tom in desperation; he's trying to hold him upright. Tom looks down, down, to the red stain spreading out across his shirt, under his fingers. I can't breathe, can't breathe . . . Tom lifts his gaze again. At first I think he's looking for me, but, no, he's looking at something behind me. I need to turn my head, need to see it, too, but I can't move. All I can see is him collapsed in Eisu's arms, hand to his heart, his wide blue eyes, the pink in his cheeks draining out—down to that crimson blossom that's getting bigger and bigger . . .

And the roar comes, shaking the ground, tearing the world apart.

Kane leaps forward across the space, shouting and grabbing for my arm, hauling me upright. My head moves of its own accord, drifting away from the look on Tom's face and up the river, toward the mountains.

A wall of water rushes straight for us, tumbling, churning, obliterating everything in its path.

Kane pulls me to my feet, but I am caught in a mess of limbs as everyone scrambles up at the same instant. Shouts from Leon's men are drowned out by the roar. We push forward, trying to claw our way up the incline, but we have no time, no time . . .

The river bursts over us like cold death.

Kane's hand is ripped from my arm as the water grabs me up, pulls my legs out from under me, and tosses me like a leaf. It drags me under, rolls me, bashes me against something hard.

And everything is dark.

17

I'VE BEEN IN THIS PLACE BEFORE. THIS ROARING hollow of black. This endless torrent of ice and pain and deafening sound.

This time, there are no Lost People to save me. I am rolled and turned and torn apart. The river is in my ears and lungs, and there is nothing I can do but let it have its way, let it carry me in its crushing embrace, race me toward my death.

And now, stillness. Like I'm floating just below the surface of this raging, wild water, and everything else moves around me: the sky and trees race past above, while branches and boulders rush by on either side.

A face appears above me, peering into the water. Her features are blurry, but her snow-white hair gives her away.

Soeur Manon.

The old healer woman, dead a season already, reaching one frail hand into the water, her brittle fingers grasping for me. They trail through my hair in a slow, sweeping motion and catch hold. She pulls me up, up, toward her. I reach for her, my body drifting slow, like a reluctant seedpod caught on a breeze.

Her hand lets go.

The violent water rushes over me. Sky and clouds and trees blur into one.

Something bites my face and squeezes the air from my chest, and I am rolled back under, rushed along the riverbed.

But deep inside I feel my heart beating out a rhythm, and I hear voices high and plaintive, lifting in song. They swirl around me, pierce straight through me. Fill me with a fire.

I strain and push and kick for the surface of the water, clawing my way to air. I'm fighting toward no one now, but the song lifts me high, and the beat of my heart is strong.

Telling me I'm not alone.

These are not my Cleansing Waters.

And this watery grave can't have me.

My eyes pop open. The white light is like searing fire. I snap them shut again.

My mouth and throat are caked with grit. I gag, trying to clear a small space to get a breath, but there's no room. Need to make space . . .

I raise my head. Sharp pain shoots through my temple, across my brow. I drop my head to one side and retch up water and mud. Blessed air fills my lungs, and my breath comes back in a ragged gasp.

I breathe deep, blinking and squinting, until the blur of color and light around me sharpens. Wet sand coats the side of my face; my right arm is bent awkward beneath me. I'm lying on the riverbank, staring at a fallen tree in the middle of the water. It's bone-white—looks like the rib cage of some giant animal, split apart and blasted clean.

Split apart.

Blasted.

I retch again. I turn my head away from the bile and press my forehead to the sand and breath deep, trying to still my mind. Trying to focus on moving my body. Can't feel my legs. And my arm . . .

I steel myself and pull it out from beneath me, gritting my teeth so I don't scream. I take a deep breath and squirm my legs back and forth, feeling a pang of relief as I realize they're not broken, just numb from the cold water and whatever rocks and trees they were bashed against. My cheek is stinging. Using one arm, I push myself up and sit back against debris that's washed ashore. My hand reaches behind for balance, and I touch something soft. Cloth. Hair.

It's not debris.

I turn, scrambling back, ignoring the throbbing pain in my head, my shoulder.

Malachi is facedown on the sand, his head turned, one bloodshot eye watching me. His body isn't sprawled in an awkward way—looks like he's resting. Waiting.

I push back in a panic, waiting for him to spring up and grab for my leg. Laboring to my feet, I look around for a tree branch or a rock. Anything to defend myself.

He doesn't move.

Standing above him now, I can see why. The backside of his head is gone. Just clean folded in on itself, like a rotten squash. No blood. No anything. Just a caved-in head and one empty eye looking at me. He's not coming after me. He's not moving. Ever again.

I turn away and retch again, but there's nothing left in my stomach. A trickle of blood streams down my chin. I press two fingers to my cheekbone, feeling a split in my skin. One hand on my knee, one arm dangling, I stay bent for a long while, listening to the woods beside the river. They're eerie quiet. The flash flood Matisa warned us about is long gone— the river is back to its size from last night. Here, it's wide and deep enough that it's silent. I straighten up, feeling a sharp pain when I breathe in, and I baby my right arm, cradling it against me.

I'm alone.

I spin and search the bank downstream. A flash of blue is caught on a branch that overhangs the river. A scrap of someone's clothing. My gaze traces up the riverbank, and my heart stutters when I see the body of a white horse. Can tell by the dappled gray marks on its rump that it's Eisu's horse. *Was* Eisu's horse.

Eisu.

Tom.

My breath leaves me.

Tom, standing there in shock, hand grasping at his shirt, blood pooling out. His eyes, searching mine . . . I told myself I'd protect him. But I didn't. I couldn't. I . . .

I stagger and drop to my knees, ignoring the rush of pain in my shoulder as I lean forward and press my head to the earth. A silent wail starts deep in my chest and moves up, pulling from something so deep within me and rushing out of me so fast that when my voice finally comes, I sound like an animal.

The sobs wrack my body, make it hard to breathe. I gasp, awash in despair so deep, it's like I'm back in the river. Feels like there'll be no surfacing this time. And I don't care who might be in these woods, who might hear me. Anything beyond the agony in my heart, right now, would be a relief.

Tom. Matisa.

Kane—

I never told him. Never told him that I still love him.

A different kind of pain courses through me, sending a roiling sickness to my belly. My arm. I look at it and wriggle my fingers, then move it about—it shoots fire in my shoulder but moves of its own accord. It's not useless and dangling, just pulsing with jagged, constant pain . . .

Rage shoots through me. I want to stop the throbbing.

And I don't care what it takes.

I pull myself to my feet and stagger to the nearest tree, grasping at it with my good hand. I wrack my brain for what Soeur Manon taught me about this kind of thing—how to tell if the bone within is broken. I can't move without pain, but nothing feels out of place.

I take a deep breath and grab the elbow of my hurt arm, pinning it to my side. I step closer to the trunk, close my eyes, breathe deep again, and start counting to three.

I throw my weight forward on *two*, driving my shoulder hard into the tree trunk. Bone-shattering pain and nausea sweep me.

Something pops.

And now: sheer relief.

I shrug, moving my arm about, daring it to protest. But the pain has disappeared.

I sit back down and cry.

I'm sitting at the table in our kitchen, looking over my little jar of left-behinds. My favorite, the little clay animal, sits dead center of the table. I watch my hands fuss the arrowheads, lining them up one after the other.

"You'll worry the sharp right off them." The voice is low, familiar. I raise my head. Pa sits across the table from me, all scruffy beard and thin shoulders.

My hands drop the arrowheads. "Pa," I breathe.

He nods at my hands. "You spent so much time collecting those left-behinds, believing they were showing you something. Who would've guessed it meant all this?"

My heart is in my throat. Now's my chance to tell him. I can tell him. "I m-m-miss you, Pa," I stutter. "And I'm . . . I'm so sorry for what happened, for—"

"Shh," he says. "Hush, now."

But I can't hush. I need him to know. "I started down this path thinking it was what I was meant to do. And I've clung to the idea that if I just trust it enough, it'll be all right in the end. But if I'd known what was going to happen, to you, to—" My words are cut off by a sob.

"My girl," he sighs. "There was only one way it could've gone. There was only ever one way."

The sun is hot on the back of my neck. I pull my head up and look around.

Malachi's body lies on the bank like a discarded June-bug

shell. The river drifts by, silent. Downstream, the blue cloth flutters in a gentle breeze.

My clothes are dry. Been sitting here—dozing?—for an hour or more.

I stand, feeling how bruised my body is now that it's no longer numb. Putting my fingers to my face, I realize that the wound on my cheek has sealed with a crust of blood.

I look upstream at Eisu's horse. Can't see anything, or anyone, else up that way.

And downstream . . . same thing.

I swallow against the panic crowding up my chest. Got nothing. No food. No medicines satchel. My knife is still wedged in my *ceinture*, somehow, but beyond that, I have no weapons. I look at my bad foot. No Beast.

I think hard on what to do. Isi and Bly followed this river east to the Keep. Mayhap my best bet is heading downstream, catching up with them. The rest might think that, too. Could be they're just a bit farther on.

Gazing up the river, I see that Eisu's horse still has its gear. Which means saddle packs.

I climb toward it, my stomach turning over. Flies have already found its eyes and nostrils. Its neck is thrown back in an unnatural curve. I stay near its rump and keep my gaze fixed on my fingers fumbling with the saddle pack. I hurry back downriver away from the animal before setting the packs down to see what's inside.

One of them was torn open in the river; it's empty.

The other contains a cloak, a bowl, and several boxes of bullets. No gun.

The saddle packs are too heavy for me to carry for long,

so I spread the cloak on the ground, put the bullets and bowl inside, and tie it up by each corner, leaving one side long to loop over my arm.

I search the banks awhile, looking for a walking stick that'll help with my balance, and finally I find one that will do—a sun-blasted piece of driftwood that fits in my hand and is near as tall as me. Won't be fast like this, but it's the best I've got.

I throw a look back at Eisu's broken horse. Shove the thought from my mind that the next person I find will look the same. Whoever I find next might need my help. I need to collect my thoughts, keep my wits about me.

I press hard onto my bad foot, feeling a pang of disappointment when it doesn't sing fire back at me. I turn and start down the shore.

18

I FIND ANOTHER OF LEON'S MEN.

His limbs are bent at unnatural angles, caught against a large boulder on the far side of the bank. His eyes are frozen open, his skin pale. He hangs like some nightmare scarecrow, staring at me. Accusing me.

The panic comes back, crowding into my chest like a hive of bees.

I turn away and take several deep breaths, trying to fight the sick feeling in my gut.

Just focus on what's in front of you.

When I straighten, I feel something cold against my throat. I fish around inside my shirt and pull out a cord. Attached is a bone and metal object the size of my thumb: the whistle Lea gave me. I remember how pleased she was to present us with them. Me and Tom.

Tom.

I push the thought of him from my mind and put my lips to the whistle and blow. Nothing. Not even the smallest of noises.

I blow into it again, harder this time. Nothing.

I scrub a hand over my face and tuck the whistle back under my shirt. Mayhap it's got river mud in it.

Or mayhap it never worked.

A raven calls from the top of a spruce near the river, and its mate answers, far off in the forest.

I continue down the bank, ignoring the dull ache of hunger starting in my belly.

I find two more horses, gear ripped from their backs. They must've been Leon's; their ribs protrude, and their coats are mangy. They're thin, underfed. Only someone like Merritt Leon would treat his beasts that way.

The picture of him meeting a similar fate—dashed against a rock or caught up in some bramble, held under and drowned—crowds into my mind, but I have to push the thought away.

Can't afford to think on Leon, or I'll think on Tom.

I'll think on Tom laughing at something, think on him practicing his aim at the settlement, think on him gazing at Eisu like he was the sun . . .

I dig my bad foot into the sand, relief surging over me as I feel a needle of pain. My tincture is wearing off. But not fast enough. I look around. Need something to harness the pain, need to put it somewhere.

My eyes are drawn by a flash of blue.

My stomach seizes.

There's another body on the far side of the river.

It's one of us—a girl? Can't tell. It's caught among dead-fall that overhangs the water. Caught and unmoving, torso just visible, back to me, head hanging at a bad angle. Like the neck is broken. The dark hair on the head is in two braids. Lea was wearing her hair that way. Amo, too.

And Matisa.

Fear grips me in a cold hand.

I look at the river. It's moving fast here, and it's deep—there's no way I'd make it across. Could try to find a shallow spot farther downstream, but . . .

For what?

It's not Matisa.

My heart hammers loud in my chest.

I squint harder. The way the hands are, they way they're twisted . . . looks like they're bound.

Amo.

I press forward, leaving the sight behind. Stumbling down the shore, tripping over slippery rocks and driftwood, I hurry, trying to put distance between me and that—

Come back.

Amo's calling to me. Calling for me not to leave him there. Calling for me to turn around, free him from that watery cage.

I clap my hands over my ears, fighting against the swell of tears. I hit my toe against a large rock and stumble, dropping my walking stick.

Come back.

Righting myself, I press onto my bad foot again, but there's no familiar, calming pain. I cast a frantic look and spot a stick—it's small, about the length of my finger, a splintered piece from a large chunk of driftwood. I grab it up in my hand and fumble with my sleeve, pushing it up to my elbow. I put the sharp point to the inside of my left arm.

Closing my eyes, I drag the stick in a line down my flesh—hard enough that it shoots pain through to my fingertips but not hard enough to break the skin. The sensation drowns out Amo's voice, but now the image of Tom, pressing his hand to his heart, is creeping in . . .

I do it again, harder.

This time, everything vanishes. The searing pain is all that's left for several welcome heartbeats. My breath is shaky with relief.

I drop the stick, swallow hard, and look up.

It's getting on dusk. The sky is turning blood-red through the tops of the trees, and night is looming like a shadowy spirit.

Can't sleep near the river tonight. It's colder along the shore and still dangerous—who knows how many flash floods the mountains have in them?—but being in the woods, unable to see what's coming . . .

Could use Hunger with me now. She always heard things long before I did.

And Beast, too.

Focus on what's in front of you.

I push off into the trees, aiming to find a place to lie down.

Before, when I was lost in this wilderness, I was with Isi and Daniel. Isi knew everything, but Daniel was young and afraid and needed help keeping his head.

I taught him to sing a song when he was getting scared, and at the time I knew I could've used one myself. Just like right now. Don't want to risk making any more noise than I have to, so I take the whistle from beneath my shirt. I breathe into it, playing a silent tune.

It's darker among the trees but warmer away from the river, so I push a little farther into the woods. Eisu's cloak is still damp, and I've nothing to use to start a fire. I'll sheer off some spruce boughs and cover myself with them for the night. It won't be like having a fire, but it'll do. I breathe in through my nose and out through the whistle as I search for trees with low branches.

I'm halfway through sawing a third bough with my knife when I hear something in the woods behind me. I step behind the tree and drop into a crouch.

It's hard to make out in the dusk, but whatever's coming at me is big, and it's aiming at something with purpose. I glance up at the spruce tree, wondering if I can climb it fast enough—

A blur crashes out of the bushes before me and pulls to a halt. It's a huge shadow in the twilight, but the white blaze on his forehead glows in the dusk. A whip of frothy sweat stands out on his glistening hair.

"Beast!"

Relief washes over me, so intense, I near collapse.

I push off the tree and stumble toward him, my hands outstretched. He doesn't shy or bolt. He lowers his head to my hands. I run them up his jaw to his brow and then circle my arms around his strong neck, pressing my face to his sweat-slicked hide, breathing in his familiar smell. His saddle is still on. His bridle, too, and the reins are still looped around his neck. I feel the cold of the whistle against my breastbone.

You can call him with this.

It must make a sound that only horses can hear.

Lea was right.

And touching Beast, feeling his warmth . . . I burst into tears.

Beast cranes his neck and nuzzles my back, his lips nibbling at the tassels of my *ceinture*.

I hold on to him like I'm holding on to life itself. "Good horse," I say, hugging him tight. "Good Beast."

He jerks his head like he's had enough of this display, and I pull away, smiling and wiping the back of my hand against my eyes.

"It's all right, boy," I say, and I pat him again. "It's going to be all right."

The ruined cabin stares at me, its sagging windows sad eyes in a rotting face. *Les trembles* move like there's a big wind, but I know something else disturbs them.

And now, a flash of movement. Darting through the dream trees. Just beyond the crumbling logs. Headed for the Watch flats.

Hurry.

Branches whip at my face and slap at my arms as I move forward, gaining speed.

Following.

Chasing.

Hurry.

19

I TWIST AND STRETCH IN THE SADDLE, STIFF
from my sleep under the spruce boughs but feeling far more
rested than I figured I would be.

Helped having Beast nearby last night. Not sure he
would've alerted me to danger, but just knowing he was there
let me surrender to a sleep I needed something desperate.
The sun filters through the boughs of the spruce above,
warming us.

When I woke, I was surprised to feel my arm pulsing with
an angry red line. And then I remembered picking up that
stick.

I rubbed at it fierce, feeling a mite ashamed, but there was
no erasing it.

Now that I know Beast survived, it seems more likely that
others have, too. And with crippling fear no longer clamoring
for my thoughts, I don't need to use pain to control them.

What I need is food. My stomach is near turning itself
inside out with hunger.

Been following the river east at least an hour and haven't found a berry or a mushroom suitable to eat. The few items from our group I found scattered along the shore were next to useless: bits of clothing, a boot and hat, a bridle, a smashed lantern— nothing that could be used as a tool or a weapon. And nothing resembling food.

I pull my knife from my *ceinture* and study it, testing the blade with my thumb. It's sharp enough—if I pressed a mite harder, I'd be dealing with a bloody hand. But I'm useless at hunting anything with a knife. Don't have Kane's aim. I'd lose the knife in the brush and spend half the day looking for it, more like.

I'm used to that dull ache in my belly from life in the settlement. It was irritating, but I knew there would be something—however meager—coming my way to eat at some point in the day. Out here, if I want to eat, I'll need to find something growing in this forest. That, or hope I run across a tree growing bowls of stew . . .

My thoughts stop there.

Matisa told me something just like that once. Told me about a tree having a fleshy underside to it that you could eat—was full of sugars. Like a treat. She said early summer was the best time—when the trees' saps were running. It's not early summer anymore, but it might still be good.

Mitosuc. That's what she called it. Said I could use the word, and everyone would know I was inviting them to go collect the tree flesh. *Mitosuc.*

And that grove I dreamt of and found her in on our journey to her people—Isi called that *mâyamito. Mito:* tree.

I pull Beast to a stop and dismount. The kind of trees

I dreamt aren't in seed anymore—they look different now. But if I can remember their trunks . . .

I stalk off into the forest, looking first to the tops of trees to find the leafy kind, and when I find a bunch growing together, I get close and examine the bark. Looks the same, mayhap?

My stomach pangs again. Dizziness floods me.

I'll have to take my chances. I drop the cloak to the forest floor and take my knife in both hands.

Carving a chunk of the bark off takes some time. When I finally manage to pull a section free, it comes off in protest. Underneath, the tree's flesh gleams white, like bone. I take my knife and begin scraping down the trunk, peeling off large strips, the way Matisa told me. I need both hands to do it, and the flesh is pulpy, dripping. I stop, grab the bowl out from the cloak bundle, and set it at the base of the tree to catch the shavings. I begin again, paying careful attention to the knife so that it doesn't skip off and cut me, and I flick off the shavings into the bowl. Soon I have a sizeable amount and sit with my back to the tree, using my hands to scoop up the mush.

It's sweet; not sweet like honey, but like the clover stems we used to chew as youngsters, and feeling it hit my belly is a relief.

By the time I'm done with the bowl, I'm no longer shaky with hunger.

I gather up my bundle and walk back to Beast, the sugars from the *mitosuc* putting new strength into my steps. The realization that I'm not helpless, that I can keep myself alive out here, pulls my chin up and my gaze straight ahead.

And as I get atop Beast, I find a new resolve, somewhere deep inside me. No matter who I find or don't, I can follow this river east to the one that winds past my settlement. It'll take me days longer than the route we were taking, but it's my best chance to see our journey through.

I've come this far.

I'll stop when I'm dead.

It's getting on afternoon when I let Beast stop and drink. I hesitate drinking the water myself. Have to assume this river is safe from the Bleed; it's the reason Leon's Keep has survived so far. Still, I'm nervous. Should probably boil it, to be safe, but I've got no way to start a fire.

The river is far shallower here, and as my eyes trace its banks, I notice a trail on the far side. It leaves the trees and widens, a mouth of trodden earth descending into the water. On our side, a similar trail emerges from the water and disappears down the bank.

My heart speeds.

Isi talked about an easy crossing a day's travel to the east. This must be it.

And I must be near the Keep.

I get back on Beast and head farther into the trees. Don't want to use the trail along the bank in case of coming upon Leon's men; better to use the cover of the trees. I urge Beast ahead, keeping alert for any signs of movement, but soon the deadfall becomes impassable. I remember when we'd approached the Keep the last time, there'd been parts of the forest ravaged by fire. Here, the trees are new, and the deadfall is overgrown. Beast stumbles over fallen logs and hummocks of grass so many times, I start to worry he'll topple me.

Ahead I can make out a clearing—the new forest gives way to a grassy meadow. Easy to traverse, if we can just get there.

I slide down and begin to lead Beast, but the fallen trees are crisscrossed at odd angles, making it hard to find safe footing between them. Soon it's clear we'll need to double back and either hug the riverbank or try to cut farther to the northwest to get through this patch of woods. I'm about to turn around and retrace our steps when movement catches my eye. It's ahead in the trees, twenty strides or more, just before the clearing. A person. One? Or two?

One.

Wearing that telltale blue.

My pulse races.

I watch as the person moves—seems to pace. A boy, surely.

I put a hand to Beast. "Stay here," I murmur, touching the whistle under my shirt to make sure it's still there. I crouch and begin making my way through the deadfall, crawling over logs and trying to keep the trees between me and the boy. My throat is tight. That blue is the blue of Matisa's people. We were all wearing it. Even Kane.

I'm so close now. I pull around the last of the trees separating us.

His back is to me, but now I can see his blond hair and pale skin.

Not Kane, but . . .

There's a rifle beside him.

I choke out a cry and leave the safety of the poplars, my heart about to burst and my thoughts all upside down. How did he survive? How did he get here—

He grabs the rifle and turns.

And his ice-blue eyes stop me dead.

"Charlie?"

The gun is raised, and he stands before me, in *osanaskisi-wak* blue, his face a mask of disbelief. "Emmeline, what—"

A thunder of hoofbeats cuts him off. My eyes snap to the meadow beyond the brush Charlie was crouched behind. Four riders are entering the clearing from the woods on the far side. Leathers, long dark hair . . .

Isi. Bly.

They're each doubling a man on their horse. Beside them, two more people are on horses and, behind the horses trying to keep pace, a dozen more *osanaskisiwak* on foot.

The first group of scouts. I dart to the side, planning to burst into the clearing so they can see me, but my painful leg makes me slow.

Charlie is far faster.

He catches me by one arm and jerks me back toward him, pulling me tight to his chest and grabbing my wrists in one hand. The other goes over my mouth. I buck and holler, trying to squirm out of his grip, but he's holding me fast. Strong. Way stronger than I remember.

The riders thunder into the clearing, their movement echoing loud in my heart, in my head, and everything in my body calls out to them.

I'm here!

They're well into the open space now. I'm fighting and struggling, but Charlie's got me firm in his arms, his hand clamped so tight over my mouth, I can't bite him. My scream is a pathetic mewling—scarce a whimper—and my body is tiring fast in his grip. But . . . no. No, I can't let Charlie be the reason they leave me behind. I need to fight, I need to—

Loud bangs erupt, and we both freeze. Gunshots.

My heart stops as two of the riders topple from their horses.

One is Bly. The scout doubling with her grabs for the reins, trying to control the horse.

More gunshots.

And three men on foot pitch forward, their arms splayed wide as the force of the gunfire lifts them off their feet.

Isi shouts and pulls his horse to a halt. The bullet storm comes again—they're getting hit from the far side of the clearing, opposite the river. There are shooters in those trees with guns that repeat and repeat, and Isi and the scouts are unprotected.

I watch, helpless, as the man behind Isi topples and his horse rears and screams. Isi pulls his horse in a circle, head swiveling as he scans their surroundings.

They're trapped: whatever or whoever they're running from is to the east, the shooters to the northwest. Their best hope is south to the river, but the crossing is upstream, beyond this impassable forest. Running in these trees is tricky; riding a horse is impossible. Isi barks at the men flattening themselves to the earth and puts heels to his horse, heading straight for us. Charlie throws his weight forward, slamming both of us to the ground.

He's heavy on top of me. Can't see anything now, but the ground is trembling with footfalls. They stop abrupt; Isi's no doubt realized the horses can't traverse the fallen logs and brush. He calls out.

I can hear them retreating.

Charlie relaxes his grip on me enough that I can push up to my knees. The scouts have fled to the riverbank. Another rattle of gunfire comes from the far side of the trees.

Now I can see Isi spurring his horse hard, leading them over the rise.

There's a mighty splashing. Isi's horse screams.

Silence. Can't see what happens next, whether they're all whisked away downstream or whether they're winning the battle with the river. I'm frozen, trying to get breath in through my nose. A sob is stuck in my throat.

Charlie is still gripping me. New fear smothers my grief. When Charlie's arms relax and he pushes off me to stand, I scramble up and away, whirling to see if he's aiming that rifle at me. I lose my balance on my bad foot and stumble, taking a knee.

He stands before me, unmoving. The rifle is on the forest floor behind him. I consider my options. I could run, but he'd have that rifle in his hands in a heartbeat. And even if he doesn't want to draw attention to us by shooting, he'd catch me straightaway. Can't run into the clearing, not with those shooters on the far side . . . I glance at the bank, picturing the fast-flowing river.

He sighs. "You'd drown."

I'm still breathing hard from struggling in his arms.

He frowns. "You think I saved you from that skirmish so I could kill you myself?"

I stare at him, trying to make sense of what I'm seeing. He's wearing *osanaskisiwak* blue. Why is he wearing that? And what does he want with me? Why *would* he save me?

I stand and back up, putting several strides between us.

"Em," he says, like he's tired. He raises his hands, palms toward me. "Not going to hurt you."

I shift my weight, wary.

"Can't you see I just saved your life?"

"H-h-how—" I stutter. "How did you know? About those shooters?"

"Been watching this fort for days. Leon's men have been waiting for First People to return since the last raid. They set up to ambush them."

The horses screaming, those men falling . . . Did Isi make it? Did his horse swim like ours?

"Wh-wh-why are you watching the fort?" I ask.

"Rebecca," he says. "She's in that Keep."

Of course. But that doesn't explain why he's in that blue. I mistook him for one of us. For . . . "Where'd you get those clothes?"

"I didn't steal them, if that's what you're thinking."

"Then where?"

"How about you tell me what you're doing here? Last I saw you, you were headed west with that girl."

My thoughts freeze. Do I tell him? Or should I pretend the rest of us are out in the trees somewhere until I truly know what he's aiming at?

"You look pretty banged up," he says, nodding at my face.

My hands go to my cheek, where a crust of blood remains, sealing the wound shut. "There was a flash flood, and—" I close my eyes against the memory and shake my head, remembering the scouts heading over the riverbank. "I have to go. I have to go see." I take a step toward the clearing.

"Wouldn't do that," Charlie says. "Leon's men'll be coming for the bodies any minute now. Soon as they're sure it's clear."

I stop. He's right.

But I don't like the way he's looking at me. Measuring me, like he's deciding something. The way he did back when we found him: an outcast from the settlement.

When he betrayed us.

My skin prickles. "Need to get my horse," I say, backing up. "Left him in the trees a ways back."

"I'll come with you," Charlie says, stepping forward.

"No!"

He stops. "Em, please."

"Why?"

He throws a look at the clearing. Back at me. He winces, like what he's about to say pains him. "Need your help."

"My help?"

His mouth pulls into a humorless smile. "Don't really have anyone else to ask."

I search his face. Charlie's lied to me before—he's pretended to be trustworthy, to forgive our rocky past, for his own gain. Not making that mistake again.

"You needed my help last time," I say. "Didn't turn out so good for us."

"Or me," he says.

The image of him tied in that grove comes over me. He was begging me not to leave him. Staring into his blue eyes now, it's clear he remembers it like it was yesterday. "What do you want?" I ask him.

"Need your help getting Rebecca back."

"Or what?" My eyes go to his rifle.

He follows my gaze. "I ain't forcing you."

"You're telling me if I don't want to help you, I can just turn and walk away this instant?" But as I say the words, I feel guilt eating at me. He betrayed us, but he also saved Kane.

"I just *saved your life*." His voice has a fire in it now.

"Did you?" I ask. "And how would I know, Charlie? How would I know, truly, what you just did? When you—"

"Here!" He backs up, reaches down, and grabs the rifle by the barrel. He thrusts the gun toward me, butt first. "Take it! Then you'll know."

I recoil, stepping back farther.

A shadow crosses his face. He sinks to his knees. "Or make damn sure I won't ask you again." He puts the muzzle to his forehead. His hands can't reach the trigger, but all at once the vision of Brother Stockham putting that gun under his chin surges over me.

"Charlie!" I gasp. "Stop that!" I slap the rifle from his hands. It thuds to the forest floor. "Quit being so bleedin' dramatic!" I stare at him, my heart beating fast.

He hangs his head. "Can't live with myself if I don't get Rebecca outta that Keep," he says, his voice broken. "And I can't do it on my own."

I stare into those ice-blue eyes, swollen with remorse and desperation. My heart twists. "I left you for dead," I say, my voice quiet.

"Don't change the fact I need you."

I think about him tied to that tree.

Don't have time for this. Need to—

To what? Told myself I'd head back to the big river alone and follow it north to my settlement, but in truth I never thought I'd have to. Was so sure I'd find Kane or Matisa if I just kept to this river, or, at the least, I'd find the scouts. I didn't, and now Bly is dead, and Isi . . . Despair sweeps me.

And the look on Charlie's face . . .

I nod at his pack. "You got any food in there? You're acting addled; let's eat something and talk." I throw a look to the clearing. Leon's men are emerging from the trees on the far side to examine the bodies. "But not here."

Charlie scrambles to his feet with a look so grateful, my relief is snuffed out by shame. And as I watch him stoop and pick up his pack, I realize he thinks he's just saved Rebecca's life. We set off into the trees, back to where I left Beast. And I realize something else.

Somehow, I knew this day was coming.

20

WE SIT UNDER THE TREES, CHEWING THROUGH the suet and berries Charlie fished out of a square of cloth. The tang of the berries cuts through the sickly lard, and though I'm real hungry, I have to force myself to eat. We're back near Beast and well out of earshot, but I picture Leon's men piling those bodies up in the middle of the field. Tossing them into the river. Can't get the ambush out of my mind, and if I don't stop thinking on it, I'm going to panic.

I turn my efforts to studying Charlie. He's different. Less certain. Being out here, alone . . . he's seen some things. But he's also probably done some things. Still don't know where he got those clothes.

"They'll be moving the women back inside the walls soon," he says. "It's our best chance to get Rebecca."

I shove down a pang of guilt. "What do you mean—moving them back?"

"They left two nights ago, all packed up, looking like they were going somewhere—just like that blond man, their leader, did a few days ago. But they just camped in the woods, waiting for them First Peoples."

"How did they know the First People were coming?"

"Not sure they bargained on those two," Charlie says. He means Isi and Bly. "Think they were hoping for revenge against them others. They sacrificed some workers as bait; pretty sure they were hoping for a bigger head count."

The others. Leon said First People attacked his Keep and took some of his workers. "You saw the first attack?"

Charlie nods, chewing.

"Could you see what the attackers looked like?"

"Plain as day. They found me first, out here in the woods." He swallows a bite of berries. "It was them First Peoples I told you about that found my camp a few months back."

Sohkâtisiwak. They must've been the ones Leon was speaking on; they attacked Leon's Keep and freed some of the captives. And Leon's men were playing at being more compromised than they were to entice them back for the rest. Isi walked right into a dispute between Leon and *sohkâtisiwak.*

"I remember," I say. "They're the people you tried to steal Matisa for."

He nods, looking uncomfortable. "Yeah, them. Anyhow, they recognized me. Shared some food with me. Even gave me new clothes."

So they're still wearing the blue of Matisa's people. I study Charlie's shirt. Was too preoccupied before, but I see it now, the small crest on his right shoulder. A hawk. He's telling the truth. "And did you tell them what had happened? That you'd found Matisa but she escaped?"

Charlie shakes his head no.

"Strikes me odd they'd be friendly when you didn't get them what they wanted," I remark.

His eyes hold mine. "I ain't lying, Em. They told me they'd try to get Rebecca out, too, but it didn't work. They only managed to free a few."

I think on this. What use would Charlie be to *sohkâtisiwak* now? Unless . . .

"Did you tell them you knew how to get to the place that cures the Bleed?" I use the words Leon's men did when Charlie was held by them, since he doesn't know how the remedy truly works.

Charlie frowns in confusion. "What?"

"When I left you at the grove, I told you that place was our settlement."

His frown deepens. "So?"

"So you could use that information to secure their help."

"That wouldn't do nothing. They already found them woods."

I sit back. "Oh?"

"Sure. But they won't go in alone. They wanted Matisa so bad because they need her with them."

"Why?"

"Said they dreamt there's something powerful in there only she can show them."

I stare at Charlie in shock. They *dreamt* it. Exactly what Matisa was wondering. I try to focus on what I know for certain. "But you knew Leon was looking for it, too. You could've used it to get Rebecca back. Why didn't you?"

"You mean make a deal with a man who keeps women against their will and slaves people?" Charlie looks at me, his face washed in disgust. "Done some stupid things in my time, but not that stupid."

He's not saying he *wouldn't* make a deal with Leon; he's saying he wouldn't trust him enough to make a deal. It's not the same as doing the right thing, but I suppose it's close enough. What would I do to get Kane back? Matisa? Or Tom—

I shove the thought away and think about the task ahead of me. Shouldn't waste any more time.

"Charlie," I say, "I need to get moving on. There's something I have to do."

His face creases. "But—"

"I'm real sorry about Rebecca, but be honest: what chance would we have against these men?"

"She's outside the walls for once! They took some of the women with them when they moved into the woods. There's about a dozen or so that aren't attached to any particular man. They're . . . for the men who don't have life mates." His cheeks go a mite red, and I realize what he's not saying. My skin crawls. I'm reminded of Kane, bringing Genya away from the Dominion men, making sure she wasn't a part of that.

I try to ignore the sudden ache in my heart, but it's there, as strong as anything.

"The men'll be fussing over the move; they'll have their guard down."

"We don't even have weapons."

"I got this rifle," he says, his voice desperate. "And a knife and some rope and—" He sees the look on my face. "*Please,* Em. Can't we just go see if there's a chance?"

His ice-blue eyes are looking on me with such desperation, I have to look away. Helping Charlie will only slow me down, and it's taking a risk for Rebecca, who betrayed us and then left us for dead.

It's foolish to even consider it.

"Been watching this Keep for days, Em. I planned to try to get Rebecca after they had their little ambush. You showing up makes me sure of it."

No. No, this is foolish. We could walk straight into Leon's men—just like Isi did—and then I'll never get back to my settlement. And if the rest of my friends don't get back, Matisa's people won't have their bargaining tool in time. The Dominion might move ahead with force—with war—and everything Matisa and I have done to prevent disaster will be for nothing.

But . . .

Walking away from Charlie doesn't feel right. Leaving Rebecca to those awful men feels worse.

Charlie doesn't seem to have a plan. He's the impulsive sort, too, which makes rescuing Rebecca less likely. But can I live with myself knowing I didn't even try?

"Em?"

The look on his face is so hopeful that my guilt from before surfaces strong.

We've all made mistakes. Some of us get to weather those with grace, and some of us don't. My own mistakes have cost me something I'm having trouble living without.

But that doesn't mean Charlie's should.

"All right," I say. "Let's go see."

‡

Charlie says the camp is east of the Keep, but going riverside is too risky, with nowhere to hide if we're accosted, so we skirt far to the north on horseback, circling at a distance. When Charlie's sure we're getting near their camp, I rein Beast in. We hop down.

"You gonna tie him?" Charlie asks.

I shake my head. "It's better to leave him free. I can call him to us."

Not having Beast's strength and speed makes me nervous, but if we want to move quiet, we'll have to go on foot. We press through the forest quick as we can manage. In the distance I can see the part of the forest that's been ravaged by fire. I remember a creek nearby—it was the one Isi and I followed to the Keep months back.

That creek had the Bleed.

Surely the men haven't camped next to it?

We climb over fallen trees and press through bramble, taking care not to snap branches as we go. We're getting close to the river again—can hear the rushing waters—when we see movement ahead of us. It's the camp or, at least, the remnants of it. Several horses are tied to the trees outside the clearing. As we approach, I can make out figures busy with tasks. The men are bringing down their tents, and the women are packing up baskets of clothes and food. One of them has a bundle strapped to her back and struggles a mite with her load.

Rebecca.

We crouch in the brush. Can see six men; two of them are armed. They're not paying too much attention to the woods surrounding, though, thanks be.

Charlie presses close to me, his voice low in my ear. "I'm going to skirt to the far side."

"Why?" I whisper.

"See if I can get Rebecca's attention. Let her know I'm here."

I don't like the look in his eyes.

"Don't do anything yet," I beg him. "We need to wait until she's alone." Charlie promised we'd get the lay of the land and then make a plan: figure how one of us could create a diversion while the other ferried Rebecca away. If we succeed, we'll head east, since it's the way I need to go to find the big river. Seeing what Charlie's endured out here alone has reignited my resolve. I'll follow the river north to my settlement and try to see this journey through.

Not too sure what Charlie and Rebecca will do. I glance at Charlie. He seems excited.

"I'll be back," he whispers, and he goes before I can reply.

Bleed it!

I should follow him, make sure he doesn't do something stupid. But if he does, being right beside him will be worse for me. Can't outrun these men, not without Beast.

I hesitate, trying to figure my next move. One of the men pulls his head up toward the trees lining the river, away from my hiding place, away from where Charlie's circling. Something's caught his eye. He mutters to the men, scrubbing a hand through his beard, and stalks off in the direction of the bank.

I scan the trees surrounding the camp. Can't see Charlie; he's good at staying hidden, at least. I move closer so I can get a better look at the women. The men continue their work; the tents are down now, and they're fussing with the ropes and pegs.

A bird calls from across the camp, a mournful tune.

Rebecca's head snaps in its direction. She pauses. The bird calls again. She sets her basket on the ground and readjusts the baby on her back, glancing around. Her eyes go to the men, but they're preoccupied.

Charlie's whistle comes a third time. Rebecca takes a step backward, toward the trees, but a woman gestures to the basket and asks her something. Rebecca keeps her face blank and bends to pick it back up.

Not yet.

And now, a shout, riverside.

The men drop the ropes and tent pegs and straighten. One of them grabs his rifle and disappears into the trees, after the first.

The remaining men venture close to the tree line. The women, too, crane their necks to see.

And no one's watching Rebecca.

My breath catches in my throat. This is Charlie's chance. Couldn't be a better one.

A ruckus draws my attention away. The man who left— the bearded one—and the man who followed him are pulling someone out of the trees.

Whoever it is is fighting hard, and the men are all over, so I can't see who it is. They throw the figure facedown. Blue sleeves become visible as they pull the arms back to bind the wrists. Must be a boy, from the way the men are treating him.

But Charlie's on the other side of the camp, isn't he? Was sure that bird call was his signal to Rebecca.

The first man grabs the boy by his wrists and pulls him to his knees.

My heart stutters.

Not Charlie.

Kane.

I cry out. The men's heads snap toward my place in the trees.

There's a pause.

And two of them start across the camp in my direction.

Kane lolls in the man's grasp. He looks dazed. My voice leaves me again.

And now the men are coming straight for my hiding place.

I'm frozen to the spot, staring at the scene, watching the men cross the space to me . . . there's a flash of movement across the camp. My gaze snaps to the women.

Rebecca is gone.

Several thoughts mash through my head at once: can't leave Kane; got a slim chance of outrunning these men; Charlie and Rebecca will need time to get away . . . I leap to my feet and step out from my hiding place, putting my hands up in surrender. "I'm unarmed!" I call.

The men venture closer. "Come on out," the first shouts, waving his gun at me.

I step forward and limp my way through the brush and trees to the clearing. Slow. I watch Kane getting jerked to his feet by the bearded man. His arms are bound behind his back, and his eyes are cloudy, dazed.

The women stand still, watching.

"I'm unarmed," I say again, keeping my hands high.

"Who are you?" the man in front of me demands. "What're you doing here?"

"I'm lost," I say. "Was traveling with my . . . my brother." I nod my head at Kane.

Kane's eyes clear and widen as he sees me. He makes a move forward, but the man beside him holds him fast.

"Brother, hey?"

"We don't want any trouble," I continue, ignoring the question there. "We're just . . ." I want to keep their gaze on me for as long as possible, and I'm not real sure what to say, so I go back to the story we told Leon. "We got split up from our family. We're lost."

The men exchange a glance.

"Well, now you're found," the one nearest me says, giving me a hideous smile. He's a hefty man with thinning hair. "Hey, boys?" He looks to the rest.

"Not much good to us," the blond man beside him says.

"Don't know about that," says another, near the tent pegs. "The wall needs rebuilding." He nods at Kane. "This half-blood looks strong. And we just lost some workers."

The heavy man beside me smirks. "And this one? Any of you like lame ducks?" He swings his head to the dark-haired man beside him. "St. Croix?"

"Shut up," the dark-haired man replies.

"Everyone, shut up!" the bearded man holding Kane barks. "I'm in charge until Leon gets back. We'll hold them till he decides." He looks around. "Get this packed up; we need to get back into the Keep before we get any more surprise visitors."

But the dark-haired man is walking toward the women now, looking them over. He turns. "There's only nine," he says. "One's missing."

The women look around at one another like they've just noticed, too, though I can't be sure they're not playing at it.

"Who?"

"That Rebecca."

"Well, get after her," the leader says. "She can't be far."

"Which way?"

They look around the woods. I think fast. What're the chances Charlie will stick to our plan? "The girl with the baby?" I ask, my face creased innocent-like.

The dark-haired man narrows his eyes at me.

"I saw her. She was headed up that way." I point north.

The man curses and hurries to his horse, which is tied outside the clearing.

"Hurry up," the bearded man says. "It'll be dark soon."

I watch the man urge his horse into the woods, in what I pray to the Almighty is the wrong direction.

"Get this packed up," he orders the rest. "And get back to the Keep."

21

MY HEART IS BEATING FAST, A STRANGE MIX OF crippling fear and joy. Kane's a foot away from me. His hands are bound; mine are free. It's clear the men don't think me much of a threat. My thoughts go to the knife tucked out of sight in the side of my *ceinture*. It's not much, but it's something.

I risk a glance at Kane again. They've stripped his shirt from him to make sure of no hidden weapons. His leggings are stiff with river mud. Apart from a blackened eye, an angry scrape on his side—a slash of red blossoming into a purple bruise—and a dozen or so small cuts on his chest, he's perfect.

He's alive.

My body aches with the desire to throw my arms around him.

He keeps his eyes ahead, risking the occasional glance at me, as if to reassure himself I'm real.

They march us forward to the Keep.

The men must be done dealing with the bodies in the

clearing. Above us, two men patrol the wall with guns twice the size of any I've seen. We pass below their gaze and through the gate. The Keep is smaller than it looks from out-side the walls. The courtyard is a few hundred strides across, with one row of buildings on the south wall and several out-buildings along the west.

I look back. The damage *sohkâtisiwak* did is substantial. The south wall is charred, and parts of it are gone entirely— chunks of burnt wood lie in piles. Two men are digging holes next to the wall. They're either scouts from Matisa's village or *sohkâtisiwak*, and they're being watched by one of Leon's men with a gun; they're not volunteering. Whoever they are, they didn't escape with the rest during Isi's raid.

"Send her with the womenfolk," the bearded man says to the blond man walking beside me.

I look around. The men are gesturing with their guns, and the women are turning to the northeast corner of the Keep, to a long wooden house with several doors—looks some-thing like our quarters in the settlement.

But it's not anything like our quarters in the settlement. And the thought of how it's different makes every hair on the back on my neck stand up. The blond man tugs on my arm.

I dig the heel of my good foot into the ground and pull out of his grasp.

His eyes narrow, and he grabs for me, catching me by the elbow. I tug away again. His eyes get a gleam, and he holsters his gun, then lunges for me, grabbing me up rough in his arms. "Hey, there, wildcat," he breathes.

I lose my thoughts. I throw myself backward, pulling him

off-balance. He fights to keep hold of me, but I start to kick and scratch at him, lashing out at whatever part of him I can find. My voice leaves me in a scream of fury and fear, and as my fist connects with the side of his jaw, he fumbles and loses his grip. I trip backward, falling to the ground with a thud.

"Don't touch her!" Kane leaps toward me, but the bearded man kicks him behind the knee, and he goes down hard on the dirt beside me. There's a man on him in a heartbeat, pushing his face to the ground.

I try to scramble up and away, but strong hands are on me in an instant, pinning me.

"Goddamn it!"

I'm flipped around, straddled, and my shoulders are slammed to the earth.

The blond man stares down at me, his weight heavy on my stomach. "You're going to pay for that," he says.

"Enough!" the bearded man barks. "Just put her in the cellar for now."

"But—"

"She needs to be locked up. Can't have her giving the women ideas."

The blond man stares at me, hate burning across his face. He sniffs, cracks his neck to the side, and gets off me. I'm jerked to standing by the hefty man, who's holding a rifle. Kane is pulled off the ground. We're forced ahead, away from the women's quarters, to a different long building with several doors. Dug into the earth beside it is what must be a cellar.

"Just put them with the other one," the bearded man says.

Other one?

The stocky man drags a wooden plank from the doors and flings them open. The darkness gapes before us, and, as we're shoved ahead, it swallows us whole. I stumble down steps into the darkness, blinded, and the smell of rot and improper preserved dry goods reaches my nose. I gag, missing my footing on the last step and falling to my knees. I hear Kane stumble down the stairs behind me.

The doors bang shut, and the wooden fast is slid across the opening.

Silence.

Kane drops to his knees beside me, and I scramble toward him. His hands are still tied, so I throw my arms around him and press my forehead into his neck, his collarbone, breathing in his familiar scent— woodsmoke and mint, now laced with sweat and fear. His skin is hot and damp from struggling with the men. The feel of him, solid, in my arms, starts my tears anew.

"Thank the Almighty," I whisper, holding him tight to me.

"Em," he breathes. I draw back and look at him. Small beams of light filter through the cracks in the cellar doors, cutting lines across his face and shoulders. "My wrists—"

"Course." He turns around to let my hands grasp for the bindings. The knots are tight—I try with my teeth, but there's no budging them. I dig my knife out from under my *ceinture* and saw careful at the rope. When the rope frays and the ties fall away, he pulls his arms forward and kneels there with his head bowed, holding his wrists with opposite hands.

Then he turns, and his hands rush for me, brushing across my cheeks and into my hair, clumsy and rough. He grasps the back of my neck, and I collapse into him with a small cry.

His voice is hoarse. "Thought you were—"

"Shh," I say. "I know."

His heart beats fast, thudding in my ear, as he strokes the back of my head with one hand.

"Why were you at the river?" I whisper.

"Followed it after that flood," he says. "Found hoofprints last night and decided I was getting close to something or someone. Saw the Keep and tried to avoid it. Didn't figure they'd be camped outside."

Hoofprints. He was following me and Beast, no doubt.

"Why are you here?" he asks.

"It's—it's a long story." I'm too tired to explain, and right now, I just want this: his heartbeat beneath my ear.

When he starts to pull his arms free, I tighten my grip. I realize now I didn't truly think I'd see him again. Never thought I'd touch him again. What if this is the last time? If it is . . .

I turn my head so my lips brush against his collarbone. He freezes. My mouth hovers a whisper away from his skin as I brush my cheek up his neck.

He sucks in a breath. His hands drop and grip my waist. Hard.

A cough comes from the corner.

We spring apart. Kane leaps to his feet. "Who's there?"

The cough comes again. "Don't mind me," a man's voice says. "Can't see much in here, anyway." Movement. Like he's standing or shuffling forward . . .

Put them with the other one.

"You can carry on with your . . . comforting ways."

But that voice. I know that voice. It's tugging at my memory.

"But may as well make your acquaintance, seeing as we'll be spending some time together."

Kane reaches back to touch me, making sure he's between me and whoever is coming forward. The way the man talks, all easy with this situation, like his mind is weak—that's what's familiar. That's what—

The streaks of light cut across his features. Scruffy hair and beard, cheeks reddened from the sun.

"Robert P. Henderson," he says. "Cartographer."

"You've been here three days, then," I clarify with Henderson, pressing close to Kane and away from the mapmaker. The moment with Kane from before is long gone; I'm shifting toward better air. We moved as far from the rotten stores as we could, but the smell is not much sweeter here. It's clear Henderson hasn't bathed in weeks, mayhap even since he first found our settlement at the start of the Thaw. We're in the darkest part of the cellar, but my eyes have adjusted, and I can make out his wild mop of hair, his bushy beard.

He's just as I remember.

"Near as I can make out," he says. "Showed up here just before they were attacked, and there's not much to do down here but sleep and try to keep track of days." He cocks his head. "Where were you two headed?"

"Back to our settlement," I say. I don't offer anything more.

"How did you end up coming to this Keep?" Kane asks. He seems grateful I'm crowding close; his body has cooled, and the flesh of his torso is pebbled from the chill.

"Ran into this bunch a few days ago to the north. They pretended to be interested in my maps, told me their man would pay top coin." He shakes his head. "Still waiting for that."

"When you found our settlement, you told us about these rogue types who were carving out their own law," I say. "Why would you come?"

"It didn't seem like they were asking," Henderson says. "And I figured I shouldn't give them reason to insist." He shrugs. "Besides, I'm a business sort. And coin rules."

Coin rules. He means he'd make a deal with whoever could give him the best one. He sounds a mite simple, but I know he's not. He's watching out for himself, no matter what that means.

"Been waiting on their boss man to get back—they say he'll decide whether my maps are worth paying for or not."

"Their boss man," Kane repeats. "Merritt Leon?"

"That's him." Henderson nods. "Haven't met him yet. They say he took some men and left two days back." He squints at us. "You know him?"

"We know him," I say. I look to Kane, wondering how much information I should be sharing with Henderson.

"He might not be coming back," Kane says. "And if I were you, I'd hope he's not."

I give Henderson a brief version of our run-in and the flash flood. I leave out the part about Tom—keep that buried way deep.

Henderson sits back and whistles. He thinks awhile. "Wonder what that'll do to the deal," he murmurs. "Wonder who's second in command around here."

"You should work on getting out of here," Kane says. "Not selling maps."

"Speak for yourself," Henderson says. "I need my maps, or I need compensation for them. Not leaving here without one of the two."

"These are bad men," I insist. "They won't give you either."

"You're underestimating my entrepreneurial spirit," Henderson says. "Haven't got this far being a terrible negotiator."

Kane glances around the dim lit space. "Did you 'negotiate' these lodgings?"

Henderson pauses, looking Kane over. He shrugs. "Said they didn't have better on account of that wall being destroyed. And they don't trust me yet. That's fine—I can turn those tables." He leans back. "I'm a people person. And their quarrel is with the Dominion."

I stare at him. He thinks he can talk this out with these men. And if he's willing to negotiate . . .

Fear spikes through me. If any of Leon's men survived that flood, they'll be looking for the place that cures the Bleed, just like I told them. And they won't need me to show them if . . . "Henderson, our settlement—it's on your map, right?"

"Of course," Henderson says. "It was one of my most valuable finds."

Kane stiffens. "How so?"

"Just so strange," he says. "All of you stuck inside those walls so long. You'll be a right curiosity to the people moving out this way."

"Please," I say. "It's important that you don't tell these men about us. Tell them there's nothing up that way. Tell them . . ." I trail off, unsure exactly how Henderson might explain marks on his map as nothing.

"Why?" he asks.

"They're bad men," I say. "We're trying to get back to warn our people about them. Just don't tell them about us." It's not the whole truth, but it's close enough, and just thinking on it makes my voice shake. "They can't be trusted. Leon—" But I can't get the words out. Can't say out loud what he did. Kane puts his hand to the back of my neck and squeezes gentle.

There's a silence.

"Henderson?" Kane says, like he's trying to prompt an answer.

Henderson lets out a long sigh.

And now comes the sound of the plank being removed from its latches.

We scramble up as the doors are jerked open and light pours into the space, blinding us. I throw an arm up to shield my eyes from the glare. For a heartbeat, the man standing in the light is a silhouette.

And as he comes clear, my heart sinks even as rage flares in me anew.

"They told me they pulled a wildcat from the woods. Should've guessed it'd be you, Emmeline," Leon says.

22

IN THE GLARE OF THE LANTERN HE BRINGS INTO the cellar, Leon is a horror. His pretty face took a beating in the raging river—his left eye is bloodred and bulging, like it was near knocked from its socket, and a giant angry scrape stretches from his right temple to his chin. One arm is cradled in a sling.

It's satisfying, seeing him like this, and it takes everything in me not to fly at him, scratch his wounded eye all the way out, pummel his broken body. The two men beside him keep their guns trained on us.

Leon tosses a shirt at Kane, who catches it in one hand and glowers at him.

"Put it on," Leon says.

One of the men waves his gun as if to emphasize the point. Kane shrugs into the shirt in a violent motion. His fingers work at the buttons as his eyes bore into Leon, fury giving them a black sheen.

Leon looks me over.

The two men with him I remember from before, and they're looking about as banged up. I wonder if only the three of them survived.

That moment I buried in my heart at the riverbank is pushing at me, wanting to come to the surface. Can't let it. I do, and I'm lost; I'll do something I regret. Need to keep my head right now.

One of the men has a large pitcher of water with a dipper hanging from the side. My throat burns, clamoring for it, but I won't give Leon the satisfaction of knowing that.

"Drink?" the man asks, gesturing to the pitcher.

Henderson steps forward, needing no second invitation.

"Emmeline?"

I force my gaze to meet Leon's.

"You must be thirsty."

"I'm not." But I am, and my eyes linger on Henderson as he takes a big gulp.

Leon notices. "Please," he says, gesturing again. "Amends for your containment."

Henderson is on his second ladle, drinking all greedy-like. But if the water's unsafe, we won't know for hours. I shake my head.

Leon looks amused. He grabs the dipper from Henderson, scoops up some water, and takes a long drink. He drops the ladle and wipes his mouth with the back of his hand. "See?" he says. "No Bleed."

I fight to keep surprise from my face. How can he read my thoughts like that? I raise my chin and step to the pitcher. I'm two feet from him. Can feel my knife in my *ceinture*, like a branding iron, searing my side. My hand reaches out and grabs the dipper. I scoop up some water, turn, and walk back to Kane, giving him a pleading look—*drink it*. His face is dark, but he complies.

Back at the pitcher, I take a drink, trying not to gulp it, and step away from the men, wrapping my arms around myself.

"Now," Leon says, looking satisfied, "I understand there's a mapmaker among us?"

"That'd be me," Henderson says. "Robert P. Henderson, at your service."

Leon smiles thin. "Excellent. My men have your parchments. I'd like you to explain them to me. Then we can work out an accord for payment."

"What kind of an accord might that be?" I scoff. "His life for his maps?"

Leon raises an eyebrow. "Emmeline, I have been a gracious host. Don't make me regret my courtesy." His voice is that violent, mild tone he was using at the river, right before he shot—I shove the thought away, but anger takes its place, burning hot and bright.

He looks at Henderson. "Emmeline and I have a history together," he explains. "We have both lost people." And the look he gives me is so insincere, I have to look away or I'll lunge for him.

"But I see your beau is not one of them," he says. I risk a glance back. Leon's eyes are raking over Kane. "You're obviously a strong one," he says to Kane. "Useful." He looks at me. "And I have men who enjoy wildcats."

Kane steps forward, a muscle working in his jaw. Leon's man levels his gun at Kane's chest and draws back the hammer.

Leon smiles. "If you'd be so kind?" he says to Henderson, sweeping aside his good arm, gesturing for the stairs.

Desperation fuels my tongue. "He's not going to pay you, Henderson. He'll get you to explain your maps, and then he'll turn you out or kill you. It's his way."

Leon turns with an exaggerated sigh. "Why are you so intent on sabotaging this business exchange?" He tilts his head. "Ah." He smiles at Henderson. "I believe Emmeline is worried she is being cut out of a deal. You see, I'm interested in a particular place up north. She offered to show us herself, but perhaps with your map, her information is not quite so precious." He clucks his tongue. "But don't worry, Emmeline, as I said before, I can still use you." He smiles and gestures again at the cellar doors. "Henderson?"

Henderson looks between us. He takes a step toward the stairs. Stops. Clears his throat. "You're looking for the forbidden woods," he states.

Kane makes a choking sound.

Leon glances at me in triumph. "You know the place."

"Been there," Henderson answers. "But I couldn't get too close. Those woods are . . ." he shakes his head. "It's like they're possessed with something."

My head snaps his way. *Possessed?*

"Too dangerous for me to get inside," he continues. "I was glad to get out of there alive." I stare at him, trying to figure what he's speaking on. "Some kind of . . . spirit or something in those trees. An ungodly monster."

It . . . it sounds like he's talking about the *malmaci*. I watch his face, trying to keep my own blank. For years we guarded our settlement with walls against a "spirit monster" because we didn't understand the Bleed. He must've heard the tale from people at my settlement, and now he's using the myth, trying to dissuade Leon, scare him off.

Leon stares at him, his face grave. The men beside him shift and look at one another.

I hold my breath.

But Leon's expression cracks, and a laugh bursts from his mouth. He throws his head back and guffaws. "Spirit!" he shouts in glee.

My heart sinks.

He hoots and hollers, laughing with genuine mirth. The men on either side of him lose their pallor and start to snicker. "Sounds like your people's tactics to deter visitors work well, Emmeline. That cure must be something special." Leon smiles at me with dead eyes. "But I'm sure I can convince them to share."

"They won't," I say. *They can't. They don't even know about the remedy.*

"No? Well, I suppose I could just follow the trail of ghosts." He looks at Henderson, amused, then levels me a look. "Don't you worry, I'll convince them." The malice in his tone makes my insides cold.

Don't know what else to do, so I pick up where Henderson left off. I raise my chin. "You think you can just walk in and take our cure? You'll be dead before you get through the woods." I lean forward and speak slow. "You've got no idea what's in those trees."

Leon searches my face.

I hold his gaze steady. I don't blink. Don't breathe.

Henderson clears his throat. "What do I get in exchange for my maps?"

Bleed it.

Leon straightens and smiles at Henderson. "You are a business partner," he says. "Of course you will be well compensated. We can work out the details in a more pleasant location."

Henderson runs a hand through his scruffy beard up into his hair, making it stick up even more than before. "And how do I know you'll keep your end of the deal?" he asks. "Your men told me you'd welcome me here, but instead I got a cold cellar."

Leon smiles, his teeth that shocking white. "Tell me, Robert," he says. "Do you have a better offer?"

"Don't!" I say to Henderson, my voice raw. "He'll kill you, anyway. He killed my friend. Shot him right in—"

"That was retribution." Leon raises his voice over mine. "Blood for—"

"Cold blood," I finish.

Henderson looks at Leon, hesitating. He gives me a contrite look, like he's a mite ashamed of what he's about to do.

Anger burns in me as I watch him shuffle past Leon's men to climb the stairs.

Leon turns to follow. He stops and looks back at me. "You know I did that Tom a favor," he muses. "A clean shot like that's a far better death than drowning."

And it's like throwing oil on the fire inside me. The words burst forth: "Your brother drowned."

Leon freezes.

Kane shifts. "Em."

"Drowned slow," I say. The anger is white hot now, and it's everywhere, in my throat and in my head. Because that moment is back, and all I can see is Leon pulling that trigger, Tom staggering back. "In his own blood."

Leon's face is white. "You were there."

"I was there," I say. "And I could've eased his suffering." I let my face twist into a terrible smile. "But I didn't."

Rage trembles through Leon's body, all over his mangled face. I swallow hard. Can see it all over him: he's going to kill me.

Kane steps in front of me, his hands raised, ready.

But Leon doesn't move. Slow, so slow, he regains control. He relaxes his stance, takes a deep breath. He smiles. "I'm not one for mindless punishment," he says. "But I will exact retribution." He holds my gaze. "I wonder how you'll live, knowing you're the reason I show your people no mercy?"

He leaves. His men follow, backing up the stairs with their pieces trained on us and grotesque satisfaction on their faces.

The doors bang shut.

The men's footsteps and voices fade away. I stand staring at the stairs, a dark panic fluttering around my insides.

Why did I say that?

Leon riding in with his men and weapons . . . The settlement won't know what hit them.

Should've kept my mouth shut.

I couldn't, though. Leon was speaking on Tom like he was nothing. He said his name like he was nothing.

My chest feels tight; my breath is coming short and fast. I can't breathe. Can't . . .

"Kane," I say, "Tom—"

"Shh," he says, his hands finding me and pulling me toward him.

But that moment is back: Tom's hand clasped to his chest, blood gushing everywhere. Guilt rolls over me in suffocating waves, and panic takes my tongue. I grasp Kane's forearms and push myself away. "I didn't want Tom to come. I wanted him to stay put, but I told myself I'd protect him! I didn't protect him, Kane."

"There was nothing you could've—"

"I should've killed Leon when I had the chance! When I was mending his wound, I could've ripped him apart. But I didn't, because I'm weak! I'm so bleedin' weak—"

Kane tries to pull me close again, but I tear myself away, staggering back a step. He drops his hands, helpless. "Em, you didn't know."

"Well, I should've!" I shout. "And now it's too late. Leon's going to kill everyone at the settlement. They won't even understand why he's there."

"We'll think of something."

"There's nothing we can do!" I pace back and forth in the dingy space. "He'll destroy the settlement, and I won't bring the remedy to Matisa's people in time. Matisa's lost. Tom's gone. All of this was for nothing!"

"It's not over yet!" His voice is fire. "Em, you can't give up."

I stop and stare at him. I'm drowning in despair and desperate for him to throw me a rope. "Why not?" I whisper. "It's hopeless—"

"It's not hopeless."

But it is. Tom won't live the life he was meant to. None of us will. I turn away from him.

"It *can't* be hopeless." He steps close and puts a hand to my back. "Please. You talked so long about your new life out here. Made me believe in it, too." His voice is raw, all smoke and knife edge. It tears into me with its honesty, forces me to turn around to see it on his face. "I need to know you're going to still fight for it."

"Why?"

"Because I need you. It wasn't right without you. Being out here." His hand presses against me. "It wouldn't have been right staying at the settlement without you, neither. I came to Matisa's people for you. And I came with you on this journey because . . ." He stops, hesitates. "Because even when I don't understand you, Em, I want to be with you."

My heart gallops; my breath comes fast.

"Because mayhap understanding every single thing about a person isn't so important. Last fall I fell in love with a daydreaming girl I didn't full understand. You were always looking somewhere else, thinking something else, hoping for something else. But I loved that about you." His hand grips my hip tight. "I love it still. I love you. And you can't give up."

My insides melt like the Thaw, and a wildfire rushing about under my skin is all that's left.

"I love you, too," I whisper.

His breath leaves him slow, like he's been holding it for days. For weeks. His hands move to the small of my back, and he pulls me close. My hands grasp fistfuls of his shirt as I lean in, so desperate for him, I know I won't breathe ever again without—

We kiss.

His mouth is exactly as I remember. Soft, hesitant and slow.

And now, insistent and searching. Making sure of me, of us. He pulls me closer, and my hands run up his chest to the back of his neck, and the feeling of his body is so perfect and familiar . . .

He breaks the kiss with a ragged breath, closing his eyes and resting his forehead against mine. He grasps the back of my neck, and I hold his forearms with trembling hands.

"I told you not to come back for me." His voice is hoarse. "But I didn't know what it would be like, living without you. Wondering how you were, wondering who you were with . . ."

"I was always with you," I say, and I lean forward again.

A sound like a thunderclap stops us dead.

23

ANOTHER BANG SHATTERS THE AIR, SHAKING the building above us. We duck and clap our hands to our ears. Dust rains down from the floorboards above.

It stops.

I pull my head up. There's a ruckus starting out beyond the cellar doors: shouts and the sound of footsteps running.

I look to Kane. "What's happening?"

"Don't know," Kane says. "But whoever was guarding the cellar will be busy." He glances around. "See if you can find something we can break out with."

It's dark, but our eyes have adjusted enough to start scouring the space. A few moments of looking, and it's clear there's nothing down here but those few crates of rotting food.

Another resounding boom from the courtyard. More shouts. Kane and I look at one another. We're going to have to wait this out and pray whatever's going on works in our favor. I grasp for Kane's hand.

And now fumbling sounds come at the cellar doors. The

hinges shriek as one door opens wide. I put my hand to my brow to make out the shadow in the doorway. The bushy hair gives him away before his voice does. "Hurry now," Henderson says, gesturing for us to climb out. We scramble for the opening, tripping up the stairs and emerging into the twilight.

Outside, men are running for horses that are tied to posts in the center of the courtyard. I hear Leon's voice from the east wall, shouting orders.

Another boom. I clap my hands to my ears, and we shrink back around the corner of the building, out of sight. "What's going on?"

"Dominion," Henderson says. "Coming to deal with the rogues. They've got something real long-range."

The Dominion. They're here, moving against Leon. Guess they didn't take him up on his offer, after all.

"They're not after us," Henderson says. "But in a battle like this, they'll shoot first, ask questions later. Get into the woods and stay hidden until this is over."

The air around us is lit up with unnatural bright light. Another boom.

"Think it's best we split up," he says, scanning the courtyard. He fumbles in his jacket. "But here." He presses a parchment into my hands. "It's my only copy."

My eyes widen. "But—"

"Got other maps of other places," he says. "I get out of here alive, I won't miss that one."

Except I know he will. He said it himself: it's his most valuable sketch.

"Thank you," I say, stuffing it into my *ceinture* next to my knife. "Did . . . did Leon ask you about it?"

He nods. "It was the only one he was interested in. And I'm not a very good liar."

"It's all right," I say. "Thank you . . . for freeing us."

"Leon would've just as soon killed me as paid me. And I know you could use the map to get home. I'm . . ." He dips his head. "I'm sorry about your friend." He glances around. "Anyway, good luck." And he's gone.

Kane looks at me, his mouth parted in disbelief.

More shouts come. No more time to think on Henderson.

We drop down and peer around the corner into the court-yard. Leon and several dozen of his men are mounted and riding out through the east gates. Men are scattered here and there, on top of the walls, in the corners of the Keep.

We retreat to the back of the building and make our way between it and the west wall, aiming for the north side. The south is too wide open for us to traverse safely; this side has buildings and tents we can hide behind while we make our way to the only entrance on the east wall. As we round the corner, we near stumble right out behind Leon's men.

They're standing, backs to us, weapons in hand, outside the long building in the northeast corner. Guarding the women. Not letting them leave.

Movement draws my attention to the right. Closer to us one unsaddled horse stands tied to a hitching post. He's dancing, skittering sideways, and pulling at his reins.

Beast! They must've found him in the woods while they were looking for Rebecca.

Kane places a hand on my arm, telling me to stay put, and creeps forward to unwrap the reins from the post. I cast a look around. Our best bet is riding straight through the hole in the east wall.

But now I see, close to the middle of the yard, with no protection at all, two men standing close together with their hands on a railing. It's the two I saw before, working at the wall. Their hands are in manacles, attached to the rail.

Bound like the horses.

Kane sees them, too. They stare back, watching Kane, quiet.

And Beast is free. Kane tugs him toward me, leading him painful slow so he doesn't make noise and draw Leon's men's gaze. We duck back behind the building, out of sight.

"Kane," I say. "Those captives." Don't know if they're Matisa's people or abandoners from Matisa's people, but it doesn't matter: we can't leave them. Don't want to leave those women, neither, but they're too heavily guarded. Trying for their rescue is impossible.

He nods. "Stay here. When I get them free, ride hard and come get me." He helps me up on Beast and gives me the reins. I urge Beast to the corner of the building and watch as Kane hurries toward the two captives. He's in full view of the men guarding the tents again. If one of them turns around . . .

An iron bar runs the length of the post and is fastened on both ends with a bolt. My heart pounds as I watch Kane examine it, keeping one eye on Leon's men. I'll wait while Kane does his best to free these two, but if Leon's men turn around, I won't think twice. I'll ride for Kane and get us out of here.

Don't turn around.

I tighten my grip on Beast's reins with one hand and keep my other one free. My breath is coming hard and fast as Kane slides the iron bar across the post. I ready myself to kick Beast forward, to run for Kane and grab him up.

A shrill scream stops me dead.

It's a whistle, a long, high shriek, gaining in volume and dwindling into—

The earth inside the far south wall of the fort explodes in a shower of dirt. The men at the tents spin. They see us, they must, but they don't seem to care. They're shouting and pointing at the wall. There's a strange smoke rising from the battered earth. A cloud. It's muddy brown, and it hovers above the ground and begins to drift into the courtyard.

The whistle comes again, grabbing up my heart and squeezing it tight in its high pitch. This orb shatters on the west wall to my right, letting out another cloud.

Leon's men scramble into action, pulling doors open and ordering the women out. They push and stumble, herding them toward the east gate, fleeing that brown mist. The men Kane has freed join them, running for the damaged wall without looking back.

I put heels to Beast, and he springs forward. Kane turns, looking for me. One hand on the reins and mane for balance, I help Kane swing up behind me.

"You on?" I ask over my shoulder.

"Go!"

I look back, watching the cloud drifting toward us, and I kick Beast hard. Kane puts his head to my back. We gallop for the gates, and Beast lengthens his stride as we race out beyond them, heading for the woods. A bright flash pulls my gaze to the river, and my breath catches.

It's impossible.

It's on fire.

The waters shine, coated with a kind of black pitch, feeding flames that shimmer and dance, reaching high for the night sky.

River ablaze. Shattering bone.

Just like Matisa's dream during the winterkill. I turn my head away as we dash toward the trees.

One of Leon's men is ahead of us, fleeing with the crowd. A shot rings out from the woods. He jerks backward, his arms splaying wide, and falls. Shots explode around us now. And I can do nothing but put my head down and pray for Beast to be fast like the wind.

Go, boy.

He stretches his neck long and opens full up, galloping hard, tearing into the woods and crashing through the brush.

The trees envelop us with their dark branches. I have a moment of relief before I realize we're headed straight into the battle. Figures, shadows of horses and men, are everywhere. There are riderless horses running wild, gunfire, shouts. And men appearing from the thick of the woods—

My breath stops.

Bulbous eyes, long trunks.

L'homme comme l'éléphant.

Elephant man.

Those masks. Those masks Isi and Nishwa turned up in last fall, worried about poison gas. The gas that'll addle your insides, turn you into a river of blood.

And now I see it, drifting through the woods, snaking around the trunks of trees: a death mist. I pull Beast hard to the left, urging him north. He crashes through the brush, tearing through the deadfall clumsy-like and leaving the poison cloud behind. As we get farther north, the gunfire gets more distant, but the forest gets denser. A bramble of brush catches Beast across the chest. He staggers to a halt.

Kane slides off Beast and looks around.

I land beside him. "Do—"

He puts a finger to his lips and tilts his head. I pause and listen. And there it is.

Movement in the trees to the northwest. Twenty strides away? Less? We're not alone out here.

We duck down as whoever it is ventures closer. As the clouds move off and reveal the moon, I realize we're not hidden. The bramble is dense, but the trees are sparse, and the moon is cutting down straight onto our heads.

"*Em.*" It's a whisper.

The figure moves closer.

"Charlie?"

He comes into view. "Thought that was you. Saw your horse's white face."

Kane stiffens as Charlie gets close, putting out an arm to keep Charlie at a distance.

"It's all right, Kane," I say. "What are you doing here?"

"Couldn't just leave you, caught."

I stare at him. "You should've left with Rebecca. I thought—" I swallow the rest of the sentence. *I thought you did.* "You were coming for us?"

"Wasn't sure what to do. Then the fighting started, and

I came to see if you made it out." He keeps his voice to a whisper.

"Where's Rebecca?"

"She's safe in the woods east of here. Behind all this. We'll need to double back around the Keep, across the river. Come on." He gestures for us to follow him.

"We're heading this way." Kane gestures to the north.

"You sure you want to do that?"

"We have to go back to the settlement," I say. "Don't have time to explain."

Kane pulls at my hand.

"Wait," Charlie whispers. "There's a dry creek bed, a hundred strides or so up that way." He points through the thick brush. "It'll take you north. You could run it, but getting there'll be tricky . . ." He looks at my enormous horse.

"How do you know all this?" Kane asks.

"Been watching this Keep. I know the forest around it well enough."

"It's true," I say. "He's helping us, Kane." I look at Beast. "And he's right. We're too slow and too loud on Beast."

"No way we'll get to the settlement on foot."

"I know," I say. "But we need to get past these men somehow." I touch the whistle beneath my shirt.

Shots ring out. And off to the east now, distant, dark figures sift through the woods.

"We need to go," Kane mutters.

"You'd best get gone, too," I say to Charlie. But my heart twists. "We can't wait for you, but you could . . . make your way back. To the settlement, I mean."

He shakes his head. "I'm done with that place. Wouldn't be welcome, anyhow."

I don't bother arguing. "Then you should head west of that cottonwood grove we parted ways in those months back," I say. "There's a village there. Good people. You'd be safe."

Charlie nods. "Obliged." He looks at Kane. "Watch out for Leon's men—these woods are crawling with them."

"Dominion, too," I say.

"Nah." He shakes his head. "They have big weapons, but I saw them move in: there's barely two dozen. Leon's got the upper hand out here." He passes me his rifle. "Take this."

I try to give it back. "But—"

He presses it into my hands. "We're even now," he says firm. He turns and is swallowed by the dark trees.

I pass the rifle to Kane, who accepts it, his face incredulous. "Think I'd better hear that story," he says.

"After." I break off a thin piece of branch from the brush at my knees and grab Beast's rein, leading him out of the bramble.

Shots again. Closer still.

"Em—"

I switch Beast's rump hard. He startles, leaping forward. And he disappears, crashing into the brush. Kane stares at me.

"He'll find us," I say, though I can't be sure, and my stomach is sick knowing I just sent him off alone.

I grab Kane's hand and tug him forward, aiming for that creek bed.

24

WE CREEP THROUGH THE FOREST, GHOSTS AMONG ghosts. The shadows to the east are ever closer, and there are more appearing to the northeast. They appear and disappear behind trees, their shadows darting forward. Silent. Quick.

The occasional shot and explosion suggests a mix of Dominion and Leon's men. They're all stealing through the woods; no doubt they're using rifles and those handheld explosives, trying to pick one another off in the dark.

The woods swap between providing perfect cover and none at all. The spruce are clustered, and their low branches provide shield. But there are bare patches and low scrub, too, and passing through those is dangerous.

We crawl and worm our way through those low spaces and use the cover of the big spruce trees to rest. I'm not as fast as Kane and surely slowing him down, but I'm far quieter than I used to be. As we pause, hidden in the trees, I spot a riderless horse racing through the woods off to our right. Beast?

Kane pulls me forward to the next bunch of trees.

A lifetime later the trees and scrub give way to hummocks of grass and thatches of willow, and I know we're nearing the creek bed. I feel a flicker of relief that we stayed the course and didn't get turned about. I put my whistle to my lips, hoping it will work and that Beast isn't too far off.

I hear something behind us, moving none too careful.

Nothing like us.

I glance back, amazed that Beast found us this quick.

But it's not Beast.

It's two dark figures. Dominion men. Coming straight for us.

We abandon our attempt at being silent and throw ourselves forward, crashing into the willows and behind a fallen tree. I fall and throw out a hand for balance, feeling a sting as my hand scrapes against something sharp. Kane pulls the rifle up and drives the bolt forward on it, slow and quiet, ready to get a shot off.

Behind us, the polished rock of the dry creek bed glows in the moonlight.

We're so close, but heading down into it now would put us in full sight of the men. Better to stay here where there's some cover. I watch Kane steady his arm on the fallen tree. He scans the brush for the dark figures. They're getting close.

There are shots off to the east again. Closer still. Kane's better with his knives. If he doesn't make good on his shot, we'll be trapped between these men and those shooting to the east, dead where we stand.

But the men come into view, staggering right toward us, and they look half-dead themselves. The first elephant man is breathing loud, near choking, like he can't get air through his mouth. He stops to lean against a tree and rips his mask away. As the clouds clear, I see bright red blood stream from his nose, stark against his white face. He coughs and spits a blackish bile down the front of his coat, onto the shiny buttons. His eyes are black in the shadows—no white at all.

The second man stumbles forward, clutching at his stomach. His shoulder hits a tree, and he sinks down, his voice leaving him in a garbled cry beneath his mask. He, too, tears at it and reveals a swollen face, mottled with bruises. His ears leak rivers of blood.

My breath leaves me.

They've got the Bleed.

Kane stands and tugs me backward to the creek bed. We're out in the open now, but it's clear that these men are in no shape to care.

The first catches sight of us and reaches out a hand, a pleading gesture. We scramble away, slipping down into the creek bed and hugging the earth wall. I'm frozen, staring up into the trees where the men are. Dying.

I feel Kane's hand in mine. He pulls me north up the creek bed, urging me into a run. As we stumble along the rocks, I remember my whistle. I fumble for it and blow with all my might. My hand is sticky, it's dripping . . .

I recall falling back against that tree now. I'm bleeding.

I grab the tail of my *ceinture* and press the cloth to my wound. A sharp sting courses through my hand, and I clench my teeth.

A shot rings out from the trees.

We duck. Kane drags me across the creek bed to a large

dark shape. A huge tree is lying on its side, yanked up at the roots by the water once rushing through here. We scramble behind it. Another shot rings out. It pings off a rock several strides shy of us.

Whoever is shooting is on the far side of the creek, in the woods.

Though how they saw us . . .

My heart is beating loud as we crouch, pressing our backs to the wall of earth and tangled tree roots. Kane's eyes widen. He gestures with his head up the creek bed. I peer around him. There's a man crouched behind a boulder on our side of the little ravine, hiding from the shots like us.

He shifts his position. The movement is jerky, painful, and I see now it's because he has the use of only one arm. His free hand is holding a gun. His other arm is in a sling. Can't be more than ten strides away. His eyes meet mine.

Leon.

I throw my body back to the fallen tree. We're tucked parallel to him; too awkward for him to have a clear shot, but if he wanted to, he could retreat a couple of paces and get us in his sights. We have Charlie's rifle; Kane could leave the cover of this tree to get off a shot.

But he can't without giving away our position and putting ourselves in the Dominion's sights.

And Leon's in the same predicament.

I risk a glance at him again.

He smiles, thin.

He knows it.

A shot comes again. This one farther off the mark.

They're getting colder. Or sicker.

Do all these soldiers have the Bleed? If so, there's no way they'll take this Keep.

There's a crash on the far side of the little ravine. A man falls out of the trees, pitching down into the creek bed, face-first. He lands on a rock, cracking one of his nightmare eyes. His mask gleams in the moonlight, elephant face staring at nothing.

My insides churn with fear. Didn't even know he was there.

Kane gestures with his head for me to look back down the creek.

An animal is moving along the rocky bed, slinking along in the moonlight.

A rush of disbelief and joy cuts through my fear. I'd know that timid little shape anywhere.

Hunger. Padding along the creek bed, her ears pricked, nose to the rocks every now and again, following the path Kane and I just traversed.

I have to bite back calling her name. She's headed straight for us. I touch the whistle at my neck. Could she have heard it? Or is she just tracking us by smell?

Good dog.

She's out in the open now. I will her to stick to the sides of the creek bed, but she's too busy with her nose. Stopping here and again. Picking up our trail. Moving forward.

But how—

My blood? Might've been leaving drops.

Oh, hurry, Hunger.

But now she's found where I stanched the cut. She draws her head up with a jerk, her ears and eyes searching for the uprooted tree, searching out our hiding spot. She knows we're here.

She gathers her legs under her and springs forward. Can see the joy in her movement as she stretches her front legs and bounds toward us—

A shot rings out from the trees. Hunger skitters to a stop and looks around.

"Hun—"

Kane claps his hand over my mouth, muffling my cry, and throws his other arm around me, pulling me back into the shadows. Another shot.

There's a silence. The bushes rustle.

Dizziness courses through me.

A man's voice pierces the air. "Did you get him?" The voice is muffled but close—too close.

I twist in Kane's grasp, trying to see, but he tightens his grip and holds me close, his voice a ragged whisper. "Don't," he breathes.

He presses us back farther so there's no way I can look for Hunger. Somewhere through my fear I realize that the men talking must be out in the open. Leon would have a clear shot. Why isn't he shooting?

A cough. "No." The other voice is clearer and closer still. "Thought I saw him, though."

"You think the rest ran off?"

"Not sure." Another cough. "There's more than we thought."

"You don't look good."

"Don't feel good."

And I know why Leon's not shooting. He doesn't have to. He knows they have the Bleed. He's going to wait them out.

"Get your mask on. Let's go."

We listen as they retreat. Branches snap here and again.

We wait. Shots again, more distant.

Kane cranes his neck, grabbing the rifle in both hands. He rises on his haunches, looking up the ravine. He curses. I peer past him.

Leon is gone.

And now more dark shapes are moving along the ravine.

We duck down behind the tree again, flattening ourselves against the trunk.

"Get St. Croix and the rest and meet at the west clearing." Footsteps crunch on the riverbed. "We'll regroup." I peer out as four men go past.

One is the blond man who pinned me in the courtyard.

"Why don't we just finish them? We've got four men to every one of theirs."

"They're dying—didn't you see that? Just need to wait them out. And they'll leave behind some damn fine arsenal."

The men disappear around a bend. We wait another long few moments.

"Let's get into the woods," Kane mutters.

He pulls me up, and I scour the creek bed. There's no sign of Hunger. We dart out into the open and up the bank, into the cover of the trees. Once we're in, I fight the urge to call her name.

And now, a new sound, clattering along the pebbled floor of the ravine.

Kane grabs the whistle around my neck, bringing his head to my throat, and blows. He hurries back to the scrub lining the ravine and parts the brush.

Beast's white blaze shines back at us.

Atop Beast, we race along the creek bed until it dwindles into nothing, emptying us into a forest of poplar. It's taking us north to my settlement, so we press on, putting as much distance between us and Leon as we can. I stare at the ground rushing past, watch the pebbled bed become soft forest floor. The moon is high by the time Beast tires and slows.

I pull him to a stop.

"We need to rest," I say.

Kane slides off from behind me and offers a hand. My legs are shaky with the effort of clinging to Beast, and as I hit the ground, I stumble. Kane catches me in his arms and holds me. There's nothing but soft wind in the tops of the trees, and a jay squawking from off in the thick of the woods. Beast nickers and bends his head to pull up some grass from the base of a tree.

I press my forehead against Kane's shoulder, drawing in a deep breath. Scrub my eyes against his shirt.

"I'm—I'm sorry, Em," he says. "Hunger might find us still."

I pull my head up. He searches my face. "Yeah," I say, "she might."

"I'm sorry," he says again.

"No. You did the right thing."

"Should we get a look at that?" he asks soft, pointing at my side.

The map. It's still tucked in the side of my *ceinture*. We won't lose any more time now that we have it, but Leon's seen it, too. He knows my settlement is north along the big river. It's clear that that faction of the Dominion didn't know how to avoid the Bleed, but the knowledge I shared with McKern's group in the valley will spread. The Dominion'll be back with more men and more weapons. If Leon survived that skirmish, and it sure seemed like he was going to, he'll be hell-bent on getting to our settlement, finding his "cure." We need to warn them.

But I can't go another step.

"It's too dark," I say. "And we need to rest."

"In the morning, then," Kane says. He tugs me over to the base of a tree, to some damp but soft moss. I sink down beside him, feeling hungry and thirsty and bone-weary but so glad for his presence. I take a sharp breath when he pulls me into his arms and wraps his body around mine. And, feeling finally safe for a moment, I let sleep steal me from him.

I'm in the forbidden woods. Rushing, rushing along, but my body is light as a feather, my breath coming fast from fear, not effort.

The cabin stares at me, its sagging windows sad eyes in a rotting face. *Les trembles* move as if in a big wind, but I know something else disturbs them.

He's in front of me, darting through the dream trees, his arm tucked into his side like it's broken.

Hurry.

I press toward the crumbling logs, gaining speed.

Following him.

Chasing him.

Hurry.

25

THE MAP IS LIKE THE ONE TOM HAD WHEN HE found us, but it covers more territory. The land between Leon's Keep and our settlement is plotted with a variety of squiggles and symbols. And words Kane can read, thanks be.

We decide we're three days from the settlement: two too many to survive without water. But we have nothing to use to boil it, and heading back to the big river means we lose any advantage we have on Leon. We decide to risk the woods, sucking the dew from leaves until the burning thirst in our throat subsides, letting Beast drink from the little creeks we come across.

We press on, using the rising sun for direction, heading along the route we were supposed to use when we left for Matisa's people months ago. I count the nights in my head and decide we've been gone from Matisa's village five days. So long as we're right about the distance to our settlement, we can still bring the remedy back to the valley in time. My dream niggles at me, though, when I think on that. Like it's trying to remind me of something.

At night Kane keeps watch until he can't stay awake any longer; then he reluctantly wakes me for a shift. We scour the woods for berries and mushrooms and chew our share slow, trying to make them last. Kane is able to get some small game with my knife but is reluctant to hunt with the gun; he's not as accurate with it, and we don't want to risk alerting anyone to our whereabouts. Got no idea who's around or who's friendly. Besides, we have no time to deal with big game.

According to Henderson's map, we should hit another ravine northeast of the Keep. If we stick to it until we reach a lake, then head north again, we'll find the woods outside the settlement.

The miles pass; the trees blur one into the next.

On the third morning we find the ravine drawn on the map, running like a rocky scar down the middle of the forest.

We're close.

Beast is laboring hard now, his coat slippery. He bobs his head with the effort of carrying us. The walls of the ravine aren't high, and I realize we're vulnerable, but I also don't want to make Beast struggle back up the incline.

Just as I'm about to suggest a rest, a flash of light catches my eye ahead. The trees on either side of the ravine are thinning, and the dry creek bed is emptying out into a small lake. It glimmers in the afternoon sun.

I urge Beast on. He pricks up his ears and picks up his pace.

The lake is small and enclosed by little hills to the north. They look like the hills that stretched out for miles beyond our forest—the ones you could hardly make out in the distance before the mountains, from the top of the fortification wall. My eyes fix on the shining waters.

Kane hops down from behind me and takes Beast by the reins, heading for the water's edge.

"Kane, no!" I say. "We can't drink."

He turns. "I thought the little waters were the danger."

I nod. "They are."

"Surely this is safe?"

"But what if it isn't?"

Kane hesitates, looking out over the glistening water. I can see the desperation in him. We drank the dew hours ago, and my own thirst is so intense, I feel half addled.

But I can't bear the thought of coming this far and making a mistake.

"We're only half a day away now," I say. "Mayhap less." My voice hitches. "Kane, we're the only two left who can see this through."

His eyes harden with determination. "All right, Em," he says.

My mouth is so dry, my tongue feels twice its size. Beast is stumbling, his head hanging low as he carries us forward. He needs water again, but the lake is far behind. And we're almost to the forbidden woods. We're almost there.

We cross through the brush, *les trembles* rustling furious about us. The wind has picked up, drying out my eyes, snaking through my hair. I lift my heavy head to look up at the leaves, flashing silver and green as they tremble.

I remember these trees so well. Remember how they used to call to me, ask me to come out this way . . .

This way.

It was all so long ago. My dreams that led me out here, chasing an apparition who turned out to be real. I remember it like it was yesterday. Finding Matisa staring at me from across the grove, chasing after her into the brush, through the Crossroads. And then she saved me, pulled me from the river. She gave me hope when it was lost. Gave me a purpose. My eyes blur, and I blink the tears away and pull my gaze forward. A girl appears in the trees before us.

I blink. Can't be.

It's my memories playing tricks on my mind.

She smiles, her dark eyes laughing, and disappears.

Wait.

Kane is slumped forward, his forehead pressed to the back of my neck. Don't have the strength to urge Beast on and can't get my tongue to work. A flash of blue and dark hair appears in the trees ahead.

Please wait.

I know she's not real. She can't be. But I can't help but call to her in my mind. She is a ray of light flashing through *les trembles* before me, and everything in me wants to follow. Wants to catch her.

But all I can do is watch, bobbing along on Beast's back. My fingers are tangled in his mane—I wove them there hours ago so I wouldn't fall.

Kane is heavy at my back, and my body is tired . . . so tired . . .

She appears again. Disappears.

And I am outside myself, watching two ragged people crumpled into one another, jostled together on the back of a tired and frothy horse on the verge of collapse. The trees blur and thin out, and we are out, out of the trees. Beast wheezes, his neck stretching out and his head bobbing furious. My skin prickles through my haze. We're somewhere I know, but the wind is hot—so hot.

No.

It's my skin that's on fire. And we're leaving the trees, but the girl has disappeared, like smoke on the wind.

We're on the Watch flats. Before us, the fortification. It's as I remember, grassy fields stretching out long and dry toward the weathered walls. Watchtower standing tall in a corner. Sharp cliffs looming across the river.

Beast staggers forward. I want to cry out, want to make our presence known, but my tongue is too swollen, my breath too shallow. And I'm listening now.

Because underneath the soft hum of insects I can hear the din from my dreams: horses screaming, people screaming, gunshots and explosions that rock the earth. I can feel it: it's coming.

And my dreams can't help anything now.

We reach the walls, and the gate opens. I see Frère Andre standing there, the journal that proved my innocence—my family's innocence—in his hand.

I miss you, Andre.

My vision blurs, and the shape lengthens and broadens. It's Luc, the scar-faced Watcher who found me in the woods that day, dragged me back to the fortification, where I was sure I'd be shot. Pulled me to safety, on Andre's command.

He has no book. He stands with his hands at his sides, staring at us. "Emmeline?" he says. *"Pourquoi êtes-vous ici?"*

And Kane goes limp and topples from Beast, dragging me with him to the grassy earth.

When you're dying, do you meet the people who've gone before? Do they come to help you cross to the other side?

Tom hovers above me, his wheat-blond hair hanging like a curtain.

My hand comes up. I brush his hair back from his face. He leans close, his prairie-sky-blue eyes wide, his eyebrows knitted in concern.

A cloth is pressed to my lips. Blessed cool water reaches my tongue.

Cooler and sweeter than anything I've known . . .

I grasp his wrist. He feels so real. Looks so real. I rub my thumb across the palm of his hand. His scars are old— they're from a life he'll never have to live again. From a time he'll never have to see again.

I want to stay in this moment. I want to tell him I love him. I want to tell him that the choices he made taught me about my own choices. That he was brave. So brave.

"T-T-Tom—"

"Shh," he says. "Don't speak." He presses the cloth to my mouth again.

And now he's blurring in my vision, drifting away like the clouds on a perfect day.

And I think he knows what I wanted to say.

He knows.

I'm staring at wooden walls; the floor is hard beneath my back. My hands reach out, touch the wool of the cloak I'm wrapped in. I'm somewhere familiar. I gaze about the space. The common room of our quarters. We shared this space with Tom's family so long ago . . .

I'm not alone. I press up on my hands, struggling to sit up.

"Go easy, Em," a voice says. "You had a rough night."

I turn my head, closing my eyes against the painful throb that follows. I can feel someone beside me.

Kane. He's sitting on the floor, arms resting on his bent knees, watching my face, careful.

"She needs more water," the voice says again. A form shifts in the corner of my eye.

I snap my head toward the sound. Eisu approaches me with a small vessel and a cloth.

Tom stands behind him.

I struggle up, screaming with the desire to call his name. It's stuck in my throat.

"I said, go easy!" He throws up his hands and kneels before me. "Here." He takes the cloth from Eisu. I watch, dumbstruck, as he dips the cloth in the water and presses it to my lips again. My mouth registers the water, and I suck, greedy, at the cloth. He smiles and hands me a cup. "Small sips," he says.

I nod and gulp a mouthful.

He frowns and pulls the cup away. *"Small,"* he says, reproachful. And smiles again. "It's so good to see you, Em." He leans forward and wraps his arms around me. And at his touch I realize I'm not dreaming. He's here.

My hands come up, gripping him tight. "How—?" I choke out.

"You thought I was a goner, right?" he says. "I thought the same about you."

"B-b-but, Leon shot you. You were bleeding . . ."

Tom pulls back. "I bled something fierce," he agrees.

"So how—?"

"Good-luck charm." Tom reaches into his shirt and pulls out two cords that hang around his neck. On one of them is the flat white stone: Eisu's token. On the end of the other is the whistle Lea gave him. He leans close so I can get a better look. The stone has a large chip in it, and the bone end of the whistle is shattered.

"Bullet hit the whistle dead-on," Tom says. "The stone was lying behind it—didn't make it through. The shards of bone pierced my skin something awful, though." He grins. "Felt like I'd been shot."

I stare at him. Shock and relief flood through me so powerful, I can't find words.

"He was lucky," Eisu says, drawing my gaze away from Tom's impish grin. "But he was a very . . . difficult wounded person." He looks at Tom with affection.

I shake my head, my mind still reeling. "But why are you here? How did you get here?"

"Took one of Leon's horses. Found it after the flood, back in the trees. I still had that copy of Henderson's map."

I frown. "But . . ." I look at Kane for help. "How would that map help you? Henderson never got as far as the mountains."

"No," Tom agrees. "But Eisu knew the hunters' trails north. And once we got close this way, I could figure the rest." He smiles at me and his eyes get full. "We looked for you, Em," he says. "But by the time I healed enough to move, we . . .

well, we decided we'd best get here." He hesitates. "Thought mayhap I could see this through in case . . ."

In case I didn't make it.

I reach out my hands and grasp his. "I can't believe it. I . . . I just can't believe it."

He smiles. "Pretty shocked myself. But you're a fighter, Em. Always knew that about you. Shouldn't have doubted you'd make it."

"Tom!" Sister Ann's voice comes sharp through the doorway to the kitchen. "Come deal with this animal! It got into the dried stores."

I look at Tom in confusion. "Animal?"

He sighs. "Your furry little tagalong." He pushes to his feet.

"Hunger?" My heart skips. Can barely dare to hope . . . I grab at Tom's arm, stopping him. "She's here?"

"Course." Tom frowns. "She was with you."

"No, she wasn't."

"Well, she came out of the woods just as we were moving you in the gates. Good thing me and Eisu were there, or Luc would've shot her. He thought she was a wolf."

I look to Kane, my eyes filling.

"She followed you all the way," Kane says, that funny smile pulling up one corner of his mouth. "Told you I know how she feels."

26

TOM'S MA CAN'T STOP FUSSING OVER HIM. NEVER seen her so mother-hen-like in all the time I've known her. She bustles from the table where we sit, back to the hearth, and again to Tom. She touches his head with affection. Tom warned me about this. He and Eisu arrived last night and haven't had a chance to explain everything to his family. With her clucking around, he's barely had a chance to get his thoughts straight.

Edith, Tom's sister, sits on his knee, eyeing me real shy.

"Come here, mouse," I say a third time, wiggling my fingers for her. She shakes her head and tucks in closer to Tom, a mischievous smile on her face. I sigh. Months are like years when you're five years old; she'll be shy for a while.

I sit back, resting my hand on Hunger's head, and look around the kitchen, at all the familiar sights and smells. Root vegetables sit waiting to be peeled and cut. The hearth is sooty and glowing warm inside the cool room. Hooks by the door hold cloaks and trapping satchels. It's all just as I remember it, except I know how Edith feels. Seems a lifetime since I've been here.

In this moment, though, this place doesn't feel suffocating. After our journey here, I'm actually grateful for these walls. Grateful for Sister Ann's watchful eyes. I feel . . . safe.

Sister Ann wasn't too thrilled about keeping Hunger indoors, but Tom thought it best she stay close. The children in particular are real curious about her, and Tom convinced his ma she'd be pestered if she was left outside.

Sister Ann ladles stew out careful, her eyes on Hunger.

"Thank you," Kane says. I nod my thanks the same.

We tuck in, burning our mouths in our haste. And again my heart pangs with the familiar taste of herbs and rabbit, all simmered together.

"Where's pa gone to?" Tom asks between mouthfuls.

"Hunting," his ma replies. "Think you gave him the idea to get good with his shot."

Kane raises his eyebrows. "Not a trapper anymore?"

"Both," Sister Ann replies. "Most people have kept their stations, but some are trying new things, too." She runs her hands over her hair, smoothing the wisps back into her bun. "Nothing to say we can't, anymore."

"Are there still Watchers on the walls each night?" Kane asks.

"There are," Sister Ann says. "Ever since Henderson told us about those rogue types, we've taken pains to make sure we're not vulnerable."

I feel a wave of relief. "And Watch is still done by the north quarter?"

"Most, yes. They're best with the weapons."

"How many people are here in the fortification?" I ask. "Did anyone leave for the east?"

"A few." Sister Ann tilts her head, looking thoughtful. "Five, six families? Most stayed. It's been easier to make a go of things now that we can venture safe into the woods." She nods at me. "And the things your friend taught us about what grows out there helps. Our sheep can graze out overnight, too, now, so they're fatter, and the ewes give birth to more live lambs." She smiles. "Things have been different this summer."

It's clear that "different" means *good*. I think on this. When I left months back, I figured the only reason people would stay inside these walls was out of fear. But hearing Sister Ann speak, I can see that that's not the case. They're not here because they're fearful; they're here because they choose it.

I feel a nudge on my elbow and look down. Hunger's staring at me. Hoping, no doubt, for a scrap. I smile. Can't believe I used to be scared of her.

"That Matisa showing up changed things for us," Sister Ann says.

"She saved my life," I say, keeping my eyes on Hunger and my voice steady. "She saved all our lives."

"Suppose that's true."

"Ma," Tom says. "We need to call Talks. Em's got some things to speak on. Things the people need to hear."

Em's got some things to speak on.

And now, in spite of my efforts, a wave of grief rolls over me. Always pictured Matisa with me for this part. Always imagined her quiet strength beside me, making me bold.

We were supposed to prevent disaster together.

I remember her showing me the remedy plant. Did she know she wouldn't be here to see this through?

Make peace with it.

I close my eyes, fighting a grief that threatens to drown me. Still, all I can think is that I need her with me; I need her strength.

A memory forms in my mind: that night in Genya's village when Matisa showed us *kânîmihitocik,* those ghosts dancing in the sky, glimmering all shades of pink and gold, green and purple. She told us they were loved ones who had died, dancing forever among the stars. No longer here but always with us.

I raise my head. "Yes," I say. "Got some things to speak on."

My breath is tight in my chest as we push into the ceremonial hall. A rush of warmth and noise greets me. The space is crowded with people of all ages, like it was for Virtue Talks a lifetime ago. But unlike back then, when we stood in silence and listened to our leader's proclamations, people are chatting and moving about.

Used to dread Virtue Talks. Used to stand in the back, making myself small, hiding away from Council's eyes. And walking into the place where the leader of our settlement fell from grace and ended his life, where my pa's life was taken from him, makes my heart beat fast. But there's a fire burning in it, too.

Things have changed, and I'm not fearful to stand in front of this crowd anymore.

Now I want their eyes on me.

Sister Ann leads the way to the top of the stairs, next to the pulpit. She calls for quiet, and, gradually, it comes. She welcomes me back into the fortification, on behalf of everyone, and asks for their attention to my words. She nods at me to step forward.

I stare out at the sea of faces, feeling everyone waiting, questioning, judging. Word spreads fast in the settlement: my presence isn't a surprise. But they don't know *why* I've returned.

Kane puts a hand on my back, gentle.

I see Tom standing beside Eisu at the front of the crowd. His prairie-sky eyes hold mine, giving me strength.

I take a breath and raise my voice to address the crowd. "Brothers and sisters, we long believed we were alone in this world, that the places beyond our borders posed danger, brought death. Last fall I stood before you here with proof that we were wrong."

Every eye is on me.

"When the mapmaker arrived this past Thaw, we realized our world was changing. We realized we wouldn't be alone forever. I've journeyed far beyond our borders, and I've seen the change that comes. Matis—" I stumble on her name, clear my throat. "Matisa's people welcomed us in peace and shared their prosperity. Other newcomers from the east did the same. But, as that mapmaker predicted, not all of the people arriving are peaceful and good. Some of them are here to take as much as they can for themselves. They will do it any way they can."

The crowd murmurs.

"We—" I steel myself. "We suffered at the hands of such people on our journey. Our trusted Watch leader, Frère Andre, and Sister Violet were sent to their Peace after one skirmish." I feel Kane shift beside me. "The First People you welcomed last fall, the people we survived *La Prise* with, are . . . in danger." I clear my throat against a sudden lump and continue. "I come on behalf of them, on behalf of their kin, *osanaskisiwak*. I ask that you consider my words, that you listen with an open heart and mind."

I look to Kane. He nods, his face full of encouragement and hope.

"This is a truly special place," I say. "Our choice about who to share it with can determine the future of this land for years to come." I take a deep breath. "There are people who will come to take this land by force. Their weapons are many and terrible. There are others who may come in peace but wish to rule us. Matisa's people will align with us against them."

I pause to let the information sink in. A murmur starts in the crowd. A man near the front takes his chance to ask, "On what condition?"

"On the condition we share what makes this place special." The chatter grows in volume. "Please listen!" I hold up my hands. "They are prosperous and peaceful. We could learn many things from their ways. They want to cooperate with us to ensure their freedom and our freedom."

"You mean freedom from the rogue types?" a woman calls out.

"Yes," I answer. "But also from the Dominion. They are parceling out this land as though it's their own."

"That mapmaker told us the Dominion was setting to move against the rogues."

"They are," I agree. "But it does not mean—"

"That mapmaker said they were bringing law."

"We already have law. Matisa's people have law," I say. "The Dominion is poised, right now, at the mouth of the *osanaskisiwak* valley. We need to help Matisa's people secure their freedom."

"Why should we?" the man from before demands. "They're not part of us."

A hot flush rushes over me. Kane steps closer, encouraging me to go on. "Because they deserve it," I say. "Because Matisa helped us, freed us, by showing us the truth outside our gates." I steady my voice. "And because helping them means a better life for all of us."

There's a silence.

"You say they'll help us," the woman says. I nod. "But how? Do they also have weapons? Will they fight for us?"

"They'll negotiate peace and freedom," I say. "They have the means."

"What means?"

I take a deep breath, trying to decide how to proceed. I hedge my bets. "These woods have long protected us from the Bleed. *Osanaskisiwak* can barter for their freedom—for our freedom—with that knowledge."

People glance at one another.

"How?" the woman persists. "How do these woods protect us?"

I look around the hall, at the men and women, the children, the grandparents, gazing at me with interest. Fascination, even. And I realize something. We survived out here because we got lucky; we've been protected from the Bleed, unknowing, for generations. But there have been far more threats than the Bleed: starvation, sickness, the killing winter. It's true that fear and untruths kept us contained all those long years, making life more difficult than it could have been, but this land is unforgiving at the best of times. These are a hardy people, determined.

And them staying here because they choose it, not because they fear what's beyond, is proof they're changing, along with our world.

Sharing the truth with them now is part of that.

I tell them everything. How the Dominion is suffering the Bleed and looking for safe places. I tell them about Merritt Leon, how I believe he will attack us because he thinks we have a cure. I tell them about Matisa's people leaving here all those years ago, how the remedy was kept secret. I tell them how Matisa figured out our dreams, how we were sure the remedy was growing here.

And I tell them how I proved it.

When I'm finished speaking, there's quiet in the hall. Foreheads crease. Heads bow. People whisper to one another.

A young girl standing near Sister Ann asks, "You did that—for them?"

They're not part of us.

My chest hitches. A rush of emotion builds, threatening to drown out my words. I clear my throat to steady my voice. "I did it for all of us," I say. "Because you're right: Matisa's people aren't part of us. They don't look like us;

they don't live like us." I take a breath. "But look." I sweep an arm around the hall. "Look at the *mélange* here. We are a mix of many different people. Some of our ancestors came out here in search of a better life; some of our ancestors fled persecution because they spoke the wrong tongue or were of mixed blood. We were not like one another. But we banded together. We relied on one another to survive. *That* is who we are." I look out over the crowd. "And anyone can be a part of that."

I catch Tom's admiring gaze, feel Kane's hand warm on my back. "We can choose for ourselves," I say. "This is our chance to prove our Virtues in the way they were always meant. This is our chance to be *true* Discovery, *true* Honesty, *true* Bravery. This is our chance to choose a new life. A chance to carve our own path."

No one speaks. No one moves.

Hundreds of pairs of eyes measure me.

Not sure what I was expecting, but it wasn't silence. My heart pounds so loud, I'm sure that everyone in the hall can hear it.

Sister Ann steps up beside me. "Emmeline has given us much to think on," she says. Disappointment sweeps me; they're not agreeing. Not yet, anyhow. "We would be wise to consider her words. I ask that all of you search your hearts for the path you believe will secure our future here." She raises her voice. "Regardless of our decision to align with Emmeline's friends, an immediate attack is of grave concern."

She points to Tom. "My boy barely made it back here

with his life. Frère Andre and Sister Violet are lost to us. These men will stop at nothing to take our settlement." She looks around. "And I need to know: who will help me fight for it?"

At this, several hands go up in the crowd. Sister Ann scans the room. Several more. She looks at me. "Emmeline, you have seen this enemy. Can you help guide our preparations against them?"

Disappointment wars with desperation in me. Got no idea whether I failed or succeeded here. If I've failed to convince them, the only thing I can do to fulfill this task is take as much of the remedy as I can and ride hard for *osanaskisiwak*—hold up their end of the bargain, at least. But then what?

Osanaskisiwak needs to be in control of the remedy; they need to be united with the settlement, especially now that I've told them the truth.

My dream niggles at the back of my mind. Rushing through the woods. Following that man . . . the man is Merritt Leon. I know it now. And in my dream, *I'm* trying to stop him.

If Leon's coming—*he's coming*—he'll be following the river. Without Henderson's map, it's the surest way to find these woods. That means he's still at least two days behind; there's time to prepare. And if he shows up soon, there's still time to get back to *osanaskisiwak* with the remedy.

If I've convinced my people to share it.

Leon might not show.

But my dream clamors loud in my head, telling me that's

not true. It's him; it's always been him, in those dreams. My breath coming fast, racing past those crumbling logs, that ruined cabin . . .

Following him.

Chasing him.

Hurry—

"I'll help," I say. "But we'll need every able body."

27

I WATCH WOMEN SCURRY TO AND FRO WITH blankets and food, stocking the ceremonial hall where the youngsters and elderly will take shelter. I see Luc and a dozen more Watchers oiling weapons, searching out metal to melt down for bullets.

As I requested, everyone able will stand on these walls and fight. Of the four hundred or so people remaining in the settlement, that's over two hundred. Leon's man said they outnumbered the Dominion four to one, and Charlie said he thought the Dominion were no more than two dozen. Surely some of Leon's men died in that skirmish, leaving him with about fifty at best, if he's bringing them all. We have a chance.

I find Tom and Kane inside the munitions shack looking over a quick sketch of the outlying woods. Tom glances up at me. "You said Leon doesn't have a map?"

I shake my head. I peer close at the sketch of the land around our fortification. "He'll be following the river." I trace my finger along the winding line. "They can't stick to the bank here." I point at the river in the south, where the walls are too sheer and the water too rough to traverse the bank. "They'll need to cut into the woods. That means it's likely they'll be approaching from here." I pinpoint the woods in the south.

"We should meet them out there," Tom says. "Keep the fight in the woods for as long as possible."

"Watchers aren't skilled at forest fighting like *osanaskisi-wak*," I remind him. "They've only ever practiced defending from the walls, with clear sight lines."

"And not knowing exactly what weapons Leon will have is worrying," Kane points out. "He might be injured, but if he brings weapons like the Dominion had . . ."

He's right. If he brings weapons like those, we won't stand a chance.

"Our best chance is surprising them," Tom says. "Looking vulnerable so they show their hand, then attacking when they don't expect it."

"Surprise would be best," Kane agrees. "Cutting back around and attacking from behind. We could push him forward to the Watch flats, where our Watchers will have a clear shot. Just not sure how we'd manage that with two horses."

"We can't," I say. "We need an army to do it. We need . . ."

We need Isi and Lea and her hunters.

The door bangs open. Luc stands in the glare of sunlight, a huge hulking shadow.

"How's the melting going?" Tom asks him, straightening up.

Luc shakes his head. *"Pas bien,"* he says. *"Nous n'avons pas beaucoup."*

The men have been melting down anything we can part with to be repurposed into bullets, but it's clear Luc's not impressed with what they've managed to produce.

"Did you take apart all the barrel casings?" Tom asks.

Luc nods. *"Chaque clos."* Every nail. *"Chaque piece de métal que nous pourrions trouver. Je pense que les maisons son prochaine."*

"Well, take apart what lodgings you have to," Tom says. "We can always rebuild if . . ."

If we survive.

We're all thinking it.

Sister Ann appears behind Luc, two women behind her. "Ceremonial hall is ready," she says. She notices our faces. "What is it?"

"We need more bullets," Tom says.

"You take apart the Hold?" she asks Luc.

"Oui."

I draw a deep breath and think a minute. Metal. Where else can we . . .

My eyes light up. "The Crossroads."

Luc raises his eyebrows.

"The gibbets—they're made of metal. We can melt those down."

The women behind Sister Ann shift.

"What is it?"

"People think it's unlucky."

"Still?"

She shrugs. "Superstitions run deep."

I suppose it's true. The women might know that there is no *malmaci*, that the Crossroads were an offering to a spirit that didn't exist, but they're still wary. It's all over their faces.

They don't want to go out there.

I remember Henderson trying to warn Leon off by speaking on the *malmaci*. I figured my people had told Henderson about it because they were explaining why our settlement was isolated so long. But mayhap they thought they were warning him.

Almighty.

"I'll go," I say, dusting off my hands.

"Me, too," Kane says.

"Moi aussi," says Luc.

I look at Sister Ann. "We'll take a few men and go retrieve them."

"It's high time for that place to be destroyed," she says. She wipes her hands on her apron. "I'll come, too."

We take materials to craft a travois—two lashed-together poles with a leather sling between them—for Beast and Tom's horse to carry the cages back from the Crossroads. Eight of the strongest men go with us, carrying wooden ladders and axes so they can cut the cages down.

The men are Watchers, but even so, they aren't comfortable with this idea. They agreed after Luc talked for a long time—rushed French I didn't full understand. Now that they're here, I'm trying my best to reassure them. I lead on Beast and give them a confident smile as the path in the woods empties us out to the red flag—the Crossroads marker. Hunger slips in and out of the trees, keeping pace with us.

I press ahead, urging Beast up the slippery incline. Tom and his ma follow on his horse. At the top of the hill I remember the day I found this place—how unafraid and desperate afraid I was at once. How my anger spurred me into this place of death.

The cages hang like brittle shells, twisting in the breeze, empty of bones. Emptied by Isi last fall. The drawings on the far coulee wall blaze out at me. The monster—the sickness—rending people with its claws and teeth and turning them into pools of blood shines in the sun. I remember those etchings coming alive, sending me fleeing back to the fortification.

Now they're still. Drawings only.

But there's a strange feeling in the air. Like this place has something to tell me if I listen long enough. I look back and watch the faces of the men as we descend into the valley. They're nervous—walking close together, they stare at the cages. One of them keeps looking behind us. We pull up before the cages, and Luc orders the men to get to work.

They hoist ladders and begin chopping at the poles. Kane and Tom work on the one closest to me.

It's late afternoon by the time the travois is loaded with the cages.

"I'll walk," I say, waving off Sister Ann's direction to get on Beast.

Kane leads two other Watchers with axes, planning to widen the path where it's tricky for the travois to pass through.

As we leave, I look back at this place, once so formidable with danger and death. The remnants of the horror are the poles that held the cages, lying helpless now on the sandy ground. Hunger crowds close to me; I let her nudge my hand with her wet nose.

Eisu stops beside me and follows my gaze. "It's perfect," he remarks.

I frown at him. "Beg pardon?"

He gestures around us. "This valley. It's perfect for an ambush."

The coulees rise steep around the space on two sides—impossible to climb without a rope ladder. The small hill that leads to this place is easy enough to traverse, and the only other exit is out the far side.

He's right: it's perfect.

We'd need to harry them this way somehow. There's no guarantee Leon's men will be on horseback, but it's best to plan for the worst; we'd need a rider to lead them.

I remember chasing Matisa through this valley that day last fall—how she seemed to appear from nowhere and re-appear, like a specter. Yesterday she reappeared because I was delirious.

Both times I felt compelled to follow.

"Come with me," I say to Eisu. "We need to talk to Tom and Kane."

We gather inside the common room of our old quarters, and I spread the map on the floor.

"That harrying technique of Huritt's," I say, "we can use that. You only need one or two horses for that kind of ambush."

Tom and Kane stare at me.

"Eisu?" I look to him for help.

He leans forward and points to the map. "We harry them into this Crossroads place and roll burning brush down on either end to trap them there. Shooters are positioned at the tops of the coulees."

"Harry them?" Kane asks.

"Lure them," Tom says, looking between Eisu and me like we're up to no good.

"But how?"

"Get them to chase us, on horseback," Eisu explains.

"And who's riding?"

"I am," I say. "And Eisu. We'll lead them there from the grove."

"The grove is to the west," Tom says. "Chances are they'll be approaching from the south."

"Yeah, chances are. But we can lead them west."

"How?"

"The *malmaci*," I say.

Tom squints at me. "Beg pardon?"

"Henderson told Leon about the *malmaci*, trying to scare him off these woods. It didn't work: Leon assumed it was us, protecting the cure. So why don't we give him what he's expecting? He'll follow something that looks like it's trying to scare him away. By the time he realizes we're leading him, it'll be too late."

Tom looks at Eisu.

"It is a good plan," Eisu says.

"No way we'll get all of them in there at once," Tom points out. "You said there might be fifty men."

"Even if we don't get them all," I say, "dividing them like that will give us a better chance. You wanted to ambush them. This is the way to do it."

Tom considers this.

"So you want us to . . . be spirits?" Kane looks at me, skeptical.

"No," I say. "I want the woods to be spirits."

Out on the Watch flats, I go over my plan with Luc and Sister Ann, describing the contraptions I envision and gesturing to the part of the woods where they should be placed.

"Make them as strange as you can," I instruct. "And make them noisy. Anything that can clink together or whine or howl in a breeze. We want the feeling of something not right. Something ghostly."

Sister Ann presses her lips in a grim line and nods. She and Luc leave to find bones and lashings. Tom has been quiet since we left the walls to discuss the plan.

"Say they don't notice the bone hangings?" Kane asks.

"That's what Eisu is for," I say. "He'll stay ahead of them, close enough that they can hear him to follow him to the grove."

Eisu nods.

"And I'll be waiting on Beast, who'll be fresh. Eisu can veer off when he reaches the grove, and I'll wait for them to see me. They'll chase me to the Crossroads, where you'll be waiting. Eisu can cut back behind and pick off any stragglers at the back."

Kane nods. "All right, I think this will work."

But Tom's eyes are worried. "Do you have to be the one riding?" he asks me.

"Yes," I say, and I've never been so sure of anything in my life. "I do."

28

I CLOSE MY EYES, TRYING TO FILL MY MIND, MY heart, with the song of *osanaskisiwak*. Trying to find my way back there, to the moment the voices and drums washed over me, protected me, strengthened me. The woods around us are still.

Beast shifts his weight and huffs out his air, like he's reminding me that we're in this together.

And we are. When we see Eisu on the far side of this grove, leading Leon's men, it'll be up to me to steer Beast to the Crossroads. And it'll be up to Beast to get there quick.

I open my eyes and gaze around the grove, thinking on the day I found it last fall. The day I first ventured out beyond the Watch flats.

That day, the fortification felt like a giant cage of watchful crows, weighing my every move, waiting to pick my bones clean. I was desperate to get away, whatever the consequences.

Today, that cage is protecting my people. Now we're fighting for it.

The signal came at midday, a thin line of smoke trailing up from the south, inside the woods nearest the impassable steep banks of the river.

Eisu spotted Leon.

And by now, surely Leon has spotted that smoke.

The settlement knows well what to do when an attack signal is given; we've been practicing for generations. The courtyard became a blur of activity. Old and young were hustled into the ceremonial hall, and new fighters hurried to their positions on the walls, joining the Watchers who'd been posted all day and night.

And we hurried to the woods.

Kane and Tom and a dozen Watchers with the best aim are back in the coulees of the Crossroads, setting up the ambush.

And Beast and I are here, ready to lead Leon into it.

It's been near an hour. I picture Eisu on his horse, luring the men through the *malmaci*'s left-behinds—the hangings of bone and blood and feather. Leading them through the ghost cries of the wind chimes. Drawing them this way like some unseen spirit.

Eisu's a decent shot and a better rider than me, even bareback. He's the best bet to lead the invaders this way and double back around. The leather of his horse's saddle creaks beneath me. I just have to keep myself on top of Beast and ride a fair straight line, but we both thought it better I have the saddle.

And now, picturing what I have to do, I'm grateful for it.

I pause and listen. *Les trembles* are tinkling, soft. A breeze snakes through my hair. For a moment, this grove feels to me the way it did last fall: a little haven, tucked away from the danger in the forest.

A strange peace settles over me, despite the fear itching at my skin, the back of my neck. And I can feel those drums, that song, murmuring beneath the wind.

And I hear it: thunder overhead. I look up to the patch of blue amid the poplars and see clouds closing in fast, dark gray and heavy with rain.

My pulse skips. Lighting the brush to roll into the valley will be tricky in the rain. But when the thunder increases, I realize it's not only the sky I'm hearing: it's hoofbeats. Pounding through the woods and toward me.

They're here. This is it.

Eisu breaks into the clearing. He sees me and veers off, pulling his horse hard to the left and spurring her into the brush. In a heartbeat he's swallowed by the dark trees.

Beast dances and strains as I wheel him around, pointing him toward the trail that leads to the Crossroads. He wants to run. I tighten the reins and look behind, feeling a fire running all over my skin.

The first rider bursts into the clearing, his shoulders hunched over his horse, who's running hard. He sees me. And I have no time to see anything else. The grove is small— thirty strides across, no more—and if I wait a second longer, he'll be on me.

I dig in my heels and give Beast his head. He springs up the trail with a breath-stealing leap and puts his neck out, stretching his legs long as I spur him again. I bend my head low, feeling his muscles strain, watching the ground and brush rush past, my pulse racing in time with the thunder of his hooves. I can hear the first man shouting, and I wonder if they're looking for a way to fan out and cut me off. They won't find it. The woods are dense here, and the fastest way through them is this path we widened for the travois.

They just need to stay on my tail.

Got no idea how many men are following me—sounds like a lot—but Beast is all fury and strength beneath me. I feel alive. Strong. Brave. I raise my eyes to check the distance and see the trees giving way ahead.

The branches above are rustling fierce now. Rain is starting. The drops pepper my skin, tearing through the poplar leaves and hitting me like fire.

The men are gaining on me; can feel them the way I once felt the *malmaci* hot on my neck.

But I'm so close now. So close . . .

Beast bursts from the woods and tears past the red flag that marks the Crossroads, laboring up the rise. I lean forward as he gathers strength and pulls us to the top. As we crest the hill, I throw a quick look behind me and count eight—no, a dozen—riders pursuing us. Closing in fast.

Hurry.

I throw my weight back into the saddle as Beast rushes down the hill, his back feet slipping in the shale. He bucks and jerks, and I grip hard with my knees so I don't pitch over his head. I'm lighter than a man, less weight to throw Beast off balance as he descends.

They'll be slower.

When Beast and I reach the bottom, we're well ahead.

Excitement rushes over me as I lean over his neck and we tear into the Crossroads, riding hard for the far side.

But the rains are coming strong now. I realize with a jolt that I can't see any smoke in the coulees. Panic cuts through my exhilaration. If the Watchers can't get the brush lit . . .

Leon's men thunder into the valley behind me.

And now, the blessed smell of smoke.

I look under my arm. The riders are dead center of the Crossroads now.

Shots ring out from the coulees, and a rider in the center of the pack falls. I see one of Kane's knives lodged in his neck as he tumbles to the earth. Another one goes down. The riders ahead of him duck, craning their necks up at the hills. They urge their horses faster, but the men at the back drag their horses to a stop and wheel them about, looking to retreat.

And now, flaming brambles are careening down the coulee walls to the east, cutting off their path. Black plumes of smoke furl outward, and their horses scream and rear.

I look forward over Beast's head, shots from the hills ringing in my ears.

We're almost to the exit. The rains are coming harder now. As Beast gallops for the far side, I scan the hills for flaming brush. Nothing. No smoke at this end of the Crossroads. My insides twist as we pass through the end. There'll be no burning brambles to trap the men on this side.

With any luck, our rifles and Kane's knives will get them first.

The rock beside me explodes with gunshot, sending hot fear all through me.

Leon's men are shooting at me now.

Beast bursts out of the valley and into the trees. I head north, planning to ride out and circle back for Kane and Tom.

But as I look back, my heart misses a beat. Four men have made it through. Can see from here, from the awkward, one-armed way the first holds the reins . . .

It's Leon.

He hollers at the others—sounds like he's telling them *not* to shoot—and urges his horse faster.

Can't stop and circle back now—I'll need to lose them in the forest. I spur Beast on but soon realize I'm in the wrong part of the woods for that—the trees here are spaced apart, the coulees are back the other way, and the riders are closing in fast.

Need to find cover somewhere.

Beast labors through the brush, straining hard at my urging, but I can feel him tiring beneath me.

We crest the next rise, and I realize I've brought us straight to a gully. And in the center, standing there, so peaceful, like the whole world wasn't turned upside down within, the cabin.

The cabin where I found Matisa, found the journal that explained my grandma'am's transgression, wiped the slate clean. The cabin where I found a truth that Brother Stockham was willing to kill me to conceal.

I'm back to where this all began.

My head spins. The men are so close behind me, and my breath is coming so fast, I don't know what to do. Where to go?

The cellar. If I can get there before them, I can hide there.

Like Kane and I did so long ago . . .

Beast gallops down the small hill, and I urge him around the building, pulling him to a stop at the door. We're hidden from our pursuers for the moment. I scramble off him, slap his rump. *"Go!"* I whisper. He leaps ahead to the hill on the far side.

I claw my way to the door.

They're coming—can hear them thundering down the rise on the far side.

I clamber inside, banging the door behind me and scrabbling for the trap door. I yank it open and throw myself into the cold, dank space.

The men's shouts are louder.

Have they seen Beast? Are they pursuing him?

But I can hear them the same way I heard Matisa and the boys last fall, pulling up outside the cabin, their beasts breathing hard and blowing out their air. And now, quiet.

Dead quiet.

My pulse is racing triple-time; my breath is ragged with fear. Foolish. Foolish! I'm trapped.

A creak. And a bang.

The door's been thrown open. They must be staying back behind the door, in case I'm armed.

I'm not armed. Not even close.

And I'm dead down here.

29

I CROUCH BACK AGAINST THE FAR SIDE OF THE cellar, in the darkest spot.

The floorboards whine above me as the men enter the cabin.

"She came in here." A man's voice I know well.

"You sure?"

"Dead sure," Leon says. There's a pause. A creak, direct above me.

The cellar door is flung open, and light pours into the space. I shrink back, gripping my knife. A big shadow blocks the glare.

"Get some light over here," Leon orders.

I'm caught, but I'm not going down without a fight.

A beam of light stabs into the cellar, blinding me against the blur of movement. A hand grabs my wrist and twists so hard, I gasp and drop my knife. I'm dragged across the dirt floor by two hands—one gripping my arm, the other knotted in my hair. My hip bangs against the hard wooden stairs, one after the other, and I'm pulled across the floor of the cabin and out the door. Can feel hair rip away from my scalp as I'm thrown to the dirt outside.

I blink and scramble to my knees, trying to see beyond the trickle of blood running into my eye. I see boots, caked with mud, and look up dirty pants past an ammunition belt and up the bandaged arm to a mangled face.

Leon, standing above me. Looking down his gun barrel with a swollen eye.

I scramble back on my heels, casting a frantic look around. Three men with guns stand in a semicircle. The rain is pattering soft.

"Well, then," Leon says. He winces as he moves his arm in the sling and shakes his head. "I guess I shouldn't be surprised."

My blood is ice water, and my breath is squeezed tight in my chest.

"But I'm done dealing with you, Emmeline," he says. "I'm real tired of it, as a matter of fact. So you can show me where this cure is—" He raises his gun. It's the one with the initials scratched along the handle. The gun I was so sure ended Tom's life. "Or I can shoot you."

I stare up at him, into his dead gray eyes, remembering the ways he's tricked me, how he's lied. Lying down now, pretending to negotiate with him so I can buy myself more time . . .

It's not my path. Not anymore.

Blood trickles from my temple into my mouth. I heave a breath and spit a gob of crimson at his feet. I meet his gaze. "Shoot me," I say.

His face contorts with fury. And something else.

Fear.

Fear.

But he pulls the hammer back on his piece, and my heart stops as I realize I guessed wrong. He wasn't lying. Not this time.

I close my eyes.

A holler, like a cry of joy and sorrow at once, shatters the trees.

Leon jerks his head up to the hills around us. I scan the rise.

They've appeared from nowhere, silent as frost.

A dozen—more?—riders on horseback. Standing on the ridge, still like stone.

We stare up at them.

They ignite: their horses leap forward, streaming down the hill. The riders holler, black hair flying out behind them like smoke, bright blue flashing beneath their leather breastplates. A rush of hoofbeats and shrill cries roar around us like a big wind.

Gunshots.

Leon screams and drops his gun, his shoulder jerking back. The men around us duck and dive for cover.

Leon scrambles back toward the cabin, and I throw myself after him, aiming for the door, but I push off my bad foot and collapse. I tumble to the earth, pulling my arms over my head.

Everywhere, everywhere, gunshots.

A thud beside me forces my eyes open. I squirm away from the dead man before I think to use him as cover. And a blur of movement to my left catches my eye. Leon. Running for the trees. He's on the far side of the cabin, and it's protecting him from the attack. He's going to get away . . .

More gunshots. I tuck my head back beneath my arms. The shots reverberate through my chest, deep down in my bones, loud, so loud it's going to split me open . . .

It stops.

The rush of hoofbeats comes again and softens to a slow patter. I can feel the beasts surrounding me, blowing hot air through their nostrils. I pull my head up.

A wall of hooves and legs surrounds me. I squint up at the horses, up their strong chests and beyond their moist noses. Above their heads, warriors dressed in *osanaskisiwak* blue are staring at me. The symbol of the hawk shines on their leather breastplates.

Sohkâtisiwak.

And the crush of horses is parting. Someone is coming through on foot. Someone determined, and I can tell by the command, can tell by the voice . . .

She pushes through and falls to her knees before me.

"Emmeline," Matisa says.

30

I THROW MYSELF INTO HER ARMS, HOT TEARS
blinding me. I hug her tight, pressing my face to her shoulder. She grips me back. My relief is so strong, and I'm so full
of love for her, it's hard to breathe.

I press my forehead to her neck. "I . . ." The words are all
caught in my chest. "I thought . . ." More tears.

"You thought we would not see one another again," she
says in my ear. "I was worried about that, too."

I hug her tighter.

"We do not have time for this," a familiar voice says.

I draw back, looking for the owner, and find Isi coming
through a split in the crowd, looking fierce. My eyes widen,
and new tears rush in.

He frowns down at me. "And we do not have time for you
to cry."

A sound bursts from me—something between a laugh
and a sob.

The rain has stopped. Matisa smiles and pulls a cloth

from the satchel slung across her body. As she presses it to my temple, I feel the sting of raw flesh and remember my hair tearing out. I'm too happy to care. I stare at her as she dabs at my wound, feeling a wave of love so intense, it makes me dizzy. And all I can say is, "How?"

"Lea and I were found by *sohkâtisiwak* after that flood," she says, peering at the wound. "They wanted my help, but I insisted on looking for you. Then two of their group found us and told us you were alive, that you'd escaped the Keep." She smiles. "We came as fast we could. And found Isi on the way."

She smiles, but the hint of sadness in it tells me she knows about Bly and the rest of the scouts who were killed outside the Keep by Leon's men.

I stagger to my feet, looking around. So Isi was coming back here on his own. Just coming, because he thought if there was a chance, he should try for it. Joy and relief flood through me. There are twenty *sohkâtisiwak*, at least. And Lea is with them.

She raises a hand and smiles.

"So . . ." I squint. "They weren't hunting you to harm you?"

Matisa shakes her head. "They don't wish to betray *osanaskisiwak*; they just believed in a different path."

I remember Charlie telling me *sohkâtisiwak* had dreamt they needed Matisa to bring them into these woods.

And she did. She followed the same path she did back in the fall—straight to this cabin. Is this why? To help us against—

An explosion stops my thoughts dead.

The warriors pull their heads up to the southwest, scanning the trees.

Distant gunshot rings out.

Leon's men. Chances of luring them all were slim—we knew that. And those remaining have found the fortification. I look to Matisa.

She guesses my thoughts. "Where are they?"

"The southwest part of the woods. But if Leon's men have the weapons the Dominion had, our Watchers won't stand a chance."

"Lea?" Matisa asks.

"How many men?" Lea asks me.

"Not sure. Could be thirty or more. We lured about a dozen into the coulees south of here."

Lea calls to the riders, gathering them into a circle around her. Matisa listens as she talks and relays her words to me: "Lea will lead *sôhkâtisiwak* and flush the men from the Keep out onto the Watch flats where your guns can reach them. They'll skirt west and ambush them from behind on foot."

"But their weapons—"

"They can kill many before the men even know they are there. And then Leon's men will have no choice but to retreat to the Watch flats. They will not want to risk being in the woods."

"*Sohkâtisiwak* will follow Lea?"

Matisa nods. "She is a respected warrior."

"Kane and Tom are still at the Crossroads," I say. "They might need help."

"We will go." She peers at my wound. "Can you ride?"

"I'm fine." I grab my whistle and call Beast. He appears at the opposite side of the gully and breaks into a trot. I draw a deep breath and gaze at Leon's men scattered around us, arrows and bullet holes riddling their bodies.

There's something niggling at the back of my mind. Some memory or sensation . . .

Isi mounts the remaining horse, and Matisa climbs up behind him.

Lea is calling to her warriors to set out. They're spurring their horses up the gully. And I remember Leon, escaping on foot to the south. I watch the riders crest the west hill, a fire of urgency rushing through me.

"Em?" Matisa calls. Isi is wheeling their horse in the direction of the Crossroads.

My head snaps her way. "I'll catch up," I say, waving them forward.

But that fire is burning bright now.

My dream. My dream of rushing through these woods. Desperate. Urgent.

Following something.

Chasing something.

Hurry.

I wait for Matisa and Isi to crest the rise. I search the ground, scanning through the bodies . . . there. I grab Leon's gun and tuck it into my *ceinture.*

I mount Beast and head up the hill.

That heavy belt Leon was wearing is cast aside in the bushes at the top of the rise. Must've been weighing him down. I press into the woods, heading southeast. Leon escaped south up the gully, but there's little chance he'll risk cutting close to the Crossroads. No. He's heading back to the safety of his men. I urge Beast on, grateful for his speed and strength beneath me but nervous at the noise we're making. I'm not fast enough to track Leon on foot, so we'll need to risk it for now, but he'll be able to hear us coming once we get close. I pause to listen again. Gunfire, closer now.

My eyes scan the bushes, looking for the kinds of signs Matisa or Isi might notice: crushed low-lying plants, broken branches.

There.

The leaves of a plant ahead are shiny with blood.

Leon's shoulder wound.

I kick Beast on.

When we hit a dry creek bed, I know we've skirted the grove to the east and are nearing the Watch flats.

A crumbling cabin comes into view—old and sagging. There are several of these kinds of ruins out here, but I know this one well: it's the one from my dreams. Beyond it, movement in the trees. Leon, limping through the forest.

I draw Beast back behind the rotting cabin, out of sight.

Could catch him in a heartbeat. He's unarmed. And he's wounded and slow. I look at his gun, tucked in my *ceinture*. I regretted not killing him back at the Flashing River. This is my chance.

Need to see this through.

I listen, trying to draw strength. Bravery. *Les trembles* are rustling soft in the wind.

No, not the wind: someone's moving through the brush behind me.

I spin in the saddle and find Matisa making her way through the trees.

"What are you doing?" I whisper, beckoning for her to stay behind the sagging walls.

She draws close. "I am staying with you," she says.

"But Kane and Tom?"

"I sent Isi." She looks at the gun in my hand. "You will shoot him?"

So she knows what I'm doing.

"I guess."

Her eyes search my face. They soften. "We will do as Lea and *sohkâtisiwak* are planning against the other men," she says. "We will flush Leon out into the open, onto the Watch flats. Take Beast and cut west and south. You can get between him and his men easily."

"I'm loud on Beast," I say.

"That is the point," Matisa says. "He is unarmed. He will try to avoid you."

"We're pretty near unarmed, too."

"He doesn't know that. Cut off his path to the south, and I'll force him east. We'll herd him to the flats."

Unease niggles at me. "You sure we should split up?"

"Yes. And we should hurry," she says.

Hurry.

"Be careful," I tell her.

She nods. "And you."

And she is gone.

I cut around the ruined cabin and head southwest. When I'm sure I'm south of Leon, I steer Beast to the east and spur him hard. Trees stream past, and a familiar sensation rises in my chest. Urgency.

I spot him hobbling through the trees. He's off balance, his arm in that sling and limping worse than before. He glances behind, and when he sees me, I spur Beast faster, making sure I cut off his route south. He shifts direction, darting to the north, but he takes only a few strides that way before he stops and switches course again.

From here I can glimpse Matisa through the trees. Appearing. Disappearing. It's clear that Leon has seen her, too. We move like this, letting him stay just ahead of us, letting him believe we're slower, for several more strides.

He breaks into a run.

I kick Beast forward, keeping to the south. Matisa sprints ahead, keeping pace with Leon to the north. He looks between us and opens up his gait. We increase pace with him, herding him east.

The trees thin, giving way to wide-open space on the far side. He slows as he makes it to the last line of trees. The gunshots are loud now. Can see from here that the fighting is moving onto the flats. Leon's men are fleeing the woods, some on foot, some on their horses. They fire at the walls and into the trees at *sohkâtisiwak*, who are flushing them out. The Watchers from the walls shoot at whoever's in range.

Leon stops, caught between us and the Watch flats. He's ten strides from me. Close enough that I can see the desperation in the way he pauses, deciding.

I rein Beast to a stop and pull Leon's gun from my *ceinture.* I extend my arm, gritting my teeth, and try to steady my hand as I aim. I'm a terrible shot.

But he doesn't know that.

He turns around, his unbound hand raised in surrender. He's holding something in it. Not a gun. Something I've seen before . . .

A handheld explosive.

31

HE SMILES. "YOU'D BEST LET ME PASS, EMME-line." He nods at his hand. "Or I'll have to use this."

"Don't move," I say. "Or I'll have to shoot you." I say the words as fierce as I can, but I'm lying, of course. I'm not half sure enough with my shot. And when I miss, he'll throw that thing.

He looks at Matisa, ten strides to the north. Back at me. "You sure about that?" And I see his thumb flick at the explosive, shedding its cover.

The gun trembles in my grip. Fury and desperation threaten to drown me in a cold wave. I dig deep for strength, bravery. I search for the memory of those drums, that song.

He raises his eyebrows, expectant.

My breath leaves me in a shaky exhale, and the gun drops from my hand with a dull thud. I meet Matisa's eyes across the space.

His face relaxes in a knowing smile. "I didn't think so."

He thinks I'm not brave enough. It's all over his smug face. But I didn't drop the gun because I'm a coward. He'll throw the explosive, anyway, whether I've got the gun or not. And I'm going to make sure it's not at Matisa.

Because there are other ways to be brave.

He takes a step, lowering the hand clutching the explosive. Which is what you do if you're about to throw it—

I don't think another thought.

I dig my heels into Beast, sending him leaping forward. Leon freezes in surprise. Beast's long legs eat up the space between us, and I gather myself. I'll dive off Beast and tackle Leon, letting Beast run clear of the blast. I'll make sure the thing doesn't leave Leon's hand. But now I see that Matisa is running, too. Toward us. Toward Leon.

No!

Leon hesitates, trying to decide who he can reach with his throw. It's a heartbeat too long. We are on him, and I do the only thing I can think of: I steer Beast straight into him. I'll only have three seconds when that explosive hits the ground to get Matisa and get out. Beast crashes into Leon with his strong chest, sending him sprawling backward. The object flies from Leon's hand as Beast tramples him and leaps free. I spur Beast hard, reaching for Matisa. I'll pull her up, I'll get her away from—

The world goes inside out. I'm in the air, weightless as a feather. Drifting. Soaring. And I'm heavy as a stone, plummeting to the earth, brush tearing at my cheeks and hands as I fall. The wind is slammed from my lungs.

Darkness. I roll and find the trees spinning bright above me.

For a moment I lie there, staring up at a circle of blue beyond the poplars, a din clamoring in my ears.

Matisa.

I push to my knees, calling her name, but I can't hear myself over the ringing in my head. Dust, thick like smoke, stings my eyes. I stagger up, sucking in deep breaths but getting no air, feeling sharp pain rush up through my side. Beast lies nearby, his sides heaving like he's laboring for breath.

I close my heart to that picture and stumble forward, searching for her.

She's four strides away, lying just inside the trees by the Watch flats. Her skin is peppered with cuts, and they're starting to make little streams that course down her face.

My dream.

My dream where Matisa's bleeding rivers, where I'm heaping dirt on her. Burying her.

It's all hot and bright in my head now.

Hurry.

I press forward, my body slow like honey, reaching for her, grasping for her.

And now sound rushes in like a big wind. Gunfire. Screams. Hoofbeats. Someone calling my name.

It's all around me, but all I can see is her. I fall to my knees and grab her to me with fumbling hands, cradling her head and smoothing back her hair.

Her eyes are cloudy—they can't find mine.

And all around me is a violent whirlwind of sound and smoke and trembling earth. I press a hand to her face. I was so sure I was healing her in my dream; so sure that my dream was showing me the truth about the soil here.

The feeling I have, when I am buried . . . it is one of peace.

Her words come back to me in a rush.

"Matisa," I whisper.

Matisa moans soft. Her eyes focus on mine.

And I near collapse on top of her with relief. She's alive.

She struggles to sit up.

"Don't!" I caution. "You're hurt."

She coughs and sinks back to the ground.

"Matisa!" It's Isi, falling to his knees beside us. He puts a hand on her shoulder, speaking words in their tongue. She nods and gestures to her arm with her opposite hand. It's hurt, bent at an unnatural angle.

"You just rest," I say, fierce. I lean forward and press a kiss to her forehead.

Isi wraps arms around us both, pressing his forehead to my neck in relief. It's a gesture that's so unlike him, I want to laugh.

I glance around and see Kane hurrying across the flats.

"Kane!" I untangle myself from Isi and Matisa and push to my feet.

Around us, chunks of debris are everywhere, wood and clumps of soil and rock and . . .

And Beast, lying on his side. I watch for the rise and fall of his chest.

Nothing. He's still.

I choke back a cry and start toward him, but I stop when I see a body lying facedown beneath the shattered trees. A twisted, bloody heap.

Unmoving.

I point at Leon with a shaky hand. Kane's gaze follows. He changes direction and heads toward him.

"Be careful!" I call.

Kane holds up a hand to reassure me as he peers close. He looks over Leon for several long moments. When he looks back at me, his face is grave. He nods.

He strides over to Beast. And when he turns back to me, he looks so sorry for me that my eyes blur and I can't take a step.

My knees feel weak, and I have to sink to them or topple.

Matisa coughs, and I turn back to her, trying to focus on the good. Beast's huge frame likely shielded Matisa and me from the worst of the blast. He saved me. One last time.

And I notice the quiet.

The sounds of chaos are gone. No gunfire. No screams. No hoofbeats.

I glance about the Watch flats. Bodies litter the space.

Tom emerges from the trees, holding his hands high and calling out so the Watchers know to hold their fire. Lea follows, and behind her the *sohkâtisiwak* warriors venture out onto the flats, looking up to the walls of the fortification, raising their hands like Tom.

And, the way they did for me, a lifetime ago, the Watchers set down their weapons and clasp a hand across their chests in the sign of the Peace.

A cheer of triumph rings out from the warriors. The Watchers raise their voices, echoing the cry.

We've won.

32

ISI AND TOM TAKE MATISA TO THE CEREMONIAL
hall until I can ready a place for her in the Healing House.
She's moving slow, and she's a mite dazed, but I can tell by
the way she frowns at Isi fussing over her that she'll be all
right.

Lea and some of the warriors leave to tour the woods, to
make sure there aren't any of Leon's men left. I stay on the
flats, picking up debris as the Watchers haul bodies out from
the woods and put them on carts to take to the Cleansing
Waters.

Voices murmur across the space, a soft melody after the
bangs and screams and gunshots. The wind blows gentle, like
it's trying to rid this place of the bitter scent of blood and
death.

"Em." Kane has appeared beside me. He has a shovel in
his hand.

Haven't walked over to Beast yet. Haven't been able to
bring myself to even look at him.

"I can carve a marker," he offers. "For the grave."

My breath hitches. "That'd be real nice," I say.

He drops the shovel and reaches out to take me in his arms. A flash of movement stops him.

Eisu is riding out across the flats. He barrels straight toward us. His horse skitters to a stop in the dust just a few strides shy of where we stand. "There's a man coming, unarmed," he says, his brow creased with worry. "He's Dominion."

The people from my settlement crowd around the gates, straining to get a glimpse of the figure leading his horse across the Watch flats. He gazes with wonder at the scene, keeping his free hand high, waving a white cloth. He comes in peace.

Kane joins me as I push my way to the front of the gathering crowd. The Watchers leave the carts. *Sohkâtisiwak* venture across the flats and file into a line, facing the man. I tug Kane forward so that we're standing beside Eisu, who has dismounted.

The Dominion man is tidy, with a clean jacket and mustache and beard trimmed real neat. His horse is groomed and looks well fed.

The people from my settlement strain to see. I can feel the curiosity and wariness pulsing through them. The man stops about six strides away and regards us, a semicircle of the strangest mix of people: my settlement in their worn and dusty clothes on one side, *sohkâtisiwak* in their battle leathers on the other. And Eisu and Kane and me in the middle.

"Good afternoon," he ventures. "We extend the protection of the Dominion to all who, uh,"—he hesitates, looking around—"are peaceful."

People exchange glances.

Sister Ann steps out from the sweat- and dirt-stained crowd. Her hands are black, and there's a dark smudge along her brow. Her hair escapes its bun. She wipes her hands on her skirts. "What can we do for you?"

"Well . . ." Again the man looks around, his brow knitted. He's trying to make sense of the scene. He looks at the fortification, at the debris. He notices the carts of bodies and squints. "Are those . . . Merritt Leon's men?"

"They attacked us," Sister Ann replies, her voice calm and measured. "We defended ourselves."

The man blinks, still staring at the carts. "Yes, of course. I'm . . . I'm pleased to see you were victorious." He looks around the flats. "One of our battalions didn't fare so well in a recent move to commandeer his fortification." His eyes sweep over and rest on the crowd. I follow his gaze and realize how dirty, how wild, we must appear to him. He gestures to our fortification. "Your people are so . . . established." He seems relieved.

"We've been here a while." Sister Ann's voice is wry, like she's had this conversation before.

"Yes." He tucks the white cloth into his breast pocket and gives us a genial smile.

"There something we can help you with?" Sister Ann asks.

"Uh, yes. Is there"—he hesitates—"someone in charge?" It's clear he doesn't figure Sister Ann could be that person.

"You can say your piece to all of us."

"Of course." He clears his throat and draws himself up again. "My superior would like a word."

"Superior?"

"He's accompanied by two other men, but I assure you, they come in peace." He points to the woods. "If I could give them indication it is safe?"

Sister Ann nods, a mite exasperated. The man steps to the side of his horse and waves his flag. Three riders emerge from the trees. Moss-green jackets and pants with shiny buttons. And the bearded man in the middle looks like . . .

My breath stops.

It's the commander from the Dominion camp: McKern.

Why is he here?

As he rides forward, his gaze skims over the carts of bodies and stops on *sohkâtisiwak*.

All at once I want to get back into the crowd, away from him. I back up slow, but he turns his head from *sohkâtisiwak*, and his gaze falls on me. My heart pounds as he squints.

And looks away.

I look down at my muddy and bloodstained clothes, feel the sweat and grime caking my skin, my hair a bloody, wild tangle. He doesn't recognize me.

He draws himself up on his horse. "We extend the protection of the Dominion to all who are peaceful." His voice rings out more sure and steady than that of the first man.

"Commander McKern," the tidy man ventures. He gestures at Sister Ann. "This is, uh . . ."

"Ann."

"A pleasure," McKern says, removing his hat.

Sister Ann isn't in the mood for niceties. "What's this all about?"

"A peaceful visit," McKern assures her. "On behalf of the Dominion. We're mapping the land and registering settlements." He gestures at our fortification. "Your settlement will be a welcome addition to our maps."

"And yet you don't seem surprised to find us here."

"We heard rumor of this place."

Sister Ann waits.

McKern exchanges a glance with his men. "So. How . . ." He seems a mite unnerved by her silence. "How long have you survived here?"

"A long while," Sister Ann replies. "Decades."

"And have you lost many people to sickness?"

"You mean to the Bleed?" Sister Ann asks. McKern's mouth opens like he's surprised. And pleased. "Not for a *good* long while."

"So you're protected from it here."

"You say that like you're hoping."

McKern looks around at the crowd again. Over at *sohkâtisiwak*. "Might there be somewhere we can speak more privately?" he asks Sister Ann.

"Whatever you have to say, you can say it here."

"Very well." He draws himself up in his saddle. "Yes, the truth is, we're hoping you have information about the Bleed. We've lost many men to the terrible disease."

"You need a remedy."

McKern leans forward. "Do you have such a thing?"

Sister Ann measures the man. There's a silence.

"The Dominion can't bring law and order to the northwest without it."

Sister Ann frowns. "Seems like lawlessness came from the east." She points to the carts of bodies.

"There are a few bad apples in every bunch," McKern says. "Our law would ensure your protection against people like Merritt Leon."

"We protected ourselves just fine."

"I see that," McKern says. "But with our law, there would be no need." There's another silence. Sister Ann tilts her head. "And if we refuse?"

"It would be in your interest to accept our rule." McKern's jaw works. "The Dominion will expand peaceably where possible, forcibly where necessary."

Sister Ann glances at the crowd. People begin to murmur.

McKern holds up a hand. "But there's no need for this kind of talk if you can provide us with the remedy. The Dominion wouldn't challenge your claim to this land."

But . . . but why is he making the exact same bargain *osanaskisiwak* offered? Why would he come all this way for the same deal?

A chill touches my neck.

"You're saying we'd be left to our own ways."

"Not exactly. You'd return to the law you left when you settled out this way, however long ago. You would be, once again, part of the Dominion. Part of us."

They're not part of us.

I listen to the murmur, look around at the interested faces, the uncertain glances.

Panic strikes my heart. Being part of the Dominion might not be so bad for this settlement, but handing over the remedy destroys any chance for Matisa's people to negotiate their own freedom. I was so sure my people would understand. I trusted them with the truth so they *could* understand. Now all it would take is one person to disclose—

"And how would we know you'd keep your word?" Sister Ann asks.

No. We can't.

"I've drawn up an accord." McKern nods to the tidy man, who reaches for the buckles of his saddle pack. The man withdraws a scroll of parchment and holds it high in his hand. "It's a simple contract," McKern explains. "Your remedy for Dominion protection."

Sister Ann crosses toward the man, gesturing for the parchment. He hands it over, looking relieved. There's a silence while she opens it and her eyes skim over the writing.

I'm frozen in place, my tongue numb with fear. Refusing McKern now requires seeing beyond our immediate gain, choosing something bigger than ourselves. I can feel *sohkâtisiwak* standing silent, waiting, after risking their necks to help us.

Please let my people see . . .

"My understanding is that First People have approached the Dominion already, with a similar accord," Sister Ann says, looking up from the parchment. *"Osanaskisiwak?"*

The surprise on McKern's face is near comical. "Yes," he says, recovering. "But those negotiations were delayed. When we heard about this place, I knew it presented us a greater opportunity."

"They didn't offer you the remedy?"

"They did. But we had no way of knowing they would keep their promise."

"Funny," Sister Ann says. "Seems it's you who's gone back on his word."

There's a rumbling in the crowd. My heart leaps. McKern raises his hands. "We haven't moved against their valley."

"But you're here."

"The agreement wasn't set in stone."

I could step forward now. I could set my people straight: tell them exactly what McKern said when Huritt and I sat in his tent and pledged *osanaskisiwak*'s help.

But it wouldn't matter.

It wouldn't stop them from choosing what he's offering.

"Look," he says. "The Dominion wishes to expand. Plainly put, these wild lands and people need law and order."

"You saying we're wild?"

"Of course not. You're clearly different."

"Different from Merritt Leon?"

"And . . . others." First People, he means.

"And how's that?"

"Well, you're like . . . us."

There's a long silence.

And now, movement in the crowd. A tall, scar-faced man pushing forward. Luc. He reaches for the parchment. Ann hands it over, and he turns with it in his hand, drawing himself up tall.

"*Je choisis mon propre chemin,*" he states, echoing my speech from the other night in the ceremonial hall. "*Je choisis une nouvelle vie.*"

I choose my own path. I choose a new life.

My breath is caught in my throat.

I watch him roll up the parchment and place it in the man's breast pocket. He pats it firm-like, turns, and crosses to where Kane and I stand near *sohkâtisiwak*.

His arm is clasped across his chest in the sign of the Peace.

And now there are more Watchers moving through the crowd, coming to stand with us. They, too, have their hands in the sign of the Peace. They file in behind us, circling us in strength, determination. And, slow, other people begin to join. Sister Ann. The man behind her. A young girl.

McKern watches in consternation as the crowd crosses the semicircle to join us. One by one, they come, hands on their chests, until we're all standing opposite the Dominion men. I glance around, back at *sohkâtisiwak*, who stand straight and proud, and I realize something.

They dreamt there was something powerful in these woods.

They were right.

I look to Kane, my eyes blurred with tears.

"You will have the remedy, but we will not submit to your rule," Sister Ann says. "You must take your bargain back to the valley and finish negotiations." Her voice rings out across the flats. "Our voice is with *osanaskisiwak*."

33

GLARING SUN, CLOUDLESS SKY.

This season is the shortest; it should also be the sweetest.

After the deadly harsh winds of *La Prise*, when your existence has been resting on a knife's edge, after the upheaval of the Thaw, when change has destroyed all that seemed so certain, summer is the respite, the answer.

It bursts with heat, with joy, with life.

My memories are rife with summer: my hair tousled by the soft night wind, skin drenched with the light of impossible stars. Drums and voices echoing my heartbeat, filling me with purpose, moving me forward to the heat of the fire. And all of it feeling like finally my dreams have been answered.

Summer is sweet.

But it is also bitter.

Parched earth and dusty fields and sun-bleached bone. Gale-force winds and wildfires eating through the flesh of trees. Days that stretch out endless, glaring light on that which should be dark.

And the things you have done, the things you've asked of others—the cost of all that lies naked in the glare.

The bodies that littered the Watch flats, speckled the woods, marred the dry creek bed, are gone—taken by the currents of a no longer swollen river.

We buried Beast where he lay.

The sweetness of summer doesn't come without sacrifice. The person you were when you slept in the icy embrace of the winterkill, dreaming of your life beyond—that person, too, is gone. Changed.

A testing season. Bitter.

But sweet.

And as I stand on the wall and gaze out, over trees now weary from a season of heat, as I remember the people standing together on these Watch flats and choosing a new path, I know that the promise of summer is like any other: uncertain but full of hope. And when you are faced with the choice to live it, despite the bittersweet, you open your arms to the glare of the sun.

You walk through its fire.

You rise from the ashes.

34

LES TREMBLES WHISPER SOFT ABOVE ME, REACH-
ing tall to the bright blue sky.

I press into the forest, feeling the murmurings of change.
Every day, the sun is less fierce. Every day, the shadows get
longer.

These trees will turn soon. Their leaves will shift into
shades of gold and orange, one last brilliant display before
they fall and carpet the earth with musty shells.

As the days get shorter, the trees will fall asleep and look
like death, brittle and stark. Quiet. But when the days get
long again, they'll know. They'll wake, bursting into existence with their urgent whisperings.

I find four soft gray-green bushes all growing together at
the base of a tree. Sinking to my knees, I pull my stick from
my *ceinture*. I dig down around the first, watchful so as not to
disturb the other plants, loosening the soil around the roots
so I can lift it. My hand grasps the moist stalk, and soil sifts
through my fingers as I free it from the earth. A shower of
dirt falls to the forest floor.

I do this for each of the plants, placing them careful in my satchel.

As I handle the last plant, I remember Isi rolling his eyes at me yesterday.

It is not a baby.

Today he chose to stay back at the Healing House to flit around Matisa. She says she's tired of his fussing, but I can tell it pleases her a mite, too. Her gaze follows him as he moves about the space, fetching her anything she asks for, helping her stand though she's well able.

But better him there than here, annoying me. Because I meant what I said in reply: *Our fates depend on this plant. I'll baby it all I like.*

I look up to the sighing branches of *les trembles*. The memory of my Lost People is heavy in these woods, but their voices are long silent. Silent, because they are no longer lost.

We have all been found.

The snap of a branch stops my thoughts.

I push to my feet, realizing I'm not alone. Something is nearby. I scan the woods. The brush is still. I pause, listening hard. Nothing but the soft wind in the poplars and the sparrow trill—

"Daydreamer!"

I cry out in surprise as strong arms catch me and spin me about. I'm pressed against a hard chest and take a deep breath of woodsmoke before I pull back and shove Kane hard with both hands. "Almighty!"

He staggers back, but he's pretending; I can't shove hard enough to knock him off balance. He grins. "Cursing already? It's not even noon."

"You scared the life out of me!"

"Did I?"

I cross my arms and try not to look at where his shirt is unlaced. It's always unlaced. Why do I even notice anymore?

"You were trying to."

"You were in your daydreaming way, is all."

"My daydreaming way."

"Yeah. You know: hearing something no one else can hear, seeing something no one else can see."

"And you snuck up on me because I was daydreaming?"

"Didn't sneak. Ran. You know I find that irresistible." His gaze travels the length of me.

I press my lips together.

He reaches out a hand. "Walk you back?"

I tilt my head as if I'm considering.

He sighs. He darts forward and grabs my hand, pulling me close. He puts one arm under my arms and the other under my knees. "All right. Carry you back."

"Kane!"

He swings me up and starts through the woods, bumping me hard with each step.

"Watch my satchel!" I cry. "The plants!" But I'm laughing harder with each bump and how foolish we must look, laboring through the trees like some off-kilter animal.

He sets me on my feet when we reach the Watch flats but doesn't let me go. His hands close around the small of my back, and his eyes get dark with intent. He leans close.

I put a hand to his chest and push back. "You could've kissed me in the woods," I say. I nod at the settlement folk sifting around the Watch flats, bringing in their gatherings and laying things out to dry. "No eyes out there."

"You think I care about an eyeballing?" Kane scoffs. He throws a glance at the workers. "We don't answer to them."

I squint at him. "Mayhap you were *hoping* for an eyeballing?"

His hands tighten around me, and my insides flutter. He dips his head close. "Let them watch," he growls, and he brings his mouth to mine.

I kiss him back, feeling reckless. I touch his face with my fingertips and then run my hands into his hair, grasping at it because I know it makes his kisses more insistent.

"Em!" A little voice stops my hands. I turn my head abrupt, and Kane's lips skip along my cheek. It's little Edith, running toward us across the flats. I pull away, ignoring Kane's sound of protest. Edith's starting to talk to me the way she used to; don't want to discourage her by seeming busy—even if I'd far rather be busy this way.

Her blond head shines as her little legs churn across the prairie grasses. "Look!" she shouts. There's something in her hand. She pulls up before us. "See?" She opens her palm and shows me a lump of clay. It's shaped like . . . well, an unfortunate-looking something, truly, though I know it's meant to be human. The eyes are made from juniper berries, so they're far too big in the tiny face, and a piece of bark is pressed into the torso for . . . clothes?

"Who is it?" I ask, perplexed.

"It's a *sogat-man*," she says.

I search her face, lost.

She frowns. "The ones who saved us."

She means *sohkâtisiwak*. I peer closer. "Oh, yes. I see now. It's um . . . it's perfect." I reach out my hand. "Is that for me?"

"No," she says, snatching it away. Her face is serious. "I'm going to give it to them when they come."

I hide a smile. Lea and *sohkâtisiwak* set out for Matisa's village with the remedy, as much as they could carry. *Sohkâtisiwak* will rejoin Matisa's people, now that the questions in their dreams have been answered. They pledged to return to us with *osanaskisiwak* leaders, including the healers' circle. The settlement's planned a feast for their arrival, and everyone has been making preparations.

Even Edith.

"They'll love it, mouse," I say.

She nods, serious. "I'll make some more." She turns and races back to the fortification. I look at Kane.

He raises an eyebrow. "They'll love it?"

I raise my hands, helpless. "It . . . *resembled* a person?"

"Well, let's hope the feast doesn't *resemble* food."

I shove his arm. "You could make life day cake. You're so good at it."

"Never making that again," he says, frowning. He tilts his head. "Unless it gets me alone with you?"

I smile, watching Edith making a beeline for the fort.

"Shouldn't they be here by now?" Kane asks, meaning Lea and the rest.

"They're coming," I say.

Matisa and Isi appear at the north gate, walking together. They're forced to part as Edith barrels straight in.

"Come on." I tug Kane forward so we meet them in the middle of the flats.

Isi is carrying a blanket and trying, unsuccessful, to put it over Matisa's shoulders. Her hair is loose and glossy, and she tucks it behind one ear as she waves the blanket away. I set her arm according to her instructions. It's still bound to her side, but she says it's not giving her pain. Isi insists on giving her the willow tea anyway.

"You're a long way from the Healing House," I say as they stop before us.

"Yes," Isi says, frowning at her. "She is."

"A week of little movement is difficult. Two weeks is enough to kill me." She gives him a sweet smile.

"You're well?" Kane asks her.

"Very well," she says. "My arm feels healed. But someone is acting like his brains were rattled."

Isi frowns. "Finally *âmopiyesîs* has to sit still," he says. "And it 'kills' her."

She laughs, and his frown fades, melting into a look so unguarded, I have to glance away.

My eyes trace the high cliffs across the river and to the riverbank, where Tom and Eisu are climbing toward us. I wave them over. As they get closer, I see that Eisu has three gutted fish dangling from a stick. Tom's hands are empty. Hunger pads along after them. She pricks up her ears at the sight of me. I smile.

"You catch all those?" Kane asks Eisu when they near us.

Eisu nods. "The sun is too hot now. They have stopped biting."

"You were fishing, too?" I ask Tom. "You didn't used to be so bad at it."

"Mostly, I was staring," Tom says. He tilts his head at Eisu. "Have you seen him when he's concentrating on something? It's . . . fascinating." Eisu smiles and shakes his head.

Matisa stretches her good arm wide and tilts her face to the sun. "It is so nice to be out here," she says.

The Watch flats stretch out around us, and the woods beyond them rustle soft. Behind us, the river drifts, silent.

It's peaceful here. So peaceful.

A loud clang pierces the air. My head snaps to the Watchtower, to the unseen person within who rings the bell. It rings once, twice, and, as people discard their tasks and straighten and turn to the woods, ten times more.

Someone is coming.

I look at Matisa, see the happy smile on her face.

And *osanaskisiwak* appear, silent, like ghosts from the trees, riding out onto the Watch flats on their tall, sleek horses. Their heads are high, their hair adorned with colorful beads and feathers. Their faces are open. They raise hands in greeting or, mayhap, victory.

Youngsters race out of the gates. Edith is among them, running pell-mell for the horses, that awful mud figure clutched in her hand.

"All is well," Matisa murmurs. "In this moment, all is well."

Matisa's valley is at peace. This settlement has the protection of *osanaskisiwak*. And, at Huritt's request, the Dominion will leave Genya's village. In this moment, all is well.

We watch as Matisa's people slow their horses. People

from my settlement crowd around them, their calls of welcome drifting over to us on the summer breeze. They urge the riders forward to the gates, chattering, laughing.

"What happens now?" Tom wants to know.

"We eat," Isi says.

"And tell our stories until people are tired of hearing them," Matisa adds, smiling at me.

"But after that?" He's not speaking on Matisa's people and the settlement—the plans they'll make. He's speaking on us—our plans.

I look at my friends.

There's still so much unknown: how exactly this land will be shared, how long the Dominion will be content with the terms Matisa's people put forth, if there are others like Leon out there who will try to lay claim.

But Matisa is better now, able to ride. She'll return to the valley and the healers' circle of her village, to be there when they pledge a new way forward. Kane is eager to get back to his brothers. And now we'll be able to return to Genya's village unharmed.

But after that . . .

Feeling my friends' love shining on me bright as the sun, a little fire starts up inside me. I think about being back out there, heading into the wilderness. Searching out new places for us, new unknowns.

Kane leans close and reaches for me. My fingertips graze the palm of his hand as he grasps it, firm.

"After that . . ." I say. I glance around the Watch flats, to the forest.

"We'll go, right?" Tom asks.

I meet Matisa's eyes. And Kane's.

"Yes," I say. "We'll go."

A soft wind courses along the flats, and we raise our faces to it, sharing the same deep breath.

And I know how it will feel when we venture out. We will feel like I did all those months ago when I first ventured into the woods. Back then, as I stood in that secret grove, my feet felt rooted to the forest floor, and the trees around me formed a haven. A place I belonged.

I can feel it around us, drifting on the late-summer breeze, drifting on the currents of the river: a knowing that fills me with hope, makes my heart beat strong.

The world is wide open. So many things to see. So many places to run.

And we will. We will open our hearts, and we will carve new paths for ourselves, discover new unknowns, knowing the choice is ours to make, knowing we belong to this land.

Knowing we belong to this life.

This new life.

ACKNOWLEDGMENTS

The Winterkill series is fantasy, and it has been inspired by narratives of the settlement of the North American West and a natural landscape dear to me. It's been my privilege to write these books: to question how the concepts of fear and hope help shape our realities, to wonder about the histories we tell ourselves, and to examine which voices are allowed to be heard. Because I don't suffer the consequences of unjust historical events, I have the luxury to reimagine the past. Because I've never been denied access to this land, I have the opportunity to eulogize its beauty. I am a newcomer, and I am extremely fortunate to be here.

My privilege includes having people in my life who have encouraged and guided me in my writing pursuits. The following people have my deepest thanks for making this book possible.

My agent, Michael Bourret: for taking care of everything, always. For helping me articulate what I need, for answering my emails in sixty seconds or less, for deciphering my acronyms YATB & IHY.

My wonderful editors, Erica Finkel at Abrams/Amulet and Alice Swan at Faber & Faber: for helping me write the end to this series that I always envisioned, only miles better. I'm so grateful to have had your guidance and advice.

Everyone at Abrams/Amulet—in particular, Susan Van Metre, Michael Jacobs, Jim Armstrong, Nicole Russo, Jason Wells, Mary Wowk, Jess Brigman, Elisa Gonzalez, Maria T. Middleton, Shane Rebenschied, and Julia Marvel—for all of your kind attention to my work.

My team at Faber & Faber, including Leah Thaxton, Grace Gleave, Emma Eldridge, Rebecca Lee, Susan Holmes, Hannah Love, Naomi Colthurst, Natasha Brown, Mohammed Kasim, Will Steele, Jack Murphy, and Helen Crawford-White: for everything, plus a fantastic relaunch.

My foreign rights agent, Lauren Abramo: for sharing my work in foreign and fancy places, and also for being open to capes.

Agents Caspian Dennis, Anna Dixon, and Kate McLennan: for taking care of things in the UK.

Dana Alison Levy, whose kind encouragement keeps me putting words to page: for being perpetually available for mulling, and talking down of Kate, and cheering up of Kate.

Rachael "Hold My Earrings" Allen, whose beta reads are legendary: for being in my corner.

My writing communities—the litbitches, the Fall Fourteeners, and OneFour kidlit—and new writer friends: for commiserating with me and for encouraging and enlightening me.

Thérèse Romanick: pour l'assistance avec le francais—je t'aime.

Carl and Reuben: for so generously sharing your expertise in Cree.

Jennifer St. Arnault: for keeping Emmeline alive when she finds herself alone.

My Rimbey girls—Amanda, Nicole, Lisa, Heidi, Christine and Liz—and my Edmonton girlfriends (including those on hiatus from Edmonton): for all of the cheers and encouragement.

My family and family-in-law: for unfailing support and love. My parents: for the aforementioned, plus reading to me when I was young. My brother, Tim: for talking logistics with me ad nauseam. Bury me with your cartoons, please (when I get Winterkilled).

Marcel and Matias and Dylan: for being proud of my work, and me. I love you beyond measure.

My young readers who are following their own paths: you make the world a brighter place.

Finally, to everyone who journeyed with Emmeline to the end and, ultimately, a new beginning: thank you from the bottom of my heart.

ABOUT THE AUTHOR

KATE BOORMAN is a writer from the Canadian prairies. She was born in Nepal and grew up in the small town of Rimbey, Alberta. Kate has an MA in Dramatic Critical Theory and a résumé full of an assortment of jobs, from florist to qualitative research associate. She lives in Edmonton, Alberta, with her family, and spends her free time sitting under starry skies with her friends and scheming up travel to faraway lands.